DECEPTION

DECEPTION

~ Haunting Emma ~

Lee Nichols

SCHOLASTIC INC.
New York Toronto London Auckland
Sydney Mexico City New Delhi Hong Kong

ISBN 978-0-545-33329-0

12 11 10 9 8 7 6 5 4 3 2 1   11 12 13 14 15 16/0

Printed in the U.S.A.   40

First Scholastic printing, January 2011

Book design by Nicole Gastonguay

DECEPTION

I couldn't see, couldn't breathe. Strapped to a chair underwater, I was shivering and my lungs burned. A moment before I blacked out, the chair rose through the icy darkness and broke the water's surface.

I gasped and coughed, but the instant I caught my breath, he plunged me under again, brought to the verge of drowning over and over.

"Once more, Emma?" he asked. "Or will you answer me now?"

I longed to tell him everything, to end the fear and stop the pain. Then the chair plunged again into the freezing water.

1

Six weeks ago, my parents disappeared.

I'd left them at the San Francisco airport at seven in the evening, nervous and excited. These were their last words:

Dad: "There's money in the bank; use your ATM card. If you get in trouble . . ." He looked at me. "Don't get in trouble. We have our cell phone. You can call us anytime."

Mom: "You know a scarf isn't a jacket, Emma."

It was a chilly forty-eight degrees—sometimes I wondered if San Francisco was really in California. I'd worn a black sweater, black jeans, black boots, and a red embroidered pashmina my parents brought back from one of their many business trips. The scarf was wound tightly around my neck and shoulders.

Me: "That's really the last thing you're going to say to me?"

Mom: "A hat helps, too."

She fingered my short, choppy blond bob—a haircut

she hadn't approved—looking like she was about to say more, but she hugged me instead.

I suppose if I'd known they were going to vanish, I would've said "I love you" and "I'll miss you." Instead, I left them at the curb and sputtered home in our ancient Volvo wagon, already planning my fall from grace: clubbing until 4:00 a.m., unsupervised shopping sprees, and maybe even a tattoo if I could come up with something good.

Hoping for inspiration, I paced our mausoleum of a house. Seriously, our coffee table was a stone sarcophagus; it was like we snacked off Nefertiti's head. My parents were overly fond of the dead, or at least the possessions of the dead. They sold antiquities from a store below our apartment on Fillmore Street, and the apartment was filled with relics and icons. Even the sofa was 150 years old—horsehair, dust mites, and all.

My family had owned the building for generations. I guess we were rich, despite the old car, my pathetic allowance, and public education. Why else would we have the high-tech security system for both the store and apartment, which required a thumbprint to get in? When we were younger, my brother, Max, and I pretended we were 007 agents. Now it was just an aggravation every time I left the house for a red-eye chai from the café next door.

You're probably wondering what kind of parents leave their seventeen-year-old home alone for God knows how long. They'd said three weeks, but my parents didn't always stick to the plan—this trip, in fact, was last minute. Still, I wasn't completely alone. They had exactly one employee,

Susan, who'd run the shop for the past ten years, and she was supposed to check on me every night.

Susan's daughter, Abby, was my best friend—emphasis on *was*. Two years older than me and two years younger than my brother, we'd grown up together, hanging out after school, obsessing over guys and our mutual lack of nice fingernails. Abby and Max were always close; he even tutored her in French. And with our parents away so often, Susan became a surrogate mother to us.

Then, this summer, when Max was home from Harvard, I discovered him and Abby having The Affair.

I'd just gotten back from the café next door when I heard noises coming from Max's room. I'd barged in without knocking and discovered them—which put a whole new spin on the French lessons.

It was more of Max's skin than I'd seen since I was a toddler, but I'd blocked out a lot from my past; it was just one more image to add to the file. And they were both happier than I'd ever seen either of them. For two months, things were great.

Then Max dumped her.

Abby was devastated, and there was nothing I could do except keep the Kleenex and chocolate flowing. I have no idea how Max took the breakup, or why he ended it, because the next day he left for his junior year abroad.

Now he was in Tibet or Timbuktu, someplace he could only be reached by yak. Which was so Max—kind of cool, and kind of cold. Breaking hearts in California so he could bring safe drinking water to remote villages in Asia.

So I wasn't completely alone, because I still had Susan. Except Abby blamed me for the breakup, or at least I thought she did. I didn't really know because she hadn't talked to me since she'd left for UC, Santa Barbara. And her mom was following suit.

While my parents thought me safe in Susan's hands, she was acting like I was her daughter's worst enemy. She definitely wouldn't be checking up on me as much as she usually did. A girl could get into a lot of trouble with so much freedom. I couldn't wait to get started.

But I wasn't exactly sure how. Clubbing wasn't the kind of thing you did alone, the shops were closed, and I was still debating the body art. So I lay alone in bed that night, with only my laptop for company. Instead of talking to actual humans, I messed around on Facebook. I caught up on how everyone was doing at college and stalked my current fixation, the painfully unobtainable Jared from school. Then I e-mailed Max:

> I imagine the yaks run on treadmills to create enough electricity for you to check your messages. Like a Buddhist episode of *The Flintstones*. Why did you dump Abby? You know you miss me.
> ——Emma

My daily pleading senryu went to Abby. She never responded, but I was nothing if not tenacious:

My brother is a dickwad
While you rock Organic Chem
Talk to me?

Abby was doing premed at UCSB and worried about Organic Chemistry, so along with knocking Max, I figured I'd send her positive energy. I wasn't sure question marks were technically allowed in senryu, but I found myself using them a lot. Probably because my life felt like one big question mark lately. Like how was I going to start enjoying my newfound freedom?

By midnight, I was zonked. I was going to have to work on my stamina if I wanted to stay out until four. I clicked send, closed my laptop, and crashed.

Seven hours later, the alarm went off. Though I'd been left alone loads of times, I never got used to the feeling of waking to an empty house. Do you know how loud your spoon sounds against your bowl when it's only you and your cornflakes in the morning?

I showered and dressed and noticed a sick feeling in my stomach. I tried to identify the anxiety. Not grades, not homework; I didn't even miss my parents yet. What made me woozy was my lack of friends. It's not like I was an outcast—I didn't wear panty hose, I wasn't the girl who drew spiderwebs all over her face—but my best friend graduated last year and I'd been the unofficial mascot of her class. So it wasn't only Abby I missed, it was everyone.

Still, I managed to drag myself out the door and my foot nudged something on the mat. A plain white envelope.

A secret admirer? A love letter from Jared?

No, a letter of resignation from Susan. Effective immediately. There were two pages of eloquent regrets, but basically all she said was "I quit."

Hmm ... what was I supposed to do about this? No reason to panic. Maybe my parents had already hired a backup employee. Or maybe they'd be coming home early, before I even had a chance to enjoy their absence.

I walked the block to the bus stop, then ran the last few feet to catch it. I found a seat, took a deep breath, and pulled out my cell to dial Susan.

She answered on the first ring. "You got my letter?"

"You can't quit now!" I said. "My parents just left for Paris. I'm all alone. Who's going to run the store?"

"You."

"Me?" But then I'd have no time for shopping sprees, nightlife, or even a tattoo. Maybe I'd just get a belly ring.

"I'm sorry, Emma. I got another job. In Santa Barbara," she said, her voice warm and motherly and completely unyielding. "I want to be closer to Abby."

I swallowed. "Is this about Max?"

"No," she said. "This is about Abby."

"I don't understand why she isn't talking to me."

After a moment she said, "I think it's better if you stop e-mailing her."

"I just—I miss her . . ." If she were still here, this whole freedom thing would've been a lot more fun.

Susan said, "I left a voice mail with your parents and I'm sure they'll come right back. I'm sorry, Emma. I really am."

Then she hung up.

The bus heaved to a stop in front of my school. I watched other students trickle off, meeting their friends on the steps. I stepped out, greeted no one, and walked into the main hall alone, yearning to be anywhere but here.

2

The next two weeks blew.

Every morning I woke in the empty house, pressed Sleep on the alarm, and phoned my parents' cell. No mysterious backup employee showed up, so either they never got Susan's voice mail or they decided I was fine on my own. They'd left me one message saying, "Not to worry, we've decided to visit Max. We'll be in touch soon." I hadn't heard from them since.

I'd lie there listening to "The customer you are dialing is out of service area," imagining all the horrors that could befall them. Snicker, because *befall* was a funny word. Then run through the litany of disasters: torture, sleep deprivation, and constant Celine Dion music piped into their cells. Though I guess it was pretty unlikely they'd ended up at Guantánamo.

They could've been kidnapped, except there'd been no ransom demand. Ritual sacrifice would serve them right for ignoring me—tossed into a volcano by some preindustrial

Andean tribe, crying out my name as they fell to fiery deaths. Except they'd probably call out, "*Maaaaax!*"

Then I'd force myself out of bed and slip downstairs through the kitchen, taking the long way to the front door because some of the antiquities were freaking me out. I hadn't been near my dad's office since the day they left. In the hallway outside his door was a jumbled collection of funeral urns, and I knew it sounded crazy but it felt as though they were missing him. The area reeked of *longing*. Those urns had always given me the shivers, so I avoided that part of the house entirely.

I stopped at the Gothic Café next door for my morning red-eye. You know you've got a problem when baristas greet you by name. You know you've got another problem when it's the warmest social interaction of your day. My parents would've been appalled at how much cash I was dropping on chais, but they weren't here to stop me, were they?

I dragged myself to school and tried for As so I could get into Berkeley, though given my PSATs, that was looking like a long shot. And ever since the Incident—a little something I no longer discussed—my parents never let me leave home. Hence I never accompanied them on their travels, and I wasn't even sure they'd let me cross the Bay to attend Berkeley if I got in—which was a big if.

Latin was the only class I enjoyed. I'd taken it since seventh grade. "Eheu fugaces labuntur anni."* It was one

---

* Alas, the fleeting years slip away.

of the few things I had in common with my parents: love for a dead language.

Lunchtime was misery.

Then I got home and opened the store from 3:00 to 9:00 p.m. On Saturday and Sunday I was there from 10:00 a.m. to 9:00 p.m. Sales were actually pretty good, but I couldn't keep up the pace. I kept nodding off during class—I mean, even more than usual.

My nights were spent sending plaintive, unanswered e-mails to Max, wanting some word of our parents, and writing senryu for Abby that I did not send.

Two weeks. Two weeks since I'd heard from my parents. Freedom so didn't rock like I thought it would. I hadn't even had time to get that belly ring. Besides, it wasn't the sort of thing you did alone.

Then everything changed.

I had chemistry right before lunch, which was a weight-loss triumph because ions and isotopes really curbed my appetite. As class ended one day, I gathered my stuff, thinking about grabbing a yogurt on my way to the library, when Natalie asked if I wanted to hit lunch.

Natalie was new but already had a social life I envied. I think she sat next to me her first day because she thought she could cheat off me—I looked smarter than I was. During the first test, she kept eyeing my paper and scribbling furiously, but when we got back the graded exams she got a B+ and I got a C.

That rattled her, but apparently not enough to turn her against me.

"Want to go to smoke?" she asked.

"Instead of lunch?" Maybe that's why she was so skinny. She was also dark haired with nice fingernails and a natural tan, and I doubted she'd turn pasty this winter as I inevitably would. "I was thinking more like yogurt."

"Oh, you poor sheltered lamb." She ushered me out the door. "You have no idea what you've been missing."

We left campus and walked two blocks to a gray building between a dry cleaner and a butcher. There was no sign, just a clear plastic box over the door filled with— you got it—smoke. I'd walked by a thousand times and had always thought it was a bar.

Inside, the place was painted a light iridescent gray, with the tables and chairs a darker gray and the concrete floor decorated with gold flames. Not a bar, a restaurant called Smoke—full of hot young professionals and some kids from school. A guy laughing in a corner booth waved at Natalie.

She dragged me by the hand toward him.

Except he wasn't just a guy. He was Jared, my fixation. The one I stalked on Facebook. Last night he'd posted a picture of himself surfing and I started to type in a comment: "Dude, gnarly Rip Curl," then realized I had no idea what a Rip Curl was, so said nothing.

Four other people sat around the table. Daniel, a Latino guy I had Latin with (I know that sounds ridiculous); Primus, the completely unoriginal nonconformist; and two girls, Maisy and Caroline, who weren't actually identical twins, despite the way they looked and acted and dressed.

Natalie scooted into a seat and said, "You know Jared, don't you?"

I eyed him as though I wasn't sure. "I think our lockers are close?"

"Oh, yeah," he said. "You're *that* girl."

What did that mean? I couldn't judge from his expression.

"Emma got left behind. Her friends all graduated," Natalie said.

I'd unburdened myself to her on the way over. Actually, she asked me why I didn't have any friends and I'd explained.

"So she's with us now," Natalie said.

I glanced at Maisy and Caroline, expecting hostility. There were already three guys and three girls. Tossing me into the mix threw off the odds. But they smiled, and Caroline said, "I hope you like shopping."

"Who doesn't?" I said.

"Let's so hit up Urban Outfitters after school," Daniel said in a girly voice.

"No!" Primus squealed. "Abercrombie is *sooo* much better."

"Shut up, losers," said Maisy. "You know we only go to Saks."

Natalie then asked me where I got my boots.

Jared eyed them under the table. "Yeah, they're hot."

This was the most conversation I'd had with kids my

age since Abby left, and I begged myself not to commit social suicide by climbing across the table into Jared's lap. I murmured something about my mother bringing them back from Europe, and took a sip of water from the glass in front of me to cool down.

"Help yourself," said Daniel. Oops—it must've been his glass.

"Oh! Ego sum rumex."*

"Haud forsit,"** he said.

"Can the Latin geeks give it a rest?" Primus said. "Unless you want to talk about togas. We were discussing where we're having our party."

I asked what the party was for and Maisy told me her brother had promised to score them a keg. They didn't really need more reason than that. Natalie suggested Primus's house.

"Not after last time," Caroline said.

"What happened last time?" I asked, as Primus turned pink.

"His parents and their friends crashed our party," Daniel said.

"They drank all the beer," Maisy said.

"And didn't even put up bucks for cups," Jared said.

Natalie and I started to laugh as three baskets of French fries and seven Cokes arrived at the table. And just like that, I had a new set of friends.

---

* I'm sorry.

** No problem.

3

The next week didn't suck.

I still spent my first rising moments calling my parents, hoping their phone would start working. I still e-mailed Max in the evenings and wrote unsent senryu for Abby. But now I actually left messages for Jared on his Facebook page. And he wrote back!

Most of the time, my fixations didn't pan out. Once I got to know the guy, I'd find he had a Wii problem or said the word *pubic* or—worst of all—he'd simply disappear from my life altogether. But Jared had yet to break the deal. And even though we'd done nothing more romantic than sitting together in a movie theater, he'd become my friend.

The whole group had, really. Daniel and I wrote skits in Latin class. Who knew how funny Marcus Aurelius could be? Maisy and Caroline and I bonded over scarves, and Primus introduced me to the pleasures of a *mocha* red-eye chai.

So things were getting better . . . until I closed shop one night, went upstairs for my cup of chamomile, and realized there was someone in the house.

When I passed the hallway that I'd been avoiding—the one with my dad's funeral urn collection—I heard a rustle of fabric.

I spun and saw a shadow of a man hovering among the urns.

I froze. You know you're a city girl when you take a deep breath and flip on the light, instead of running away shrieking.

There was no one there. Had he slipped into Dad's study? A breeze wafted toward me from the hall. Maybe I'd left a window open and that rustle of fabric I'd heard was the curtains—that could sound like a person lurking in the hallway.

Right?

I didn't want to check, but it's not like I could sleep upstairs wondering if someone was in the house. Maybe I should've dialed 911, but if this turned out to be nothing—all in my head—the cops would find out I was staying here by myself. I wasn't sure what they'd do, but I knew it'd be nothing good.

Especially since the murder. Some poor girl, five or ten years older than me, had been slaughtered in her apartment a few months back. Nobody knew exactly what happened—the police weren't saying—but gossip at school said the killer carved every inch of her dead body with strange designs.

They called him the Curlicue Killer. The whole thing sounded like an urban legend to me, like alligators breeding in the sewers or wild parrots living in Golden Gate Park—oh wait, that was true. Still, if there was a kernel of truth, the cops wouldn't let me stay here alone, so I had to handle this on my own.

Besides, I was sure this was nothing. Definitely nothing. Completely and absolutely nothing.

A mantra ran through my head: *No one here. No one here. Ooohm. No one here.*

As I stepped down the hall, voices whispered behind me, strange, wordless sounds. There was an almost familiar tingling in my body. I yelped and turned but saw nothing except a wisp of smoke wafting from one of the funeral urns like a cobra from a basket.

I blinked and breathed and closed my eyes—willing my imagination into submission—but when I opened them a dozen more spirals of smoke curled toward the ceiling from the other urns.

The spirals wove together in braids, forming a thick billowing rope. It twisted toward the end of the hall and wound itself into a figure, like a mummy formed from snakes of smoke, twisting and thickening. It drifted toward me with a slow, malicious purpose. I opened my mouth to scream and tasted ash; I couldn't make a sound.

The whispering sounded like a thousand snakes hissing in my ears.

Eosssss, eosssss . . .

I couldn't move. My feet were buried in ash and I sank

deeper, the ashes dragging me downward like quicksand as the figure crept closer.

Neosssss, neosssss . . .

Panic rose in my throat as I furiously tried to free my legs. The smell of the smoke mummy smothered me as it staggered toward me. I held my breath until my vision blurred.

Then I woke in bed. The clock said 7:03 a.m.

A dream?

Of course a dream. Here I was in my pajamas, staring at my empty teacup on the bedside table.

But in the bathroom as I brushed my teeth, the taste of ash was still in my mouth. I swirled water and spat into the sink. *Oh God. Oh God.* I stepped, trembling, into the shower and turned the heat to scalding, pretending the smoky figure in the hallway didn't remind me of the terror of my childhood, the man from the Incident.

A man who wasn't there when I was seven years old. Who couldn't possibly be here now.

I pretended until I almost believed.

At lunchtime, I followed Natalie off campus, wishing she were Abby.

I really liked Natalie—she was funny and smart and freakishly self-confident—but I wasn't comfortable telling her about my nightmare. About my problems and my fears. Not only because I'd seem like the head case I actually was, but because what could she say? That maybe

I'd walked in my sleep and dug into the urns before returning to bed? And tasted the ashes of the dead?

Too gross to consider.

Maybe I didn't know what was real anymore, but there was no way I would tell someone as together as Natalie about the Incident, or that I was thinking of calling my old doctor. That I'd actually gone through my mother's papers, looking for his number, wondering if he'd remember me and help me, or just drug me.

She wasn't Abby, so I didn't tell her about that stuff. I told her about my parents and Abby's mom leaving instead, and she gave me a comforting squeeze.

Inside the restaurant, I eyed the smoky motif nervously, my mind wandering until Natalie said, "So this is news. Emma's living all alone."

"For how long?" Daniel asked.

"Indefinitely," Natalie told him.

"Party?" Primus asked.

"Private party?" Jared said with a half smile.

I melted inside but said, "No parties! My parents would kill me."

There was a fair amount of cajoling and kvetching, but I didn't give in. And then I thought . . . why not? Maybe this was exactly what I needed to forget about school, the store, and my nightmare.

So I said, "Okay, party on!" and immediately regretted it. I lived in a mausoleum, remember? If anything happened to one of my parents' relics—well, we'd finally know for sure how little they cared for me.

Everyone else was beyond thrilled, so maybe it wouldn't be as bad as I thought. At least I could pretend I was a normal teenager, hosting a bash while her parents were away. Which is exactly what I'd wanted. Right?

On Saturday, I found myself alone in the shop, opening and cataloging the packages that arrived during the week. Not exactly a thrilling weekend, yet I eagerly checked each return address for some sign of my parents' location.

No luck—they were all shipments from a previous trip. Well, except for a package from Periwinkle Antiques on Charles Street in Boston, which contained the paperwork for an internship Max had finished. And there was one box from a London dealer.

I opened it and found a mask concealed under layers of foam peanuts. It was stark white plaster, with no holes for the eyes or ears. The invoice read: *Death Mask, 1700s, Anonymous.* Apparently they used to make wax casts of corpses for keepsakes and, although this went out of vogue for some inexplicable reason, the masks were now prized by collectors. Well, *some* collectors.

I stared at the mask, wondering what the dead person would think about winding up as a sculpture in an antiquities store. Some macabre rich person would probably hang him over the toilet in their powder room.

The mask felt surprisingly heavy. I rubbed the outside with my fingertips, the cheeks and forehead, then the inside. The part that touched the person's dead face.

A shiver ran up my arm, a little thrill of horror as I felt the urge rising in me. Then I placed the death mask over my face.

The mask suctioned to my skin like plastic wrap. My body began to tingle and I felt light-headed. I couldn't see and couldn't breathe and the world twirled away from me.

There was a great whooshing sound and I felt as though I were spinning. Around and around, until suddenly I stopped and could see again. I lay in an antique bed. My arms were withered like pitiful twigs and my skin had faded to cracked parchment. I was somewhere in the past. Someone else's past.

I smelled rot and sweat and cloying perfume. I couldn't speak or move, and this definitely wasn't my body cloaked under the terrible weight of memory, of frailty and disease. I felt claustrophobic and suffocated. I clawed at my cheeks and yanked the mask from my face.

That huge whooshing noise again, then I was alone— still in the store, breathing heavily, the mask in my shaking hands. I plunged the eyeless plaster beneath the foam peanuts like I was trying to drown it. Then I dragged the box into the farthest corner of the storage room and slammed the door.

4

I was still shaking when Natalie walked in. I stepped unsteadily away from the storage closet door as she wandered through the store, her fingertips trailing over a rare bronze statue of the Persian god Mithras. She paused there, interest flickering in her brown eyes, then she spotted me and smiled. "So this is where you lurk when you're not failing chemistry."

"Hi," I said, my heart still hammering from what had happened.

Natalie wove between display cases of Roman vases and ancient Greek jewelry. On good days, the place looked more like an art gallery than an antique shop. She stopped at the mummy of a cat. "Um. Is this a cat mummy?"

"Yeah," I said.

"People *pay* for this stuff?"

"Ha."

"I'd never sleep again."

"Heh," I said.

She finally noticed my inability to say anything but monosyllables and crossed the room toward me. "Emma, are you okay?"

No. No, I wasn't. What was happening to me? Slipping into the past of someone else's life had seemed so effortless, so real. But that was impossible.

I tried to wipe the goose pimples from my arms. "I'm just cold."

"Oh, here." She took off her black cardigan and draped it around my shoulders. "Is that better?"

I nodded. "Thanks."

"I stopped by to talk to you about our party." She cocked her head. "You *sure* you're okay?"

"I'm fine. Um, about the party? I've changed my mind. Natalie, my parents would kill me, and with everything else I've been going through . . ."

Natalie's eyes narrowed. "What else have you been going through?"

"Nothing." How was I supposed to explain about the ashes and the death mask? She wouldn't believe me, even if I did tell her.

"You just need to chill," she said, pulling a flyer from her bag, with "CATSAWAY PARTY" in letters cut from a magazine. The date and my address were handwritten in a Gothic font. I recognized Primus's arty hand. "Cool, right?"

"Except you spelled *castaway* wrong," I said, frantically trying to figure how I could get out of this. "And don't expect palm trees."

"It's not *castaway*, Emma," she said. "It's *cat's away*. As in, the mice will play. This is going to be the best party our school has ever seen. Kids from Uni are coming."

"What?" Uni is short for Unity, the private high school in Pacific Heights, full of self-important posers. Max went there. "How do they even know about it?"

"The flyers are everywhere, Emma. There's no turning back now."

"Wait," I said. "This is today!"

"Don't worry, we have six hours to get ready."

I guess six hours were enough, because by midnight the house was thumpin'. I'd like to think it was because I was so popular, but I'm pretty sure it was the kegs.

Actually, I wasn't sure, because I was Elmered to the front door all night, with my thumb pressed to the security print. Every time I tried to step away and assess damages, the doorbell rang again.

The Natalie gang arrived first with the kegs. I hadn't seen any of them since they set up in the kitchen. You'd think at least Daniel would've swapped Latin verses with me. And where was Jared? I wore my black miniskirt and no leggings just so he'd notice my boots again.

But the only one who noticed was a senior from Uni who said, "Sexy boots," right before he yukked next to them. That's when I left my post at the door and searched for Natalie.

I found her in the living room. With Jared. Making out. On Nefertiti's head.

As I stood there, mouth agape, a hand snaked around my waist. "Baby, we're all hooking up. I get you."

I spun around and found Primus leering at me. I shoved him. "No, you don't."

"C'mon. Jared gets Natalie, Daniel gets Maisy."

"That leaves you Caroline," I said.

Primus pointed to the corner where Daniel, Maisy, *and* Caroline were locked in a threesome. I wanted to be blasé and cool with it, but I sort of felt: yuck.

And this whole time, the doorbell was ringing and dinging and driving me insane, and Natalie suddenly broke away from Jared and looked at me. "Why aren't you answering the door?"

"Party's over, Natalie! Some guy from Uni just puked in the hall!"

"Don't be silly, everyone's having the best time." Natalie slid a proprietary hand over Jared. "Especially me."

Jared didn't even look at me—he was too entranced with Natalie. I'd always hated his Rip Curls anyway, whatever they were.

The doorbell continued to jangle. "Let them in," Natalie told me.

"No."

"Then I will," she said.

I followed her down the hall. "How are you going to open it without my thumb?"

"That can be arranged." She sidestepped the vomit. "Ew." At the door, she turned to face me. "I know you

didn't want this party, Emma, and I'm sorry. About everything."

"You are?"

"Yeah, but I'm not done yet."

She opened the door, the alarm wailed, and the police
were waiting outside.

5

The cops weren't here about the party. They came because they got a report that I was living alone. Standing next to me in the doorway, Natalie became someone else. That bitchy girl who's inexplicably always hated you.

"That's right," she confirmed. "She doesn't even know how to get in touch with her parents."

"I do too," I blurted. "They're just on vacation! Natalie!" Why was she doing this to me? What had I done to deserve this?

Natalie smiled sadly. "Oh, Emma, don't lie. They can check."

"We already have," the cops said. "Child Protective Services is on the way."

They let me stay long enough to clean the floor and make sure that nobody walked off with one of my mom's Day of the Dead dolls. But they didn't let me spend the night. Instead, they took me to a halfway house.

Halfway to what? Nowhere I wanted to go. The only good thing was that I didn't dream—not about death masks or ashes or ghostly figures.

Probably because I was already in hell.

The next afternoon, I met with my CPS caseworker, a cadaverous man who looked way deader than anything in our apartment. Plus, his office smelled like formaldehyde, as if the embalmment had recently begun.

"You have two options, Miss Vaile," he said, his voice devoid of inflection. "The first is—"

"Can't I just phone my parents?" I asked.

"You may place a call, Miss Vaile, but according to the file, you don't have your parents' contact information."

"But I do! It's not like they've abandoned me." Saying the words made me sick; it was *exactly* like they'd abandoned me. But I summoned a weak smile. "They're just on vacation."

The Cadaver opened a manila envelope and pulled out my cell phone, confiscated at the door of the halfway house. I guess they worry you'll order out pizza . . . or crack.

I dialed, then paused as if listening to a ring, then said, "Mom! It's me. No, things are fine. How's the beach? What? No, that's Max, you know I don't like paragliding." How come my mother preferred Max even during imaginary conversations? "Listen, I lost the information—when are you getting back exactly? Tomorrow night? That's great, because . . ." I covered the mouthpiece and whispered to the cadaver. "I don't have to tell her about all this, do I? I'm gonna be in *so* much trouble."

"Hand me the phone," Cadaver said.

"That's okay, I'll tell her," I said. "Mom, don't panic—"

Cadaver plucked the phone from my hand. And listened to "The customer you are dialing is out of the service area."

"I guess she went through a tunnel," I said.

He didn't bother arguing. "Your first option is to stay in the halfway house until your parents are located."

"No way. And those other kids shouldn't have to stay there, either. Don't you have better options for them?"

"Yes, there's the street," he said.

"Well, I don't think that's a better . . . oh." Irony from the Cadaver.

"Your second option is to be placed with a foster family."

"My parents are coming back." I began to panic. "Why can't you understand that?"

Cadaver shuffled papers on his desk. "You're in luck. The Belcher family is available. They specialize in children with behavioral problems."

Behavioral problems? What exactly was wrong with my behavior? It's not like I set fire to the halfway house. "Is this about the fake call to my mom?"

"If you are unaware of what—" He stopped when the phone on his desk rang. He lifted the receiver and listened a moment. "For Miss Vaile? I find that hard to believe. Paperwork? Well. Send him in." He hung up and told me,

"There's someone here for you. He claims he's your legal guardian."

Dad! They came back for me! Except no, Cadaver would've said my father was here, not my "guardian."

Oh, maybe it was Max—he *would* pretend he was my guardian. Unless he really was my guardian, because Mom and Dad were . . . I swallowed hard, fighting back tears, and turned as the door opened.

It wasn't Max. It was Bennett.

"Hello, Emma," he said. "I—are you crying?"

"No." I wiped at my eyes. "Just the last twenty-four hours . . . they haven't been great."

"I'll see what I can do to make things better," Bennett said.

"My hero." I would've fallen in love with him then and there.

Except I already had.

I met Bennett two years ago, when he came home with Max on spring break. He was my picture ideal of what a Harvard freshman should look like: half preppy, half bohemian in faded polos and ripped khakis. His dark wavy hair fell perfectly across his brow, and every time he looked at me he seemed to be smiling. Max, on the other hand, had taken to brown plaid shirts and stovepipe corduroys—a look that suited no one.

Meeting Bennett was like meeting destiny. When he'd appeared behind Max, something had clicked. I couldn't look away. I just *knew*. Maybe we weren't meant to be together right then, but one day our lives would join.

He only stayed a week, yet my insides resonated every time he entered the room, like the right chord on a piano. So in a way his sudden reappearance simply felt right, after two years of fantasies. Of course, in my dreams Bennett wasn't saving me from a foster family, but I wasn't the type of girl to turn down a knight in J.Crew armor.

Except he wasn't my guardian. He was just a friend of my brother's. He wasn't even distant family. Guardian *angel* maybe, with a tilted halo, not looking quite as innocent as he used to.

"I'll need to examine your papers," Cadaver told him.

"Of course." Bennett handed them over and flashed me a look. The smile was still there, and so was his preppy-hippie style. He wore a white button-down, tattered blazer, dark-wash jeans, and loafers. His eyes were bright blue and thick lashed, and I forced myself to look away before the Cadaver realized I was hot for him. He wasn't going to let me go off with the sexy guardian, like in some steamy romance novel.

"Does that mean—" I stopped. I didn't want to say too much in front of Cadaver. "Have you seen my mom and dad recently?"

"No. Emma, I'm sorry. We arranged the guardianship before they left. You've heard from them though, right?"

"Well, they're outside of cell reception so I can't call them back. They're with Max now—"

Bennett's frown stopped me, and I recalled why he

disappeared two years ago. He and Max had a blowout fight, some apocalyptic argument, and Max refused to speak of him ever again—even though a certain sister pestered him until he locked her in the bathroom. I'd never found out what they'd fought about. Now was my chance.

"Speaking of Max. Why did you two—"

Cadaver interrupted. "The paperwork *appears* to be in order. Still, one cannot be too careful." He showed me the papers. "Look them over, Miss Vaile."

I checked my parents' signatures. My dad's looked absolutely real, but I noticed a faint dotting of the *i* in *Vaile* on my mother's. She never dotted her *i*'s. Still, the papers had been notarized, so Cadaver had no reason to doubt them—and I wasn't going to live with the Belchers.

Plus, I didn't have any reason not to trust Bennett. Not yet.

"That's definitely their signatures," I said. "Everything looks right to me."

"You now have a third option," the Cadaver told me. "The halfway house or the foster home, as previously discussed, becoming a temporary ward of the state until . . ."

I tuned him out as I gazed at Bennett. What was he doing here? How had he known to bring fake guardianship papers? Did he counterfeit the signatures himself?

And what exactly was that shade of blue in his eyes—cobalt?

Cadaver's voice penetrated my reverie. "And your decision?"

"I choose Bennett."

6

On the drive home, I planned how it would play out: Bennett would transfer from Harvard to Berkeley and move into Max's room. We'd meet for study breaks and candlelit suppers. His family also sold antiquities, so he'd help me with the shop, and in no time my parents would return and Bennett and I would be in love.

In reality, I worshipped him like a god the entire ride home in his Taurus rental and he, apparently, knew he was divine because he rebuffed me like Apollo spurning a lowly shepherdess. Although after spending the night in a halfway house, I did look as though I'd rolled with the sheep.

Still, despite the urge to pick straw from my hair, I was relieved to be home. And grateful. Only . . . how had he known to come?

Suddenly unsure, I paused with my thumb over the security print. "Why are you here? How did you know I was in trouble?"

He flashed a crooked grin. "Always a safe bet."

"Hey! I'm never in trouble—I mean, except now. And that's not what I meant. How did you know where to find me? And those fake papers—"

Bennett's phone jingled. "Saved by the iPhone," he said, and stepped away.

I stood there with my thumb hanging out, watching him. He eyed me as though I were trying to eavesdrop, which I was, so I went inside and tried to eavesdrop from there.

I heard him murmuring, but couldn't make out the details. He said either "love you" or "you, too" before hanging up. Was he talking to his girlfriend?

He came inside and said, "I've gotta run."

"The last time you left," I said, "you didn't come back for two years."

He took my hand and looked at me with his cobalt eyes. "So you *did* miss me."

"That's not—" Okay, yeah, that's exactly what I meant.

He grinned. "I'm not going to leave you again, Emma."

Then he told me to stay out of trouble—like I was ten—and disappeared. My hand tingled where he'd touched me. After staring dreamily at the doorway for a few minutes, I pulled myself together. What was it about him?

I wasted the afternoon cleaning up from the party and avoiding the hallway outside my dad's study, still not wanting to think about the scary smoke or the death mask in the shop downstairs. Truth was, I wasn't sure I didn't belong in some sort of home. Was I really going crazy?

I ate leftover chips and salsa by myself for dinner, wondering when Bennett would be back. I didn't light the candles on the table, figuring that'd look desperate. I did, however, devise a revenge strategy for the traitorous Natalie that involved shaving her head of perfect hair—I just wasn't sure she'd let me get close enough with the razor.

The doorbell rang late that night, as I was steeping my chamomile. I brought my mug to the front door and let Bennett inside. He looked tired and almost solemn, with his jacket rumpled and his hair mussed. I, on the other hand, had applied some discreet lip gloss and donned my gray silk robe, trying to look effortlessly chic on my way to bed.

I intended to say something sultry and sophisticated, but instead blurted, "Where have you been?"

"Why?" he asked, his eyes suddenly keen. "Did something happen? Are you okay?"

"Um . . ." My mind blanked, startled by his burst of interest. God, he was gorgeous when he gave a damn. "No, I'm all right. Nothing happened. Well, except someone turned my dad's Indian oil lamp into a bong."

"That's so Bollywood," he deadpanned, though he looked relieved that it was nothing more serious. "Get some sleep. Tomorrow's a big day."

Ugh. Tomorrow was Monday. How was I going to face Natalie and everyone?

"Our flight leaves at two, so you can pack in the morning," Bennett continued.

"Our what?"

"It's direct, straight to Boston. You can take three suitcases."

"Massachusetts?"

"I believe that's where it's located, yes."

I ignored the sarcasm. "When I agreed to your guardian thing, I didn't know you were gonna drag me to *Boston*."

"Well, you can't have thought I was going to move *here*."

"No," I said, in a small voice. "What about school?"

He looked at me for a moment, and I thought maybe he'd take my hand, but instead his eyes just grew tired again. "You've been accepted at Thatcher Academy, a private day school in Echo Point, where my parents are trustees. It's just north of Boston and we have a house nearby. You can stay there."

"With you?" Maybe this little fantasy of mine could still work.

He pulled out his iPhone and started scrolling through messages. "No."

I nodded, trying to keep the tears at bay. "Just for the record, this really sucks."

He brushed past me down the hall. "Yes."

But did it suck more than going crazy? More than living in a halfway house?

No. No, it didn't.

So I decided to stop being emo and went to bed. I slept

better than I had in years. He may have been distant and dictatorial, but the idea of Bennett sleeping on the other side of the wall comforted me.

I woke early and set to packing. After watching my mother do it so often, stuffing my own suitcases was second nature. I was ridiculously excited about the plane ride—I hadn't left San Francisco since the Incident, when I was seven. Pre-Incident, my passport looked like I'd been adopted by the Jolie-Pitts, but one doctor had said, "She needs stability," and my parents had anchored me to the city.

The thought of Bennett sitting beside me curbed my enthusiasm. He'd be all cool and jaded about flying and I'd have to pretend I wasn't thrilled during takeoff so he didn't think I was acting like a child. Plus, his current demeanor—chilly and polite—was sort of a drag.

My wardrobe looked incomplete as I plopped it into the suitcase, so I decided to raid my mother's closet. I found a few scarves and snagged two cashmere sweaters before pausing at her jewelry case.

My mother had amazing jewelry. I tried to lift the lid, but it was locked. Good thing I knew the key was taped to the back of the dresser. Sadly, she'd left only the glittering gems, nestled in the pink satin, that were too dressy for everyday. I rifled through, looking for a piece that would remind me of her, but nothing was quite right. My finger caught on the bottom of the case and the satin lifted and I found a little carved pendant underneath. Hmm. Had it fallen through the seams or was she hiding it there?

It was the size of a quarter, a delicate art nouveau design made of green jade. Though I'd never seen my mother wear it, for some reason it reminded me of her. I strung it on a gold chain and clasped it around my neck. I smiled, knowing I had something of my mom's to take to Massachusetts, then locked the case and returned to my room.

As I passed through the hall I heard Bennett rustling around in my father's study. I sidled past the urns and found him standing in the middle of the room, his arms in a defensive position. He wore a black polo, fraying khakis, and yesterday's loafers. His skin was lightly tanned, probably left over from sailing in Nantucket all summer. God, I bet he looked great on a sailboat. Great with his shirt off. Great with—

He made one final motion then stopped, breathing deeply.

Something felt out of place in the room, but I didn't know what. I glanced at the musty old tomes in the bookcase about ancient burial rights, séances, and necromancy. Everything looked in order. Well, except for the obsession with the dead. I wished my parents would mix it up a bit and show some concern for the living every now and then. Even the *dying* would've been an improvement. Max had read every one of these books, but they'd told me to wait until I was older. Like I was eager to raid the library. If I wanted to commune with the dead I'd go graveyard-hopping with my friends.

Well, if I still had friends.

Bennett saw me in the doorway and dropped his arms.

"Tai chi?" I asked.

"What?"

"You were doing tai chi, right?"

He cocked an eyebrow.

"Or qigong or something," I said.

"Tai chi, right." He mimed holding a ball of energy, then tossed it into the air. "That's the beach ball pose."

I laughed. "No seriously. What are you doing in here?" But the question I wanted to ask was "Do the funeral urns freak you out?"

"I heard something in here, and I—"

"You heard him, too?"

"Who?" he asked.

I hesitated to reveal my imaginary smoky-snake guy for obvious reasons, but if Bennett thought he heard something, then maybe . . . Maybe what? He had nightmares, too? "Um . . . just the curtains in the breeze. I'm pretty sure that's all I saw. I mean, with our security system—"

"Don't play games with me, Emma. What did he look like?"

What games? I didn't know what Bennett wanted to hear. He couldn't know about the Incident, could he? If he knew and he was teasing me, that was just cruel.

Anyway, I wasn't going to tell him about my nightmares. So I said, "When do we leave?"

Bennett checked his watch. "Right now."

"Great," I said.

Takeoff was nothing special. I didn't get excited or any-thing.

I said: "Omigod! Here we go—woo-hoo! The front wheels are off the ground. There go the back wheels. We are officially airborne. We are *in* the sky. Look at all the tiny buildings. Hey! There's boats and fields and . . . We're in the clouds! Oops, nope—we're *over* the clouds. Wow. It's like a whole new world up here."

Bennett spoke nothing but monosyllables the entire trip, like something was bothering him. Possibly me. But since he said no more than "yes," "no," and "mmm," there was no way to tell for certain.

I knew people flew every day, but I still found it amaz-ing to wake up in San Francisco and go to sleep in Boston. Of course, not as amazing as putting on someone's death mask and reliving their dying thoughts. Or being smoth-ered in your dreams by ashes in your father's urn collection.

But those were delusions. Right?

We arrived in Boston late. Well, maybe ten at night, my time, but it still felt like one in the morning. Guess I was already adjusting. I'd never been to Boston—they really do have those crazy accents. I sort of loved it.

"Where did you pahk?" I asked Bennett.

He finally looked at me, struggling along with the luggage cart.

"I hope you didn't pahk the cah too fah," I told him.

A tiny smile finally escaped his stony face. "That's the worst Boston accent I've ever heard."

I felt a warm satisfaction at his tiny smile. And a warmer one when he relieved me of the luggage cart. We trekked to long-term parking where Bennett stopped at a decrepit Land Rover.

"You drive *this*?" I said.

"What's wrong with it?"

"Looks moody and irritable," I said, giving him a meaningful look as he tossed my bags in the back.

"Not at all," he said. "Totally trustworthy."

I started for the passenger seat, then stopped. "How come the wheel's in the wrong place?"

He got into the right side and me the left. "It came over from England," he said, pulling out of the spot. "It's my lucky car."

"Why? Because it's where you got lucky?" I glanced at the back seat, trying not to picture the kind of girls he liked. Abercrombie & Fitch models. With their tops off.

"Well . . ." There was a spark in his eye before he remembered himself and frowned at me. "How old are you again?"

"I'm seventeen."

"Just a kid."

"You're only twenty, right?"

"I wouldn't say 'only.'"

I would, because that meant he wasn't too old for me.

"I signed you up for junior year," he said. "If you're seventeen, shouldn't you be a senior?"

"I started school late." Actually, I repeated a year, but that required more explanation involving the Incident.

Instead, I laid my head against the seat and watched the scenery. I counted five Dunkin' Donuts—which I'd never seen in San Francisco—before giving in to exhaustion and letting my eyes flutter shut.

When I woke, we were pulling into a long drive lined with maple trees.

"We're here," Bennett said.

He stopped the car in front of a museum. A four-story house with columns, a solarium, multiple chimneys, and extensive grounds.

A sign in front read:

Welcome to Stern House Museum
A Federal period home
Designed by Adam McIntyre

"Here where?" I asked. "I thought you were taking me to your house."

"This is it."

"You live in a museum?"

He snorted. "Like you can talk. I've seen your house."

He stepped out and I followed him to the back of the Land Rover, where he was retrieving my suitcases.

"But—this really is a museum," I said.

"Only in the summer. You'll be gone by then."

Gone where? Everything hit me at once. What was I doing in Massachusetts, staying at Bennett's museum? I didn't really know Bennett, or why Max hated him now. And where were my parents? Why hadn't they called?

I'd been ignoring my feelings of abandonment, the panic and the rejection, just refusing to think about it— like I refused to think about so many things. Yet now it all hit me, and I slumped into the house behind Bennett, feeling more alone than ever.

My only consolation was that I no longer had to avoid the funeral urns at home. That and, well—the place was spectacular. There was a sweeping staircase with a gleaming mahogany banister, two adorable parlors, a cozy library, and more bedrooms than I could count. The decor was mostly sea greens, yellows, and blues, invoking a classic sense of sun and ocean wherever I went.

"And you'll like this," Bennett said, throwing open a set of double doors in the middle of a wide hallway.

I stepped through. "A ballroom?" I twirled across the floor. "This is gorgeous. You know, it turns out I throw a *great* party."

"No," he said. "No, no, no."

"I'm kidding!"

He eyed me suspiciously. "I can never tell with you."

We wandered into the north-parlor and after admiring the white bas-relief mantel and mosaic tile floor, I caught Bennett's eye in the gold mirror over the fireplace. "Do you think they're dead?" I asked. It was getting harder to come up with any other excuse for my parents' lack of communication.

"Of course," he said.

"That's not funny."

"What else would they be?"

When I saw he was serious, I fell back onto an embroidered silk couch. "How—how do you know?"

"What?"

"My parents are—"

He looked stricken. "No, no! Your *parents*? No." He sat beside me. "Emma, I have no idea where they are, but I know they're not dead."

"How? How do you know?"

After a brief pause, he said, "I just know."

His tone was so confident that the tightness in my chest loosened. "Then who did you mean? Who's dead?"

He shrugged. "The people who lived here, back in the day. My ancestors, their servants."

I glanced around the room, looking for photos, portraits, some evidence of anyone who'd once resided here. There was nothing but paintings of seascapes and schooners. "Why would you think I was talking about them?"

He stood. "You're tired."

"But—"

"I'll show you your room."

My new bedroom waited at the end of a wide hallway on the second floor. Behind the thick cherry wooden door I found a surprisingly bright room, even at this time of night, with long paned windows and pale yellow curtains.

A teal blue Shaker dresser lined one wall and a matching wardrobe fit snugly in the opposite corner. There was an adorably minuscule fireplace and a raised four-poster bed frame with pineapple carvings and white linens.

I flopped onto the bed and the room seemed suddenly crowded by the presence of . . . I don't know. Of history, I guess. The antique furniture, the nickel doorknob polished by hundreds of hands over hundreds of years. The generations of Bennett's family who'd slept in the bed.

But mostly, I was conscious of the proximity of Bennett. He looked as unyielding as his last name—Stern—and unhappy to be here or maybe just unhappy with me.

"Why pineapples?" I asked, looking at the bed frame.

"They're a symbol of hospitality in New England."

"That doesn't make any sense," I said. "They don't grow in Massachusetts. They don't belong here."

But I wasn't really talking about the pineapples.

Bennett dropped my suitcases inside the door. "They're expecting you at school tomorrow. There's a uniform in the wardrobe, I guessed on the size. You're not due until ten."

I nodded, too exhausted to think about starting a new school while wearing some horrible uniform. I did have one question, though. "Bennett, why? Why did you come for me?"

He leaned in the doorway, his khakis wrinkled and eyes weary. "I don't know . . . yet."

. . .

I fell asleep the minute my head hit the pillow. The room was completely dark when I woke to a scraping noise from the corner.

"Bennett?" I murmured.

C'est moi. Stoking the fire. Rest easy.

I sighed back into slumber.

When I stirred again, hours later, dying embers glowed in the little bedroom fireplace. And I remembered the voice in the middle of the night. It wasn't Bennett.

It was a woman.

7

Sunlight streaming through the window woke me. I climbed from bed, disoriented. The ormolu clock on the mantel said 9:25 and I couldn't remember when Bennett said I needed to be at school. Ten o'clock?

I stumbled down the hall. "Hello? Bennett?"

No answer. He was probably downstairs, whipping together a breakfast of blueberry pancakes with warm maple syrup, and couldn't hear me over the sizzling of the pan.

I found the bathroom and took a *freeeezing* shower.

"There's no hot water!" I yelled downstairs, as I stomped back to my room.

I put on underwear and raced to the wardrobe. Grabbed the uniform and shivered in front of what was left of the fire. I slipped on the navy plaid skirt—minuscule—and the white button-down and navy wool blazer—snug. My God, Bennett thought I was a preteen. There was a striped tie, but I had no idea how to tie it, so I knotted it around my neck like a scarf. Even with the heat of the banked fire, my legs were goose pimpled. I glanced out the window at the cold, cloudy day, wondering if I'd ever be warm again.

I found gray thigh-high tights in my suitcase and pulled them on. They stopped an inch below the skirt. I slipped into my boots and examined myself in the wardrobe mirror. I looked like a Catholic school slut. But there was no time to worry about it. My pancakes would be getting cold.

When I arrived downstairs I found no pancakes. No Bennett. No strange woman attending the kitchen fire.

Nothing but a note on the table:

Called away. Didn't want to wake you. Go to school.
Make friends.
     Bennett

No "love" before the Bennett?

"Called away." Everyone in my life got called away, and nobody ever told me why—and then they didn't return. Just once, I wanted to be the reason someone got called away instead of the person they got called away from.

I shredded the letter and scattered the pieces over the kitchen table, which made me feel a little better.

I found a strawberry yogurt in the fridge and snagged a spoon and my wool coat on the way out the door. Last night, Bennett told me the school was only three blocks up the hill. I dug into my yogurt and started walking.

The neighborhood was sweet. The houses were

shuttered Colonials shoved too closely together with wrought-iron fences surrounding little gardens filled with late-blooming pansies and mums. Maple trees shed russet leaves and Indian corn was tacked to front doors. Everything looked picture-perfect New Englandy.

I stopped to pet a black Lab and asked his owner for directions to the school. The dog slobbered on my spoon and the man told me to keep going. "You'll know it when you see it."

The man moved on, oblivious that his dog now had my yogurt container in his mouth, and I was left alone in the cold with a dog-licked spoon. What was I doing here? My parents gone, my friends gone—losing my mind and stuck three thousand miles from home.

I wanted to curl into a ball and never unwind myself. But I remembered Bennett saying "I don't know . . . yet."

That little *yet* pushed me forward. I'd give him a reason for rescuing me, for keeping me out of a halfway house. I'd go to school. I'd make friends. And I'd live in Bennett's museum until he knew I was worth saving.

My newfound resolution didn't falter until I found myself in front of a tidy blue house at the top of the hill. I reached for the doorbell beside the black lacquer door and stopped.

What was I doing here? This wasn't the school. My feet just led me to the door, the way you don't have to think when you're walking home. Except I'd never been here before. I'd never even been to Massachusetts. Yet there was something so familiar about it.

A chill touched me. Maybe there was something really wrong with me. I mean more than nightmares and a too-lively imagination. My parents abandoned me, then Natalie betrayed me, and Bennett took me away. That was enough to throw a sane person, let alone one who was digging into ashes of the dead.

Maybe I had a brain tumor. That would explain a lot.

As I debated my sanity, the door opened and a tall woman with short dark hair and a slight smile said, "Emma Vaile?"

"Oh! Yes. Um . . . hello."

"I'm Dean Grant. Bennett Stern told me to expect you." She frowned slightly. "Is the doorbell broken?"

"No, I just—is this the school?" Because it looked more like a cottage than a school. If I was going to be home-schooled, what was I doing in this jailbait uniform?

"Dean's office," she said. "That's the school."

She gestured next door toward a stone wall with a gated entrance. I couldn't see anything but the tops of trees behind the massive wall, which implied that the school was at least school-sized. From the outside, it looked like the sort of place that required a uniform. And a chauffeured car.

"My intern will walk you up," the dean said.

She disappeared into the cottage and returned a moment later with a tall dark-haired guy wearing the boy version of my uniform—only his fit—and his wiry frame and deep green eyes made it look good. Bennett used to go here. I wondered if he'd looked as cute.

"This is Coby Anders," Dean Grant said. "He's got your

schedule and will make sure you get to class. If you have any questions, you know where to find me."

Coby held out his hand to me. "Nice to meet you, Emma. Welcome to Thatcher."

"Uh," I replied, dumbfounded. Guys at home mostly gave me a halfhearted "Hey," and never a handshake. And Coby wasn't even performing for the dean's benefit, since after introducing us, she'd closed the door behind her.

I took his hand and said, "Pleased to meet you," feeling like a complete impostor. I followed him to the front gate, wondering if all the kids were going to be like this. If so, I was going to have a hard time with Bennett's "make friends" request. I'd left my copy of Emily Post back in San Francisco.

"This is your schedule." Coby gave me a sheet of paper from a folder he carried. "Thatcher doesn't offer all the courses you were taking and we have some different requirements, so it may seem a little weird at first."

I didn't respond. Because if we were talking weirdness, I wanted to know why I felt like I'd been here before.

We walked down the cobblestone drive, past sprawling lawns and crooked apple trees, and I recalled the crisp taste of the low-hanging fruit, the soft patch of grass perfect for a picnic, and a stolen kiss in the shadowed gazebo.

"Are you all right?" Coby asked. "You look a little flushed."

"It's the gazebo," I said.

He turned toward the corner of the lawn. "What gazebo?"

"Right th—" I looked again, and the gazebo was gone. "There. That looks like a good place for one. Don't you think?"

"For a gazebo." His tone was teasing.

"Yeah. I think it'd really . . . um . . . tie the lawn together." I giggled, slightly hysterically. "Maybe I'm a little jet-lagged. And hungry. A dog stole my yogurt on the way here."

Coby pulled an apple from a branch overhanging the path. "You want an apple? One a day keeps the . . . Well, my dad's a doctor. He says it keeps you regular." He cleared his throat. "I don't know why I said that."

"Thanks," I said.

I took a bite as we rounded a curve and saw the school: pale stone and paneled windows, with marbled steps leading to a grand entrance. Not a cottage, not a house— a mansion.

We mounted the steps and the crunch of the apple sounded in my ears; the sweet juice flowing in my mouth tasted so familiar. And my feet on the steps were even more so, as though I'd climbed them hundreds of times before. Then there was that great whooshing sound—

The world spun around me, like a merry-go-round, when everything speeds up and twirls and you can't see anything except a blur of color and motion. Then everything stopped. I pressed a hand to my cheek and found myself wearing a blue dress with puffy sleeves and a long full skirt. I felt wrong—constricted and short of breath. I couldn't breathe.

Panic rising, I began to pant. I fingered my rib cage and discovered a corset. The day was suddenly night, with torches illuminating the path and families in fancy dress stepping from carriages, through a gauntlet of uniformed footmen into the mansion. I'd been transported to the past again, just like I had with the death mask.

I yanked at the dress, fighting to breathe, desperate to return to myself. I couldn't tear the thing off. I started at the top button and—

Whooosh!

I lay on the ground, with Coby kneeling over me.

"Are you all right?" he asked.

"I'm back."

He nodded. "You fainted. Well, after you started unbuttoning."

"Oh God."

The blouse I wore under the slutty uniform was undone to my navel. I felt myself blush and clasped the shirt together over my bra, then quickly buttoned up.

"We should go to the nurse," Coby said. "Or if you want, I'll call my dad."

I shook my head. "No, I just . . ." What was I going to tell him? That I was transported back in time? "It's only jet lag. And I'm a little nervous about starting a new school."

"You do look a little . . ."

Scared? I was terrified. What was happening to me? Who was I supposed to tell? The dean? Bennett? A psychiatrist?

". . . pale," he finished.

"I'm fine," I said. "Just majorly embarrassed."

"Yeah," he said, pulling me to my feet. "Nobody wants to spend their first day passed out on the front steps. That's for prom night."

"Oh God," I said. "You think I'm a drug addict."

"No, no. Just a drunk."

"I'm not!"

He laughed. "I'm kidding." He laid a hand over his heart and flashed a boyish grin. "I promise not to tell anyone."

For some reason, I trusted him.

"C'mon," he said. "I'll show you to your first class."

We stepped into a foyer that rose two stories high, a chandelier illuminating the pale glow of white marble. Two medieval French tapestries hung from the walls, depicting scenes of pastoral countryside with manors in the distance. A grandfather clock stood at the foot of the stairs, grander than I'd ever seen. Off to the left was a reading nook with chairs and settees arranged around a large hearth.

I was a long way from public school.

Coby noticed my expression. "Kind of cool, huh?"

"You could roast a pig in that thing," I told him, eyeing the hearth.

"My friend Harry and I tried once."

"What? Really?"

"Didn't go well." He sighed. "The pig escaped."

My laughter echoed off the walls. "It was *alive*?"

"We didn't have the heart to kill it."

"So it was more of a theoretical exercise," I said.

"Exactly." Coby led me toward a hallway. "You know, I think you'll like it here."

"I think you're right," I said.

Because as I trailed Coby through the historic halls of Thatcher, I felt as though I'd come home.

8

The feeling didn't last. Roaming the halls of my new school, I felt as if I'd wandered into a play and was distinctly unprepared for the lead role.

The setting: Thatcher Academy. Once a grand mansion, the institution still maintained its charming Georgian decor, open rooms, distinguished portraits, and marble floors. The classrooms and corridors were elegant and refined, the student body even more so.

Enter Emma Vaile, the new kid.

My mom took me to a play a few years ago, a period piece involving class issues. The lead character, a young maid, always dressed differently from the rest of the cast. If they were done up for dinner, she was in her nightclothes. When she was gowned for a ball, they were in riding costumes.

That's how I felt walking into my first Trigonometry class. I was unprepared for the lack of . . . well, students. There were only ten, in addition to me and Coby, who led me to a quaint wooden desk before finding one himself. Was he going to shadow me all day? I wasn't exactly an invalid who needed to be wheeled from class to class— although given my fainting spell, I could see why he thought maybe he should stick close.

"You don't need to stay," I whispered to him. "I'll be fine."

"Homework, please," the teacher, Mr. Sakolsky, said.

Coby grinned and pulled a notebook from his backpack. He handed his homework to the student in front of him who passed it on.

"Oh," I said. He was in the class.

"And let's all welcome Emma Vaile," said Mr. Sakolsky.

"Oh," I said, louder, as everyone turned to stare at me.

Yes, we all wore the same uniform, but somehow I looked ready for a costume party, dressed as the slutty schoolgirl, while the other girls appeared ready for their close-ups in *Elle*. And it wasn't just my minuscule uniform. They were the epitome of chic, with carelessly blown-out hairstyles, artfully knotted ties, eclectic jewelry, and oversized leather bags in place of backpacks. And the guys weren't all that different—well, less jewelry maybe.

"Hi!" I said with an idiotic wave. "I'm Emma."

"Yeah, we got that," a petite blonde said with a well-mannered sneer.

"Britta," Coby warned. "Don't bite."

"I never bite," she purred at him. "I only nibble."

So I hated her already.

I inwardly sighed. How come when you started at a new school you couldn't suddenly become someone else? Smarter or prettier or more popular? Maybe a magnet to cute guys instead of the idiotic waver. I glanced at the clock on the wall. It took me all of twenty minutes to become the same girl I'd always been.

I actually liked math, so I tried to concentrate, but everything conspired to distract me. How different the kids looked and how few of them there were. It'd be impossible to disappear into a crowd here, which made me nervous. And the classroom itself looked like some fancy English club: walls of dark paneled wood, the ceiling ornately carved, and an Oriental carpet under the teacher's antique desk.

As Mr. Sakolsky blabbed on about inverse functions, I tried to take notes, but none of it was making sense. I couldn't stop thinking about what had happened outside. How I had felt like I'd been here before. The gazebo and the vision of a previous time. What was happening to me? I'd rather be boring old me than the new girl who went insane her first week at school.

I glanced at the equations on the board, and noticed another teacher standing at the front of the room, a tall man in an old-fashioned brown suit, watching me intently. He was thin, a little stooped, and had a dramatically receding hairline. A frown creased his brow when he saw that I'd noticed him, and he greeted me with a little wave.

I lifted my hand in return.

"Yes, Emma?" Mr. Sakolsky asked. "You have a question?"

"No, I just—" I stopped when the man in the brown suit shook his head sharply. And I realized that nobody else in the room saw him.

Perfect. This time, I hadn't even felt that whooshing feeling, or been transported into a vision. I was just sitting here in the classroom with Coby and Britta and the other kids turning to look at me.

I wanted to scream, *Don't you see him? He's standing right there. He waved to me!* Instead, I gritted my teeth. Must not completely freak out my first day at school. "I, um, no, I—"

"Do you need the little girl's room?" Britta asked, fake sweetly.

The man in the brown suit pointed to a word on the blackboard: *Homework.*

"I kinda missed the homework assignment," I said, and the man in the brown suit nodded in satisfaction.

"Yeah, 'do the problems on pages forty-five and forty-six' is pretty complex," Britta said.

"Emma's been working from another text," Mr. Sakolsky said, a little sharply. "Perhaps you might help her, Britta."

Britta rolled her eyes, and Coby said, "I'll show her."

The girls in the class exchanged significant glances, but Sakolsky seemed oblivious. "Fine, fine," he said.

It was only my first class and I was already making all

the wrong moves. I might have been more concerned if I wasn't worried my sanity was slowly crumbling apart.

In the hallway outside the classroom, Coby took me aside and said, "This is the tricky part." He flipped to page forty-five in my book. "There you go! And I'm pretty sure page forty-six is somewhere nearby."

"Very funny."

"Do you want me to dog-ear them for you?" he asked innocently.

I glared at him.

He grinned. "Seemed more like you were spacing than you didn't understand. You probably wouldn't be taking Trig if you couldn't find page numbers in the book."

Yeah, if I spaced any more—seeing imaginary brown-suited men—I'd launch into orbit. I was saved from answering when a striking chestnut-haired girl turned the corner.

"Hey, Sara," Coby called to her. "You've got Fencing now?"

She glided over, her skirt flipping slinkily around her thighs. "Yes," she said, her voice deep and raspy, like one of those sexy old movie sirens. "Why?"

"This is Emma. Emma, Sara."

"Um. Pleased to meet you," I said.

Her laugh, while also deep and raspy, was maybe a little too polished. "Likewise, I'm sure," she said.

I couldn't tell if she was mocking my attempt at manners or being truly polite, so I gave an uncertain smile.

"Can you take Emma with you?" Coby turned to me. "Then you've got lunch. Just follow everyone. There's only one cafeteria."

"Wait, did you say *fencing*? Like . . ." I waved an imaginary épée in the air, a word I only knew because my father was obsessed with crosswords. "Swords and stuff?"

"We call them foils," Sara said dryly.

Coby glanced at his watch. "Coach will kill me if I'm late for practice. See you later." And he jogged down the hall, leaving me hanging with the gorgeous, sexy-voiced Sara.

"How'd that get on my schedule? I don't fence."

"It's tradition," she said, sauntering down the hall.

She didn't bother to wait for me, so I galumphed after her in my big boots, trying to keep my skirt from riding higher and my thigh-highs from dropping to my shins.

"Everyone learns to fence at Thatcher," she said, leading me around a corner.

"I guess I should be grateful it's not horseback riding," I said.

She looked at me. "You don't ride?"

"Not if I want to walk the next day."

She laughed, this time without the edge of supercilious politeness. "You're funny."

"Thanks?" I wasn't quite sure if that was a compliment, so I changed the subject. "What does Coby play?"

"Football."

"They practice in the middle of the day? And isn't he kind of regular sized for that?"

"Not if you're the quarterback. And they get PE credit for it. When they get closer to games they practice after school, too."

"Let me get this straight." I made ticks with my fingers. "The dean's intern, a perfect gentleman, a doctor's son, a quarterback. So basically, Coby's the all-American boy?"

Sara smiled, though she didn't look happy. "Yes."

She led me down another hallway and introduced me to a crowd of kids lounging in a room that looked like you needed a membership to enter. There were leather club chairs and built-in bookshelves and potted palms. Along one wall was a row of mahogany wooden lockers. Everyone greeted me with the same effortless ease that Coby had, and I smiled, nodded, and immediately forgot everyone's name. Fidgeting in my uniform and glancing around warily for people who weren't really there, I felt completely out of my element.

At the end of a corridor with an arched roof, we went down a flight of narrow stairs into the locker room which— amazingly—looked like a regular locker room. Sara found me a fencing costume and a locker and left me to my own devices.

I slipped into the canvas jacket, knickers, and knee socks and once I'd connected the protective vest around my chest and propped the mask on my head, I felt good. Formidable. I was ready to slay the errant dragon or two, when Sara came around the lockers and giggled at me.

"Close," she said.

She removed my vest and put it on frontways and Velcro-ed it in the back. Apparently, I had the mask upside down, too. She, of course, looked completely stylish in her uniform, like she'd had it tailored.

"C'mon," she said, dragging me through the doors to the gym. "This is going to be fun."

If your idea of fun is being stabbed repeatedly by a pointy sword that even though it has a little protective ball at the end *still hurts*, then I had a blast.

9

I nursed my bruises through the lunch hour, whiled away by myself in an empty classroom. I couldn't handle the lunch crowd—not while trying to suppress my panic about all the terrifying strangeness in my life. Plus I had forgotten to bring lunch.

After my last class—World Literature, in which half the kids read the books in their original languages—I slunk out the side door and, instead of going straight home, wandered through the pretty little coastal village. I didn't get back to the museum until after four.

As I pushed through the gates, I caught a flash of motion among the maples. Behind an ancient tree, I found a patch of bare ground. There was a circle drawn in the dirt, cleaned of fallen leaves but scattered with acorns. No, not acorns. I leaned down and grabbed one. Marbles, little clay marbles. I didn't even know marbles *came* in clay.

Next to the circle was an old-fashioned slingshot, left

behind by some kid. I gathered it, along with the marbles, figuring the museum had a lost and found. I got halfway to the door when I saw him. A little boy, maybe ten years old, lurking in the bushes, watching with sad eyes. I couldn't see much more than his thin, pale face, but that was enough; he was afraid I'd confiscated his toys and he'd never see them again.

"Are these yours?" I called.

The bush rustled, but he didn't say anything.

"Don't worry," I said, smiling to reassure him. "I know what it's like, losing your marbles."

He still didn't answer. Shy kid. So I left the marbles and the slingshot on the ground, and headed for the entrance. I turned at the door in time to see him grab his toys. He shot me a huge smile from his grimy little face.

Now if only I could charm an errant guardian.

I let myself inside and instead of yelling, "I'm home! Did you miss me?" I quietly combed the house for Bennett.

He wasn't there, but I found further evidence that he thought of me as a child on the kitchen table—he'd left a snack of cheese and crackers and a sliced apple. He'd even peeled the apple, just like my mom.

I inhaled the snack and drank a huge glass of milk.

"Thanks," I told the empty kitchen. "Though you could've packed me a lunch."

I stumbled upstairs for a much-needed nap. Trig and Fencing had been just the beginning. I didn't start Latin until tomorrow—which I was actually looking forward to—but I'd taken a beating in Advanced Biology and Western Civilization, in which I suspected I was the only student who identified with the plebeians.

In my room, I discovered the bed neatly made, with the pillows fluffed and the coverlet turned down. Strange, because Bennett didn't seem like the bed-making type. And despite wanting to cuddle with him under the covers, it felt odd to have him make it first.

I tossed my school uniform over the easy chair in the corner, slipped into black leggings and my favorite wool sweater, then flopped onto the cream bedspread. I closed my eyes and waited for the oblivion of sleep—so of course my mind raced.

The nightmare of ashes in San Francisco. The death mask. The vision today when I'd worn the old dress and corset, and the man in the brown suit. I finally admitted to myself what I'd known all along: this was all related to the Incident.

But that ended ten years go. Why was it happening again now?

The Incident.

Three weeks after turning seven, my parents committed me to the poof. That's the sweet, powder-puffy way of saying "children's mental hospital." I didn't remember much about that time, just a few scattered and unsettling images, but I did know why I'd spent three formative months there.

Because I'd had too many imaginary friends.

How many is too many? I saw them everywhere.

I couldn't wander the grocery store without make-believe clerks offering me Chips Ahoy. A Chinese grandmother ran my bath at night and clucked her tongue at my scrawny frame. At least twice a week I had a sleepover with a twelve-year-old redhead named Katie. And I always stood on the trolley, avoiding the "empty" seats occupied by people nobody else saw.

Then one day my imagination went too far.

I'd been drawing chalk rainbows on the sidewalk in front of the store when a pair of black shoes stepped onto my purple and blue. I peered up at the man—tall and rawboned, with wet lips and bright black eyes like a crow. I remembered his long hands, spiderwebbed with veins, stroking a brown leather dog leash. They looked so much older than his face.

"Have you seen my little dog?" he asked. "My little white dog?"

I shook my head. "Sorry."

"My poor lost Snowball, all alone." His voice sounded mournful. "She's very frightened. Will you help me find her?"

I said, "Sure."

I brushed the chalk off my palms, leaving pastel streaks on my jeans, and followed him down the street . . . and into an abandoned storefront. I'd felt a sick sense of wrongness in my stomach. The moment we were inside, surrounded by bare shelves and ominous stains on the floor, I'd known there was no little white dog.

The man stood between me and the door. "You have something I need," he said.

I whimpered and shook my head.

"You must take your clothes off," he said.

"I don't want to."

He raised his hand and spread his spindly fingers. "Then I'll help you."

He stepped closer, blotting out the daylight. A stench rose, of rotting food and mildewed mud. His bone white teeth glinted as he pulled a gleaming blade from his pocket and swiped at me.

I raised my arms to protect myself, and his knife struck my forearm, leaving a frozen ache behind. A splatter of my blood arced through the air. He caught my blood in the cup of his left hand, a glossy red-black that dissolved into his flesh as he moaned with animal hunger and—

"Emma!" My mother burst inside, somehow looking both hesitant and fierce. "Tell me, what do you see?"

"The—the man!" I trembled with fear. "The man!"

She scanned the wreckage. "Where? Where is he, Emma?"

"He has my blood." I'd sobbed and pointed at the man, knowing she couldn't see him, knowing she couldn't help me. How do you protect someone from a nightmare?

The man smiled at my mother with a terrifying, hungry pleasure. Then he said, "Your blood tastes like power."

"He can't hurt you anymore," my mother said, pulling me close. "He's gone now."

"No!" I hid my face against her. "He's right there. He's laughing."

"God help me," my mother said, with real fear in her voice. I'll never forget that.

She dragged me at a run back to the apartment, through the security system, into Dad's office. "Nathan! Nathan, we can't go on like this." I remember the streaks of tears on her face.

By the next evening, I'd been committed. I remember the stuffed elephant they sent with me to the hospital, the taste of lime Popsicles, and the scent of the man in the shop. The doctor told my parents I needed stability—and that I needed drugs to keep me from hurting myself.

And they'd fixed me.

But now, ten years later, I felt myself falling into the same nightmare. I lay on the bed in Bennett's museum, staring through the window at the cold blue sky. My mind brimmed with too many questions: Where were my parents and Max? Why did they all leave me? How did Bennett know I was in trouble, and why did he bring me here?

And most important . . . why was I seeing things again?

I felt a bleak certainty that I didn't want to know the answer. You start seeing things, then you start hearing things—and then they send you back to the poof. It had been bad enough as a child—I didn't want to think about a mental hospital for teens. For one thing, they probably didn't give you lime Popsicles.

So, I'd pull myself together. Forget the craziness. Go to school. Make friends. Just like Bennett said.

I woke in the dark, groggy and confused. It took a moment to realize I was in my bedroom in the museum—and there was someone in the room with me. I sat up abruptly and clicked on the light, but I was alone. Then I heard noises from downstairs. Finally, Bennett had returned—hopefully with pizza.

I went into the bathroom to fix myself. I splashed cold water—the only kind available—over my face and tried to cover the shadows under my eyes with concealer. It only seemed to highlight them, so I washed my face again, then brushed my bangs toward my eyes, hoping Bennett wouldn't notice the raccoon rings underneath.

In the kitchen, I didn't find Bennett or pizza—though I could smell some kind of roast that made my stomach rumble. The light flashed on the old-fashioned answering machine on the counter and I pressed Play.

"Emma," Bennett's voice said. "Sorry I'm not there. Things are taking longer than I'd hoped, so I asked Martha to look after you 'til I get back—you'll like her. Please don't break the house." He paused a moment. "Please don't break Martha, either."

Beeeep.

"I miss you, too," I told the answering machine.

What things? Wasn't he supposed to be in school? I got the distinct impression Bennett was trying to avoid me, exactly when I wanted nothing more than to drag a few answers out of him. At least he hadn't completely forgotten me. On the other hand, *Martha*?

Who was she? Some old lady to babysit me? She'd probably want to make me warm milk, read me bedtime stories, and tuck me in at night. Actually, that didn't sound so bad.

Then I realized that's who must've made dinner. I called out, "Martha?"

No answer. I followed the scent of comfort food into the dining room and found dinner waiting. My meal was laid out on gold and white china with a swirly pattern. The utensils were real silver with the soft patina of constant use and an etched crystal glass was filled with ice water. A fire danced in the massive brick fireplace, gently illuminating the soft green walls and creamy woodwork. The table was mahogany and looked as though it would seat thirty.

And I was completely alone. "Martha?"

I checked the entire downstairs, then looked in the driveway. No car. No nothing.

So I sat down at one end of the long table, feeling like a ridiculous movie cliché—the solitary billionaire dining alone in his castle. Though given my life lately, it was more like I'd wandered into Wonderland. I couldn't decide whether I was Alice or the Mad Hatter.

Dinner was oddly old-fashioned: pot roast, peas, and

boiled potatoes. I'd pegged Bennett as more of a takeout sushi kind of guy; no way he chose the menu. I hardly knew where to start—this wasn't exactly California fare.

I devoured it.

When I finished, I took my dirty dishes to the kitchen and ran a sink of sudsy water. I left everything soaking and did my homework in the sitting room by the front door, so I'd hear Bennett when he came home. My Trig homework was the most difficult. You'd think two pages wouldn't take forty-five minutes and it was after ten before I got through the Sophocles assignment for World Lit.

Jet-lagged and stuffed with pot roast, I felt my eyes begin to droop. Where was Bennett? I'd vowed to pounce on him before going to bed—with *questions*, that's all— but I couldn't wait any longer. I climbed the majestic staircase, brushed my teeth, and slept like the dead.

10

Early the next morning, the pale light of dawn glowed through my bedroom curtains. It was far too early to be awake—and far too chilly to leave the toasty cocoon of my comforter. As I snuggled back to sleep, I glimpsed a slim woman hanging my uniform in the wardrobe, her red hair backlit by the dawn. The mysterious Martha. Not at all how I pictured her.

She saw me watching and put a finger to her generous, smiling mouth, shushing me back to sleep. I returned her smile drowsily and somehow comforted by her presence, drifted immediately back asleep.

When I woke again, the dawn had passed into morning and a fire blazed in the little hearth. Charming and romantic, but I wish someone would find the central heating. I shivered in front of the flames before dashing into the bathroom for another freezing shower.

Did Bennett ever stay here? Had he simply not noticed

there was no hot water? I vowed to look for the furnace when I came back from school.

Downstairs, I found the kitchen sink empty, the dishes put away and a meal waiting in the breakfast nook. After wasting ten minutes looking for Martha . . . or Bennett . . . or anyone, I sat down to eat. Freshly roasted coffee, with white toast and a soft-boiled egg in a hand-painted egg-cup. Actually, I didn't know it was soft-boiled until I tried to roll the peel off like a hard-boiled and the innards oozed all over my plate.

"Yuck." I dumped my plate into the sink. "I only like scrambled." I wrinkled my nose at the coffee. "And tea."

Not that there was anyone there to hear me. All alone, as usual.

I buttered the toast and tried to jump-start a romantic daydream about Bennett cooking for me and starting the fire and setting the table with candles and roses. But it was undoubtedly the elusive Martha who was doing all the work.

I finished my toast, opened the fridge to make lunch, and found a small wicker basket on the top shelf. Packed tidily inside were a little tomato tart, slices of cheese, grapes, and a wedge of pound cake.

"Well, hello!" I said. "Much better."

I left the house in my ridiculously snug uniform, black leggings, and my requisite boots. I'd fiddled in front of my wardrobe mirror for twenty minutes with accessories, trying to emulate the chic looks of the other girls, but it was useless. My mother had been right about my hair being too short. And I'd never been good with makeup, so I'd just run product through my hair and glossed my lips.

My only jewelry was my mother's jade pendant tucked into my blouse, a sort of touchstone for home and family and everything I'd lost. My mood soured as I thought about that and I trudged the three blocks to school, resenting the sunny, crisp day for not reflecting my dark temper.

I found Coby and Sara sitting on the steps of the dean's office with a dark mop-haired guy who somehow looked both completely well-groomed and utterly sloppy at the same time. They stood as if they'd been waiting for me.

"Hey," I said.

"Hi, Emma," Coby said, as we all headed to the school gates. "You look—"

"Pissed," Sara finished. "Or is that how you always look in the morning?"

If possible, her voice was even rougher today, like it hadn't quite woken up yet. Her hair and makeup, though? Flawless. Along with her red wool coat, black suede boots, and bag suited for an LA starlet.

"I was going to say spunky," Coby said.

"Even better," I said.

Sara giggled. "That came out worse than I meant it to."

"It's okay." Actually, I was sort of pleased that someone noticed my mood. "I'm still settling in."

"You're living at the Sterns'?" the new guy asked.

"This is Harry," Coby said.

"Harrison," he corrected, and unlike everyone else at Thatcher, he didn't offer to shake. Instead, he thrust his hands into his pants pockets, looking like a brooding upper-class poet with a hangover.

"Harry Harrison?" I asked.

"Harrison Devereaux Armitage the seventeenth," Sara told me.

"The *fourth*," Harry said.

"Just call him Harry," Coby said. "Everyone does."

"He's such a Harry." Sara pressed a finger to Harry's chest, like she was sticking something to him. "Face it, you're stuck with it."

Harry arched an eyebrow and brooded silently. Were the three of them just friends? Sara was too hot for Coby and Harry *not* to be interested.

"I hope you're not bruised," she told me. "From fencing yesterday."

"Oh, how'd that go?" Coby asked.

"I was a pincushion," I said.

"Sorry about that," Sara said with a crooked smile. "We've all been taking since freshman year."

"Can't have been worse than Trig," Coby said. "Did you do the homework?"

"Yeah." I frowned. "How long did it take you?"

"An hour." He groaned. "Sakolsky always assigns too much. It's not like we don't have other classes."

I'd only spent forty-five minutes. We'd see if I got any of the answers right.

We passed through the apple orchard and I noticed

Coby eyeing me, probably wondering if I'd start un-buttoning my shirt again. But nothing happened: no whooshing, no memories, no nothing. And walking with the three of them into the grand foyer, my mood began to lighten. Bring on the sunshine.

Turned out Harry had Latin with me, so I followed him to class. He showed his first bit of politeness by gesturing me into the classroom before him, but I couldn't help feeling he was mocking me. Then he partnered with me for dialogues and immediately started a conversation that had nothing to do with the verb tenses we were meant to be practicing.

"Vestri velitatio est brevis."*

"Ego non animadverto."**

And it went on from there. My blouse was too tight, I might pop a button—I had nice legs, but I should learn how to knot a tie. I'm not even going to repeat what he said about my lips. I should've been offended, but I was a tiny bit pleased instead. Back home, I wasn't the girl a guy flirted with like that, and I definitely wouldn't have flirted back. But now I toyed with my hair and just barely stopped myself from nibbling seductively on the cap of my pen. With my luck, the ink would've spilled all over my face.

---

* Your skirt is short.

** I hadn't noticed.

Through all of this, Harry maintained his attitude of ennui, absently taking notes on a sheet of lined paper. The teacher, known as Mr. Z, wove between desks, checking in on conversations, offering suggestions and corrections. Then he stopped and peered over Harry's shoulder. "And what have you two been discussing?"

I panicked, but Harry simply shrugged and showed Mr. Z his paper. "Just getting to know each other."

Oh my God. He hadn't written all that down, had he?

Mr. Z frowned at the page, and I leaned forward to read Harry's notes. In perfect grammatical Latin he'd detailed a conversation about my life in San Francisco and his in Massachusetts. Apparently, I liked long walks on the beach while he was into sailing. It was all perfectly banal and innocent.

I smiled at him, stifling a laugh. Forward, rude, and sort of brilliant. As good as I was at Latin, I couldn't have had one conversation and written down another. I found him impossible not to like.

After class, he escorted me to the second floor, murmuring a steady stream of arch comments about the passing students. A freshman boy helplessly in love with his best friend's older sister, despite that she only dated college guys. A student who ran away from home when her parents divorced. Some faceless kid who'd gone to rehab last year.

"A blackout drunk," Harry said with uncharacteristic venom. "A real waste of space."

"Did he stay clean?" I asked. "That's all that matters."

"You didn't know him."

"True. And as someone without a *single* fault, I'm happy to judge him."

Harry inclined his head, like he was granting the point, and left me outside my Trigonometry classroom. I watched him for a moment, then went inside—and stopped short. The man in the brown suit stood at the window, gazing toward the apple orchard. The morning sun cast stripes across him, through the blinds.

I looked to the floor for his shadow. No shadow; the stripes of light were uninterrupted. Then back to him. Then back to the floor again.

"You look like a bobblehead," Britta the brittle blonde said from her desk.

"What? No, I'm just—thinking."

"Me, too. I'm thinking you need a neck brace."

The man in the brown suit noticed me looking, and gave me a little formal bow. I settled into my desk, pulled out my homework, and ignored him. If I didn't know any better, I'd say he was a ghost. But I did know better. At least, I thought I did. I wasn't sure about anything anymore.

Coby sat down next to me. "How's Latin?"

"Ego sum rabidus."*

"I have no idea what you just said."

"Good." I glanced toward the man in the brown suit. "Um, there's only one teacher in this class, right?"

---

* I am crazy.

"Right," Coby said. "Unless you've got another stashed in a gazebo somewhere."

"That's funny," I said, not laughing.

I kept my eyes averted from the window. If the man in the brown suit didn't stop showing up, I'd fail this class. I couldn't concentrate with him hovering there. So I ignored him as Mr. Sakolsky started going over the homework. Halfway through, I glanced toward the window, and the man in the brown suit was gone. I exhaled in relief, and when we finished giving our answers, only one student had scored 100%.

"Emma Vaile," Mr. Sakolsky said. "A fine addition to our class."

I didn't know what to say. That never happened to me before.

"Oh, so you're that girl," Coby said with a quick grin.

"Yeah," I said. "I get that a lot."

In fencing class, the teacher—a middle-aged woman with incredibly muscular calves—partnered me with Kylee, a nearsighted girl with twig arms who weighed maybe ninety pounds and only came to my chin.

She thrashed me soundly. She really seemed to enjoy herself. In fact, her triumphant laughter was so infectious, soon the whole class was giggling along.

When it was over, Sara peeled me from my vest and dragged me to the dining room for lunch, promising to show me some moves.

"At least a little defense," she said. "So you can keep a toddler from stabbing you with a lollipop."

The cafeteria was a large room with lofty ceilings and a wall of windows overlooking the playing fields. Round tables with white cloths dotted the floor, and instead of the scrape of plastic trays I heard the tinkle of silverware against china. There wasn't even a vending machine. Everyone brought their own gourmet lunches in techno lunch pails and charming little bento boxes—at least I had my picnic basket.

Sara and I sat with Coby and Harry, and the three of them were witty and smart and warm. I liked them far too much, but didn't feel I could trust them. Not after what happened with Natalie. I wanted to be part of the ease they shared with each other, but the friendship was too new and I was afraid of getting burned again.

Besides, how could I trust them, when I couldn't even trust myself?

11

I couldn't face the empty museum, so after school I just opened the front gate to drop my backpack inside. Then I stopped short. The little boy with the marbles and slingshot was loitering inside, whittling a stick.

He saw me and froze, like I'd caught him playing hooky, then shot me a cheeky grin.

I laughed. "You hang out here a lot?"

This apparently struck him as the height of humor, and he erupted in silent laughter.

"Toss my backpack at the front door, would you?"

He nodded, so I handed over my backpack and watched him trot toward the house. I don't know why I trusted him, but I did.

I closed the gate behind me and walked into town. The village was tightly packed with Colonial houses and reminded me of neighborhoods in San Francisco with Victorians snug up against each other like they were huddled for warmth.

The houses in Echo Point were less ornate, but still cozy and colorful, in yellows and blues and greens. Piles of leaves stood beside swing sets and kitchen gardens, and half the houses had plaques dating them to the 1700s, built by men with names like Elbridge and Jeremiah and Abner. Antiques were everywhere. Maybe that's why I felt so at home, winding through cobblestone lanes toward the harbor.

Or maybe it was more than that.

I passed an upscale toy store, an Italian restaurant, and a corner grocery before my feet stopped outside the Black Sheep Bakery. I don't know why I paused; maybe I identified with the name.

The door swung open with a jingle, and a wave of nostalgia hit me as I stepped inside. Before I could stop it, my body began to tingle, my vision blurred, and I felt the whooshing.

Then the bakery spun around me, and I found myself standing in the center of the store, but not in the present time. I didn't panic—maybe because I was still in my school-slut uniform instead of a corset—but I did examine the room carefully. A wooden counter had replaced the glass case, the floor was covered in sawdust, and the walls were white instead of the lavender they'd been when I walked in. And there was a different woman behind the counter than the girl I'd seen before. She had rosy cheeks and a flour-covered apron, and smiled brightly before offering her help.

But I was too panicked to answer her. I backpedaled, overwhelmed by sensations. I shut my eyes, willing away the memories, willing myself back to the present. When I opened them again, the girl frowned at me from behind the glass case of pastries.

"Are you all right?" she asked.

I glanced around the shop. The walls were again lavender, the floor polished pumpkin pine. "Was this always a bakery?"

She pointed to a plaque on the wall. "Two hundred and fifty years. We've still got the brick oven in back. What can I get you?"

"Nothing," I croaked. "I don't want any of this."

I shoved through the front door and stumbled down the steps, racing blindly along the crooked narrow streets. I didn't stop until I reached a pretty little pond not far from the harbor, with ducks paddling near a spindly sculpture. I flopped onto a bench and stared at the rippling water. This had to stop. I couldn't keep running. Something was seriously wrong inside of me, something deeply broken. Whatever I'd survived as a child, whatever I'd overcome, had returned with a vengeance.

And this time, I didn't have anyone to protect me. Not my father. Not my mother. Nobody.

After a while, I wandered over to inspect the sculpture. It wasn't a sculpture at all, but a heavy wooden chair latched to a beam that pivoted over the water, to rise and fall into the pond. A plaque underneath read:

Welcome to Redd's Pond, named for Echo Point resident Elizabeth Redd, accused in 1682 of "detestable acts of Witchcraft and Sorceries wickedly, mallitiously and felloniously used, practiced & exercised." Redd and four other women were executed on this spot, 1682–1697.

The whole thing was chained shut for safety—but just looking, I felt a charge in the air. Had they used this chair to torture those women? Drown them? I shivered and walked on, trying to shake the feeling of death. I walked for hours through the old winding streets of Echo Point, until the sun dipped toward the rooftops, and the shadows turned to an inky black.

And in the growing darkness, the world suddenly changed. My body tingled with fear as black shadows crept toward me from every corner.

I pushed on, pretending the shadows didn't remind me of the smoke creeping toward me from my father's urns in the hallway back home. The wind rose from the harbor and tossed a mass of leaves against a garage door. The rustling sounded like a strange hiss. *Eossss.*

A squeaking weather vane spun on a rooftop: *Eossss.*

The shadows followed me from street to street with disembodied moans: not *Eos*, but *Neos, Neos, Neos.*

I *shoved* the shadows away with my mind as I began to run. I sprinted for half a mile, up a hill through the village, looking for signs, until I realized that the darkness was just darkness, the shadows, only shadows.

I slowed to a walk and caught my breath. I realized I was only a block from the museum, so I sped up again until I stepped through the front gates and felt an encompassing sense of safety. I exhaled, then breathed in the scent of maple leaves and fresh-cut grass. The windows of the museum glowed with welcoming light.

My backpack lay on the table in the museum's foyer, and the sight of it made me feel like a high-school kid again. Books and homework assignments and all the boring, stable, comforting routines of normal life.

Grabbing the pack, I called, "Bennett?"

No answer.

"Bennett? Martha? Anyone?"

Still nothing, as I crossed into the kitchen. A pot of stew bubbled on the Wolf range. A plate of shortbread cookies sat on the counter.

"I don't want food," I said under my breath. "I want *company*." I raised my voice: "Bennett! Bennett, are you here?"

Silence as I crossed into the dining room. The table was set beautifully, with fancy china, candles, and polished silver.

Set for one again. For me. Alone.

I screamed in frustration. "How can he not be here?!"

I stomped upstairs and found my bed made and my pajamas laid neatly on top, like some maid had snuck in while I was gone. Could that be it? But wouldn't the mysterious Martha at least leave a note?

I peeled off my wretched uniform and picked up my flannels, an unbecoming but completely comfortable red plaid. I wouldn't be caught dead in them in front of Bennett, but since that seemed completely out of the question, I cozied into them.

Still cold. "Wish I could have a *hot* bath," I muttered.

Back downstairs, I served myself the stew and sat at the head of the long formal table, pretending I was normal. Just your average girl, eating stew from Limoges china and monogrammed silver.

After dinner, I grabbed a couple of cookies and went into the ballroom to do my homework. The walls were a warm shade of yellow, the parquetry floor was polished to a high gleam, and the tall windows were perfectly proportioned. I pulled the pale blue silk curtains shut against the night shadows that I worried still hovered outside the gates. The museum wasn't quite so comforting now that it had grown completely dark outside.

I crossed the floor to the grand piano and played a few notes. The sound tumbled around the room, rich and resonant. It was the perfect place for a wedding—a string quartet playing, the French doors open to the rose garden . . .

I shook myself, worried I'd feel a sudden whoosh and find myself in some dead person's wedding. So I grabbed a silk feather pillow from a settee and tossed it to the floor. Then I emptied my backpack and lounged on the pillow as I finished my assignments.

The clock struck nine but I wasn't ready to sleep.

Despite all the antiques and history, I'd discovered the house had wireless, so I fired up my laptop. Every time I checked my e-mail I hoped there'd be a message from Max or my parents, or that Abby was done with the silent treatment. But I found nothing but school reminders and spam.

When I got bored with celebrity blogs, I flipped my computer shut and paced the room. I was dying for music, but the speakers on my laptop sounded ridiculously tinny in this ginormous ballroom. I riffled through the built-in cabinets along one wall and found a stereo almost intimidating in its high-techness. There was a Bose iPod dock as well, but my parents refused to get me an iPod, saying, "You already have a computer." I know that makes no sense, but they'd refused to budge. Don't even get me started on my cell, which might as well have been purple and green. And called Barney.

Elton John was the only thing other than classical music in the entire cabinet, so at random, I chose Vivaldi's *The Four Seasons*. I put on Concerto No. 3 ("Autumn") and listened to the violins reverberate through the room. I felt a strange sensation on my face, and realized I was smiling. This music, in this ballroom, just made me happy. The dread that had colored everything lately began to wash away.

I glided over the parquetry floor, daydreaming about flowing silk gowns and fancy balls, a time when guys didn't just sway back and forth while trying to grope you. I curtsied to a make-believe suitor, fluttering my fan as he took me in his arms and spun me around the room, twirling and breathless.

Right into the arms of Bennett.

"How long were you standing there?" I spluttered. "It's not what you think. I was . . ." *Of course* he'd finally return to find me dancing like an idiot by myself, dressed in my red plaid pajamas with cookie crumbs down the front.

Maybe he'd just think I was elfin and childlike.

Maybe that was worse.

He grinned and touched my mouth with his forefinger.

I shut up.

We were standing maybe six inches apart, and I felt the warmth of his body through the space separating us. My lips pulsed where he touched them. So did my body as he laid one of his hands on my hip and pulled me closer.

He clasped my right hand in his left while his other palm slid along my hip to my waist to my back. I shivered, breathing in his scent, like cold fresh air. I couldn't look away from his blue eyes and I wanted nothing more than to kiss him and press myself further into him.

The music rolled around us, and at a cue I didn't hear, Bennett moved and pulled me with him. He spun me around the room in a European waltz.

My free hand rested on his shoulder and I felt his heat and muscle through the thin cotton of his shirt. We'd never touched before. Not like this, not like we were the only two people in the world. Spinning and spinning and spinning.

Then the music stopped, and a moment later, so did we.

We stood there in the silence. I'm not sure for how long. I didn't want the moment to end—not ever. In that ballroom, in his arms, everything felt right.

Well, until Elton John's "Bennie and the Jets" started blaring. So maybe I'd slipped that in the CD changer. Sue me.

We stepped apart and I said, "That was . . ."

"Unexpected," he finished.

I'd been hoping for "amazing" or "sexy," but maybe he was talking about the change in music. "Yeah."

"It's getting late," he said. "You better go to bed."

"With you? I mean, are you staying with me tonight— I mean, *here*. In the house—in your room." Ugh.

"Have you been lonely?" he teased. "I'm sorry I've been gone so much."

"What've you been doing?"

"Trying to take care of some . . ." The warmth faded from his eyes. "Some family business."

"Well, I need to talk to you."

A sudden stillness took him. "Are you okay?"

No, I'm not okay. Where have you been? Why did you come for me in San Francisco? Why did you bring me here? What's happening to me? Am I losing my mind?

But he looked so tired and spent that I didn't press it.

Well, I also hesitated to ruin the brilliant moment we'd just shared, when all I wanted to do was laze in bed and dream. "I'm fine. We can talk tomorrow."

He turned off the stereo while I shoved my books and laptop into my backpack. We walked up the grand staircase together, and I cursed my dowdy flannel pj's that made me look ten years old. I wasn't sure how far I wanted things to go between us—at least not right *now*—but I definitely wanted *him* to want things to go pretty far.

"Where's your room?" I asked at the top of the stairs. I'd snooped around and found his parents' room—he'd said they were in southern France—but I hadn't found Bennett's.

"The door at the end of the hall," he told me.

"Isn't that the attic?"

"Yeah." He shrugged. "It's peaceful up there."

"This is *literally* a museum," I said. "It doesn't get much quieter."

"Well, when my sister lived here . . ." He shook his head, smiling softly. "Never a moment's peace."

"You have a sister?"

"I did," he said.

We'd stopped outside my door, and I guess I'd been hoping for a good-night kiss. But now I didn't know what to say. He *did* have a sister? So . . . he didn't anymore? Was she gone? Disappeared like my family? Dead?

Before I could respond, he kissed me.

On the forehead.

"Good night," he said, and walked away.

12

I woke early the next morning and went through my daily ritual. My parents were still out of their calling zone—you can imagine my surprise—and I sent Max an SOS message in an e-mail.

For the first time in ages, I texted Abby.

```
I need u!!!!
```

I waited a moment, but didn't get a response, probably because it was only 3:00 a.m. her time.

```
Chk ur eml.
```

And I started to write. I told her about everything, from Natalie to Bennett, from the ashes to the death mask, from San Francisco to Echo Point, from visions to nightmares, to what I really thought was happening to me.

I was seeing ghosts.

Crazy, right? But lying in bed last night, still feeling like I was twirling in the ballroom with Bennett, I'd pieced it together. My imaginary friends when I was a child were too real, too complex for a seven-year-old to make up. Plus, my parents pretended not to notice, but the ones in the house moved things, started showers, and made cups of tea no one asked for.

And everything else that had happened: the smoke and ashes at home, the death mask, the flashbacks from someone else's life I'd been having since I'd come to Echo Point, the man in the brown suit who cast no shadow. They all led back to one thing.

Dead people. I saw ghosts.

It felt right, the pieces all clicked, but it was *insane*. That's why I e-mailed Abby. She knew me better than anyone—better than myself, sometimes. She'd know what to think about all this. Maybe she still blamed me for the breakup with Max, but when she read the e-mail, she'd respond. As I clicked Send, I heard stirring downstairs: definitely Bennett this time.

I couldn't face him in my plaid pajamas, so I slipped from bed and warmed myself by the fire for a moment before dashing into the bathroom.

I started the shower and braced myself for the icy coldness—and a cloud of steam enveloped me. Warm water!

I laughed in pleasure and showered for twenty minutes. A total luxury. And having finally revealed the truth to myself, I felt the tension that had accumulated over the last few weeks begin to loosen.

After the shower, I did the best I could with my hair and makeup, then made a face at myself in the mirror. If only I looked more like Sara—or even Brittle Britta. Back in the bedroom, I dressed in my uniform, adding black tights and, of course, my black boots. Harry had openly wondered if I owned other shoes, or I was just hiding cankles.

For the record, I did own other shoes, but didn't like any of them. And my ankles were fine, thank you very much.

I stomped downstairs into the kitchen and found Bennett in the breakfast nook. He was reading a book while eating scrambled eggs and toast. I may have been spotting ghosts on every street corner, but the hot shower and the sight of Bennett first thing in the a.m. did wonders for my mood.

"Good morning!" I said.

He stopped cold, toast halfway to his lips. "Good *lord*."

"What?"

He gestured with his toast at my skimpy uniform. "*That*."

"You have no one to blame but yourself. Anyway"—I pirouetted, allowing him to see just how short the skirt actually was—"I'm already known as the school slut."

"You don't look slutty," he said, repressively. "You look juvenile."

I narrowed my eyes at him, but he went back to his book. Evil.

I poured myself some coffee. Took a sip and made a

face, then set the mug down. I reached into a high cabinet for a breakfast plate and in the reflection in the glass door, caught Bennett checking me out.

Ha!

When I turned back, he was innocently reading his book. I hummed a little tune as I filled my plate and sat down beside him. I pronged a few forkfuls then looked at the title of his book: *Integrative Research Methods in Criminology*.

"You're studying criminology?" I asked.

"No," he said.

"You're grumpy in the morning."

He looked at me. "I find you distracting."

"Good," I said. "Now put the book down, we need to talk."

"Sounds ominous," he said, setting his book aside.

"Yeah. Well." Now that he was listening, I felt suddenly nervous. How do you tell someone that you think you see ghosts? "You're gonna think I'm nuts."

"Nuttier than dancing in the ballroom by yourself?"

"You're so comforting." I took a breath. "Okay. Do you ever . . . *see* things?"

"I see a girl in a uniform that's too small."

I shook my head. "No, I mean things that *aren't* there. Things that couldn't possibly be there—like . . . visions?"

"Gee, no," he said, dripping sarcasm. "That *never* happens to me, but thanks for asking."

"What? I only—you don't have to be mean," I said in a small voice.

"I'm not being mean, I just wonder when you're going to start trusting me."

What did he think I was trying to do? This was hard for me. He must know I had no one else to turn to, even if he didn't know I was going to tell him I saw ghosts.

His iPhone rang and he pulled it from his pocket.

"Don't answer it," I said.

He glanced at the text message. "We'll talk later." He shoved his book into his cargo bag, and was out of the nook in a flash.

"Bennett!" I followed him into the front hall. "Don't go. I'm not done."

He slipped a black canvas jacket over his T-shirt. "This can't wait."

"When will you be back? Things are happening to me that I can't explain. That—"

"What things?"

"I don't know. Things that aren't—that shouldn't be—I don't *know*, that's the problem!"

"C'mere," he said, and took my hand.

Now he was going to kiss me? Probably just to shut me up—but I wasn't complaining.

He pulled me in front of the hall mirror and stood behind me, my back against his chest. I held my breath and watched his reflection: the deep brown wave of hair, his impossibly blue eyes.

He slowly unwound the tie from my neck. "Like this," he said.

He laid the tie over my shoulders and showed me an

intricate loop and knot. There was something so sensual about him manipulating that slip of silk against my bare neck. The way he caught my eyes in the mirror. I leaned against him and just about swooned.

"Much better," he said, straightening the knot. "We'll talk later, okay?"

I nodded dumbly, and stood there as he left. I listened to the engine of his ancient Land Rover ignite and the wheels crush over the gravel drive. When I managed to collect myself, I returned to the kitchen for breakfast. I sat in the little nook contemplating what had just happened. First he's sarcastic, then he's flirtatious. Did Bennett have feelings for me? He was probably just trying to distract me. Anything to avoid actually talking to me.

"Well, it's not going to work," I said aloud. "He'll see that sort of behavior gets him nowhere." But I knew it was a lie before I'd even finished saying it.

I bit into my toast and poured a cup of tea from the little pot in the center of the table. Wait a minute. Scrambled eggs instead of soft-boiled? And tea, in addition to coffee?

At least *someone* was listening to me. "Thanks," I told the empty kitchen, raising my teacup in a toast.

On the way to school, I passed through the campus gates and Harry fell into step beside me.

"Hey," I said.

He eyed me critically. "Bedroom hair."

"What? Shut up." I furtively checked my hair. "Where's Sara and Coby?"

"Why?"

Because I flirted with you yesterday in Latin and now I want a buffer. But you can't possibly expect me to tell you that.

He grinned wickedly. He *did* expect me to tell him that.

"Never mind." I hooked my arm through his. "Tell me something I don't know."

"Anything in particular?"

Anything to occupy my mind through the apple trees, because I'm not in the mood for an imaginary corset. "Just something interesting."

"My dear Emma," he said. "Could I be anything but? All right, you see the girl with the headband? She's in love with Maddy—over there—no, the Amazon with the unfortunate bob. Maddy, sadly, is only in love with herself. And that's Peter," he finished, "the third side of the triangle . . ."

He kept up a murmured recitation all the way to Latin class, and I found that I couldn't stop smiling. He'd even started looking less goofy and gangly. Maybe it was his voice, which was low and full of self-confidence, or maybe I was just getting used to good breeding.

"How come you know everything about everyone?" I asked, as we took our seats.

"Perhaps I'm lying." He waved his hand airily. "Who tied your tie?" he asked, changing the subject.

I fingered the knot at my throat. "What, this?"

"You're blushing."

"No, I'm not." I felt the blush turn three shades brighter. "How do you know I didn't tie it?"

"That is an Oriental knot," he said, managing somehow to lounge in his wooden chair. "Beyond your capabilities, I'm afraid."

"There's this thing called the Internet," I bluffed. "Maybe you've heard of it?"

He pondered a moment. "I'm thinking Bennett Stern."

"What? No. Well, yes. He helped me a little. How did you know?" Did Bennett make a habit of tying girls' ties?

Harry arched an eyebrow significantly. "He used to date my sister."

"And I suppose he tied *her* ties, too! I hate your sister."

"Ah, so it's like that." Harry grinned at my jealous outburst. "I only asked because Bennett always wore his with an Oriental."

"I wouldn't know," I said sourly. Great. Now he knew I liked Bennett.

"So, unrequited love, is it?"

"I'm not even going to pretend to know what you're talking about."

"Oh, you're pretending, all right."

My only recourse was to shush him fiercely as class started.

The man in the brown suit didn't appear until after Trigonometry.

"Sorry I didn't call you back last night," I was saying to Sara, who'd left a message on my cell. We were standing in the hallway, chatting with Coby before he left for practice and we went to Fencing.

"Doesn't matter," she said. "Just wanted some girl talk—and Coby was busy."

I giggled, and Coby spread his hands and looked skyward, as if appealing to a higher power for patience.

"I like that you're new," Sara continued. "It gets so incestuous around here. We've all been in the same schools since we were kids. The closest we get to a fresh perspective is—"

And that's when the man in the brown suit materialized two feet away. I yelped and bobbled my Trig textbook onto Coby's toes.

"Ow!" he said. "Emma!"

"Sorry!"

"You should see her with a foil," Sara said.

"First she breaks my heart," he said, mournfully, "then she breaks my toes."

I didn't respond, too distracted by the man in the brown suit. He'd never stood so close before, or looked at me so intently. And somehow it was different, now that I knew what he was.

"You coming?" Sara asked me, a little curtly. "I promise not to mark you with an *S* this time." Yesterday she'd practiced her Zorro skills on me.

"Um, in a minute. I've got to, um . . ." I watched the man in the brown suit lay a hand against his forehead, feigning illness. "I'm not feeling so well?"

The man nodded in approval.

"I'll take you to the nurse," Coby said.

"Would you stop?" Sara told him. "Every time she sneezes, you want to take her to the nurse. But then you always did like playing doctor."

"We were *nine*!" he protested.

"Coach would kill you anyway," I said. "Just point me the right way."

Sara gave me directions as Coby headed off—right through the man in the brown suit. He rolled his eyes and straightened his lapels.

I started toward the nurse's office—not quite sure why—and halfway there the class bell rang. I felt a pang about the detention I'd get for cutting.

Anyway, the hallway was empty—the man in the brown suit was gone. This was ridiculous. I turned back toward the gym, when he reappeared right in front of me.

"Ack! Warn a person, would you?" I scolded.

The man looked not at all chastened. He gestured toward a closed door nearby, asking me to head inside. In the dark room, there was a stack of broken chairs, boxes of chalk, and rolls of toilet paper. Wooden shelves lined two walls, and one of those retractable world maps hung in the back. Great. The ghost had led me into a storage closet. Now what?

The man in the brown suit wove silently through the cluttered room to the back wall, and pointed at the Indian Ocean.

"Um," I said. "The Indian Ocean. Okay. Thanks?"

He seemed to sigh, shaking his head at me in despair.

"Oh, everyone's a critic. You're a ghost. You're not even *alive*."

He pushed his hand through the map, and mimed opening a doorknob behind it.

"Fine," I said.

I tugged at the map, trying to ravel it back into the bar at the top. It didn't move, and when I looked closer I saw that it'd been permanently stuck in the down position. I glanced at the ghost, and he pretended to squeeze into the eight-inch gap between the map and the wall. Which was a little disturbing, because he didn't squeeze well. Half his body still appeared on my side of the map.

Still, I got the idea. I scooched between the map and the wall, and felt a doorknob back there. The door opened with a theatrical squeak, and I shoved a little harder at the map to squeeze through.

Then I thought: *What am I doing?*

Apparently squeezing through a long-forgotten door into a dark, empty hallway that a ghost revealed to me. I didn't know what else to do. It was time I stopped running from my visions of ghosts and confronted them. I needed answers. And I sensed this ghost was trying to help me.

Still, that hallway was really dark and really empty. I looked to the man in the brown suit for reassurance— which, I know, wasn't my most rational moment—and saw him closing the door behind us.

"Wait," I said. "You can do that? Move things?"

He waggled his eyebrows at me. Some reassurance.

I took a breath and started walking. The farther I went, the darker the hallway grew. Just when I decided there wasn't enough light, the man in the brown suit began to glow.

"Oh, you've got to be kidding me," I said.

He grinned in his luminescent way. The glow touched both sides of the narrow corridor, exposing the dust accumulating on the floor and cobwebs hanging from the exposed beams.

I've never been what you'd call brave. I wasn't the first girl to jump off the high dive, I've never sat all the way through a Wes Craven film—heck, I was still worrying about cutting class. But I didn't have the luxury of cowardice right now. I saw ghosts and I was hoping this one was trying to help me figure out why. So I said, "All right. Lead on."

Twenty paces down, we came to a staircase, and a tingle started in my spine. I flashed to someone else's memories. I knew this place. In busier days, it had bustled with activity: boots for polishing, linen to launder, trays of food carried from the kitchen—

"This leads to the servants' quarters," I said.

The man nodded.

We climbed until we reached a door with an old-fashioned latch. Beyond, I found an enormous attic, with light streaming through tiny windows in the slanted roof. Dozens of old bed frames were stacked against one wall and there were wooden crates everywhere. Two massive brick chimneys straddled the room from floor to ceiling. I smelled mothballs and cedar and straw. Dust bunnies had quite the little neighborhood going on, and I waded through their grimy warren looking for any clue as to why the man in the brown suit brought me here. Speaking of which, where was he?

I turned circles in the room, but he'd disappeared. And that's when I caught sight of myself in the mirror.

Only it wasn't a mirror. It was a painting leaning against the far wall, with a white sheet pooled around its base.

And the woman in the painting looked exactly like me.

She wore a French blue dress with tiny buttons down the front and a corseted bodice: the dress I'd worn during my first flashback on campus. She looked a little older— stronger and more confident, her features were sharper and her eyes both steely and amused. Her hair looked darker, too. Guess they didn't have highlights back in the eighteenth century.

For a long moment, I just stared. My brain couldn't make sense of this: a picture of me—well, not me, but someone who looked exactly like me—in the attic of a prep school in Massachusetts.

I knelt before the painting and found a plaque attached to the bottom of the gold frame.

Emma Vaile, 1773–1801.

I gasped and stumbled backward and fell across one of the old cots. A cloud of dust puffed around me.

What was *my* name doing on that painting? Was this

all some elaborate hoax? Yeah. Someone was drugging me so I'd have psychotic flashbacks into dead people's memories and see imaginary people hovering everywhere.

Sure, I was so important, there was a conspiracy after me.

I wished. Because I knew the more logical answer. Nobody was trying to drive me crazy. I already *was* crazy. They hadn't fixed my insanity in the children's psychiatric hospital—they'd just driven it below the surface.

"No," I said. "No."

I didn't believe that. I knew what I really believed, what I'd long suspected and finally felt in my heart to be true.

And, suddenly, I also knew that I needed to get out of here. Now. Before my mind spontaneously combusted. Because while I'd been telling myself I could see ghosts, I hadn't really believed it. I'd still hoped there was some logical explanation.

I wiped the dust from my face and shoved through the door, then stumbled down the staircase and fled along the dark hallway, which was a lot scarier without the glow-in-the-dark man in the brown suit. I stopped at the door with the deadbolt, imagining myself trapped here in this nightmare.

But the bolt moved easily, and I squeezed from behind the map and caught my breath. I stepped back into the hall, and a minute later bumped into Coby.

"Hey!" He shot me a quick smile. "There you are."

I opened my mouth, but nothing came out.

"I was looking for you," he said. "The nurse said you never showed."

"Oh. No. I felt . . . better."

"Is that why you skipped Fencing?" he asked. "So you'd *keep* feeling better?"

His sheer normalcy soothed me. "Are you calling me a coward?"

"Well, you're obviously not a germaphobe."

"What do you—" I glanced down and found myself covered in dust bunnies. I sighed. "Do you ever get the feeling that maybe you're not who you always thought you were?"

"Emma, are you sure you're okay?" He looked at me with so much concern that I felt my eyes watering.

"Um." I blinked a few times. "I might've passed out again."

"That's not good."

"Maybe it really is a brain tumor." I started giggling, slightly hysterically. "That'd be brilliant. I could really go for a tumor about now."

"Emma," Coby said. "You should see my dad."

I stopped laughing. "Do you think—" I glanced up at him: solid, gorgeous, kindhearted Coby. "Do you think you could just take me home?"

He didn't hesitate. Didn't complain about skipping class. Didn't worry about leaving campus or missing lunch. He walked me home and didn't even talk on the way, just let me be alone with my thoughts.

We stopped at the gate. "Don't make me wish I'd called my dad," he told me. "If you're in real trouble . . ."

"I'm fine," I said. "I promise."

"You're alone here?"

"Bennett will be home soon."

He showed me a crooked grin. "Way to reassure me."

"What?"

"Nothing. You take care of yourself."

"I will. Now go—you'll be late for class. I bet you have a perfect attendance record, too."

His cheeks turned pink. It was adorable.

"Go!" I said.

"I'll call you later then." And he turned and jogged back to school, his uniform jacket fluttering in the wind.

13

I went straight to the ballroom as though drawn by some magnetic force. It felt not unlike arriving at the dean's office, my feet leading me there unconsciously. I tossed my books onto the grand piano and sat on the bench, then ran my fingers over the keys, playing a simple Mendelssohn melody I'd learned long ago in piano lessons. As the last note faded, I saw a man standing just inside the French doors.

I didn't have it in me to be scared, despite his commanding presence. He wore a blue dress uniform, had windswept dark hair, a carefully groomed mustache, and a saber at his hip.

He strode forward like he owned the place, his dark eyes boring into me. I finally understood what they meant in old books when they wrote about a *rake*: he was the dashing seducer, a fallen angel.

At the grand piano, he stopped and glowered at me. He stared for a long time, and I met his gaze—the two of us a motionless tableau at the piano. Finally, he nodded curtly.

"I'm glad I meet your approval," I said, and patted the seat next to me.

Ignoring me, he leafed through the sheet music and turned to the opening of a piece.

"Oh, I don't play," I told him.

He scowled and gestured to the sheet music again.

"No, I really don't. I just know that one melody."

He rose and stalked toward the French doors, clearly disgusted.

"Wait!" I said. "I don't understand what you want! Don't leave!"

After a moment, he turned, with a chilly correctness.

"You're a ghost, aren't you?" I said. "I see ghosts."

There was a sense of sadness in his eyes, and he inclined his head.

"Well, nice to meet you." I looked through the window at the treetops. "I mean, it's not like I *want* to see ghosts. Better than going crazy, though, right? Except maybe it's the same thing." I looked back to him. "Am I insane? Is this all in my head?"

A hint of a smile appeared on his stern face as he shook his head.

"I'm asking an imaginary rake if I'm crazy," I told him. "I think that's the definition." I plunked a few piano keys. "I only wish—I wish they hadn't all left me. My brother, my mom and dad. I wish they'd cared enough to stay. I wish I had someone to tell, someone to trust. But

I don't. Not my friends, not Bennett." I felt tears on my cheek. "I'm all alone."

He crossed the ballroom floor and knelt beside me, like a man proposing. His face looked so strong and so sad. He put one hand over his heart, and bowed his head, the gesture unmistakable: pledging himself to me.

"Thank you." I turned away, blinking back tears at his kindness. A complete stranger, a *ghost*, offering me the support I so badly needed. It was wonderful and terrifying at the same time.

When I finally turned back, he was gone.

I swallowed. Ghosts. I saw ghosts.

The man in the brown suit. The dashing, tragic rake. The woman from the death mask. And the other Emma Vaile, whose life I lived from the inside: her stolen kiss in the gazebo and her pretty blue gown with the stifling corset.

Ghosts.

For a long time, I sat there fiddling with piano keys. Then I stood. Might as well get this over with. I started toward the kitchen to find whomever—or whatever—was cooking my meals and lighting the fires.

But when I turned toward the door, I found that they'd come to me.

Three of them standing in line by the door, as if awaiting my inspection. A man, a woman, and a boy.

I stepped cautiously forward. A shock of white hair rose above the man's ruddy face, and he had a curly mustache of impressive proportions. He wore chef's whites and held his floppy hat in his hand. Beside him stood a flirty-looking redhead in a black dress and white apron, with a little white cap pinned to her luxuriant hair. I recognized the hair from that early morning in my room, when she stoked the fire in the hearth. And I knew the boy, too—the kid with the clay marbles and slingshot, dressed basically as Oliver Twist, with a pale face and big mischievous eyes. Frankly, seen in the light, they all looked like some low-budget period piece from *Masterpiece Theatre.*

I stared at them, from one to the next and back again, and they stood with gazes lowered. They clearly wanted something from me, but I didn't know what.

"Thank you," I said, finally.

The boy raised his head and grinned at me, and the maid elbowed him softly. He lowered his gaze to the patched cap he was wringing in his hands, then stuck his tongue out.

For some reason, this gave me the courage to continue. "You were there for me when nobody else was." I looked to the chef. "You're the one cooking dinner and packing me those lunches? I don't know what you put in the cookies, but they ought to be illegal." At his expression, I quickly added, "That's a compliment!"

The chef bowed slightly, beaming under his mustache.

"Setting out my clothes for me every morning and looking after my room," I told the woman, "you've made me feel at home here, thank you." I looked at the boy. "And you! I don't even know what you do, sweep the chimneys?" Smiles blossomed on their faces, and the boy mimed something to me. "Oh! You fixed the furnace?"

The boy nodded shyly.

"Then you're my hero. Thank you all. I, um, I'm new to this and—" I stopped, catching sight of myself in the reflection of the big window, alone in the empty ballroom. "Hoo boy. I'm in for a long stay in a padded room."

My footsteps echoed as I crossed the ballroom to the window. Maybe the ghosts didn't appear in the reflection, but I did—and nothing confused me more than myself. Nothing alarmed me more.

I saw ghosts.

Every day, here in Echo Point, I saw them more easily, and more clearly. The harmless, helpful ones, like the man in the brown suit, the maid, the chef, and the urchin.

And the others. The looming figure braided together from burial ashes, the whispering shadows in the village that had ached with hunger and crept toward me with malicious intent. *Neossss*. The man in the storefront, who'd cut me all those years ago.

I turned back to the room and the three ghosts were gone. Very discreet, leaving me alone with my feelings. Like good servants, they'd been trained to remain in the background.

Grabbing my backpack from the piano, I headed to the front door—I needed to get out of here.

I stopped short in the the hallway.

Another ghost stood at the bottom of the stairs, surrounded by antique luggage, an old steamer trunk, and a capacious velvet bag. She looked like Mary Poppins, with a white ruffled shirt peeping from under a trim black jacket that brought the word *bombazine* to mind. Her steel gray hair was pinned into a soft French twist.

Her face caught my attention, because her expression was so sweet and kind that I wanted to throw myself into her arms for a comforting cuddle. Except I'd probably pass right through her ghostly form and smash into the wall.

So I just smiled. "Glad to meet you."

"You must be Emma," she said warmly. "I'm so happy to—"

"You *talk*!" I squeaked.

"One of my many talents." She laughed. She even had a Mary Poppins accent that was faintly English.

"Really? What else can you do?"

"Well, my dear, I've been known to coddle, tease, manage, advise, and—I'm sorry to say—even *gossip*." Her eyes twinkled at me. "I've run households and raised children. Never my own, though."

I goggled at her, amazed to meet a talkative ghost.

"For you," she continued, "I'll manage the staff and perhaps even teach you a few things. And, I dearly hope, be a friend to you in this difficult time."

"Who—who are you?"

"I'm Martha," she said. "Did Bennett not tell you I was coming?"

"Oh! Oh, he did, but he didn't—"

"Well, he's distracted these days, poor boy." Her eyes creased with concern. "Still mourning his loss, and—"

"Wait!" I said. "You're *real*."

"Pardon?" she said.

"You're not a gh—not a—I mean, you're really *here*. Finally." I squeezed her arm, and yes—she was flesh and blood. "I'm so glad to meet you."

She inspected me, and behind her sweet face I sensed a keen intelligence. "I'm struck by an uncomfortable feeling that we owe you an apology," she said. "In any case, I'm sorry I'm so late in arriving—everything's at sixes and sevens back home."

I had no idea what that meant. "Well, you're here now. Can I help with your bags?"

"Relax," she said. "Nicholas will do it."

"Nicholas?" I asked. "Who's—?"

But there he was, the urchin, carrying her sea chest upstairs, his back bowed under the weight . . . grinning happily.

"Oh," I said. "Um."

"Surely you've met the staff?" Martha asked me.

"Um," I repeated. She saw him, too? So he wasn't a ghost?

"Better with a footman, of course, but the Sterns prefer a small staff." She beckoned me toward the kitchen. "Well, they did when they were in residence."

"Are the Sterns gone? I mean, for good?"

"For the foreseeable future," she said, filling the teakettle with water. "The whole family is still in shock."

"What happened?"

She sighed and bustled around with the tea bags and honey. "Nothing good, I'm afraid. A few months ago—"

The front door slammed open, and Bennett called, "Martha?"

A warm smile rose on her face. "In the kitchen!"

A moment later, he strode in and, without a glance at me, wrapped Martha in a fierce hug. "You look beautiful," he said.

"I look the same as always," she said, stepping back to eye him. "*You* look pale and exhausted. And too skinny." She turned to me. "Is he not eating?"

For some reason, his pleasure in Martha, his clear affection for her, made me crabby. Maybe I was jealous, or maybe . . . well, okay—I was jealous. Not of the affection, so much, but of their smiles and shared history. I felt like the outsider I was, like I'd never know him as well as she did.

"He's too grumpy to eat," I said.

"Grumpy? My sweetest little boy?"

Bennett looked at me, a laughing appeal in his eyes. "If she breaks out the baby pictures, I'm begging you—*run*."

I refused to be charmed. "We *still* need to talk."

"I haven't seen Martha in two months, Emma, I—"

"Bennett," she interrupted. "I'm not going anywhere."

He sighed as he looked at me. "The day's warming up. Let's go in the garden."

Bennett and I strolled through the now-barren rose garden, toward the red sumac and the Japanese maple.

"So," he said. "I'm listening."

This was it, the moment I spilled all my dark secrets. After which Bennett would call the men in white coats.

But I didn't care; I couldn't keep this bottled up any longer. I took a breath.

"Emma?"

"I know," I said, and kept walking. "I'm going to tell you."

"Good."

"Here goes." I paused in the middle of a row of dying roses. "Okay."

"Okay?"

"I see ghosts!" I blurted.

He nodded. "Yeah, you told me."

Not the reaction I'd expected. "No I didn't. When?"

"'You see things,'" he said, in a bored tone. "'Imaginary things, visions.'"

Okay, yeah I'd said that, but I hadn't expected him to believe me. "No, I *really* see ghosts. I mean, the spirits of the dead. Walking around in period costume." I took a shuddering breath. "I thought I was going insane, I was so afraid, and I . . . I can't believe this, but knowing they're ghosts is a *relief.* Because I'm not crazy. I really see them."

He eyed me speculatively. "Uh-huh, you really see them. Anything else?"

"You want *more*?"

"I want everything," he said.

We turned at the end of the row, toward the brilliant stand of red sumac. "Fine," I said, "strap on your straitjacket." And I told him about the ashes and the death mask. "And since I came to Echo Point, I'm seeing them more and more. And I'm . . . I don't know, reliving the memories of a previous life."

He frowned at the last part. "Hmm."

"*Hmm?* That's all I get?" Could he act normal for once? Why wasn't he trying to calm me down or offering to get help? One of us needed to be rational here and it certainly wasn't going to be me.

"Well, I don't understand the shadows and the ashes. That's not possible, but I suppose you're still learning how to—"

I couldn't take any more. I screamed, "Stop it! I see *ghosts*, Bennett! Stop humoring me."

"You really don't know, do you?" There was an incredulous expression on his face. "I can't believe they didn't tell you. I thought you were playing games, pretending you didn't know, keeping secrets from me and—"

"What? What is it that you think I'm supposed to know?"

"Emma, I'm sorry." He put his hand on my arm. "Let's start at the beginning. Why do you think you're seeing ghosts?"

"Because the house is haunted?"

"Mm. And are you afraid of them?"

"Uh, *yeah*. They're ghosts."

"How afraid?"

"Well, terrified that I'm losing my mind. But the actual ghosts? The man in the brown suit, the servants . . . no. Not scary, actually." I turned that over in my mind. "How can I not be afraid of ghosts? They're all haunty and ghoulish, right? And Bennett, why are you taking this seriously?"

"You're a ghostkeeper, Emma."

"Yeah, well, you're a jackass."

He surprised me with a laugh. "No, I'm serious. You're a ghostkeeper."

"Not funny. I need your help. I can't concentrate at school, I'm having flashbacks. I don't want to go back to the poof."

"The poof?"

We walked to a bench beside an arbor and sat silently for a time. Then I told him about being committed to a mental institution. I told him about the stuffed elephant and the lime Popsicles. And the heavy sluggishness in my mind, seeing the world through a dirty film, all the color and brightness faded.

"Oh, Emma," he said, his voice so appalled that I felt myself suddenly blinking back tears. "How could they do that to you?"

I shrugged. "They didn't know. They were afraid I'd hurt myself." I absently rubbed the scar the man with the knife had given me.

"No, something isn't right—we're missing a piece."

Martha stepped from the rose garden, carrying a tray of sandwiches and iced tea. I felt suddenly shy, falling silent as she arranged the food beside us. Bennett seemed to understand, and he just smiled and thanked her.

"Sometimes," she murmured to Bennett, "we just need to know that we're not alone."

I glanced at Bennett after she left. "What did that mean?"

"She wants me to tell you about me."

"What about you?"

"I see ghosts, too, Emma," he said. "I'm a ghostkeeper."

"Why do you keep saying that? *Ghostkeeper.* It's ridiculous."

"Remember when you caught me in your dad's office? You thought I was doing tai chi?"

"You were gh-ghostkeeping?" I could barely say it with a straight face.

He nodded. "I sensed something—something not good."

"It was probably those funeral urns."

"I swear to you, Emma. This is real."

"Fine," I said. "Prove it."

He smiled. "Love to."

14

I crossed my arms and waited expectantly—any minute, he'd start laughing and phone the insane asylum.

"C'mere." Bennett took my hand and dragged me into the middle of the garden. "Good. Now close your eyes."

"This is silly," I said, but did as he asked.

Fallen leaves crinkled under my feet, and I smelled the damp earth and felt the breeze on my face. Holding his hand, I didn't want the moment to end.

So he immediately dropped my hand. "Can you feel that?"

"Not anymore," I said.

"What?"

"Never mind. What am I feeling for?"

"You've felt this before," he whispered, his breath tickling my skin. "You were born with the gift—you don't only see ghosts, you *call* them."

"How? I don't know what I'm supposed to—" Then a pins-and-needles tingling started in my spine, spread to my arms, and extended in tenuous threads into the garden. "They're here," I said. It was hard to explain, but I could feel ghosts present in the garden with us, like when you know someone has walked into a room behind you. All I had to do was see them in my mind and turn their shadows into fully formed beings.

"You're good," he said. There was respect in his voice. "Open your eyes."

I did, and he was smiling at me. When I managed to look away, I saw the ghosts. They were just as they'd appeared in my thoughts: a woman and child near the wall, dressed in nineteenth-century finery.

"Describe them to me," I said. Then I'd know he really saw them, too.

"She's a plain woman with brown hair and freckles, in a green dress with a . . . what's that called? The thing in back?"

"A bustle."

"And that's probably her son, in a blue jacket with knickers. Missing a few of his baby teeth. They look like something out of a Victorian movie from the fifties. Ghosts always look like they're wearing bad costumes, nobody knows why."

I stared in awe. "What do they want?"

"Nothing," Bennett said. "You called them, so they came. Ghostkeepers each have one gift. *You* can summon them. I can sense that they're there, but unless they come forth on their own, or another ghostkeeper summons them, I can't see them. Echo Point is a nexus, and your powers are coming back."

"What's your power?" I asked.

He hesitated. "I can't summon them. That's why I needed you to do it. I can only dispel them."

"Like in my father's office. The tai chi."

"Yeah. I thought you were playing dumb. I didn't know—"

"That I really *was* dumb?"

"Well . . ." He didn't bother denying it.

"Dispel—what does that mean?"

"I send them back to their mortal forms."

The breeze turned cooler and swept leaves across the garden as the Victorian ghosts started to twitch and fidget.

"What are they doing?" I asked.

"They're afraid of me," Bennett said. "They know what I can do."

Instead of watching the ghosts, I watched Bennett. What was that expression on his face? Shame? Or pleasure? What did he mean that he could "send them back to their mortal forms?" He could kill ghosts?

Then the tension in my chest started to loosen. "They're leaving," I told him. "Can they do that?"

"Unless you compel them to stay—which you can't. That's another power entirely."

"Okay," I said. "So instead of being a crazy person who thinks she can see ghosts . . ."

"You're a crazy person who *can* see ghosts," he said with a grin. Then, more softly, "And you've got a lot to learn."

"This can't be happening," I said. "I can't wrap my mind around it."

"Tell me more about those shadowy things. And feeling like you're reliving a previous life."

"No." I shook my head. "I can't do this anymore. Not now."

He stepped in front of me, and I expected him to argue. To scold me, to tell me to grow up. Instead, he threaded an overblown peach-colored rose—the last of the season—through a buttonhole on my school jacket. Then his gaze flickered away, watching Martha cut across the garden toward us.

"She looks done in," Martha said. "The poor child."

"She didn't know, Martha," he said. "How could she not know?"

"Hello, I'm right here." They were talking about me as though I'd wandered off.

"Well, of course you are, dear." Martha wrapped a motherly arm around me and ushered me into the house. She smelled of fresh lemons as she led me upstairs, murmuring comforting nothings. When we passed the red-headed maid in the hallway, she curtsied to both of us.

"You see them, too," I said.

"Yes," she answered.

Inside the bathroom, a steamy bubble bath waited.

"You've had a long day," Martha told me. "A long few weeks. But you're not alone anymore."

I sank into the bubbles and let my problems float away.

Back in my bedroom I found the bed turned down and a Wedgwood plate on the bedside table. The Oriental bird pattern was covered by grapes and little tea sandwiches of cucumber and watercress.

I demolished them. Delicious.

Then I fell into a refreshing and dreamless sleep. When I woke up, the sky outside my window had turned to gray and there were flames in the fireplace. I wondered if the little ghost urchin had started it.

My favorite skinny jeans and a pale blue cashmere sweater of my mother's lay across the dresser. Comfortable and comforting—exactly the right things. Though odd that I wasn't sure if I should thank Martha or the ghost maid for suggesting the outfit.

There was a knock on the door as I finished getting dressed. Martha beckoned me downstairs to meet Coby, who was waiting in the foyer. We went down the grand staircase together and I asked, "Did you lay out my clothes?"

"No, that's one of Celeste's duties," she replied.

"The ghost maid? They can do things?" Well, of course they could. Like light fires and cook meals. I shook my head.

"The precise physics is a bit . . . complicated. Much depends on how they passed away, and when. Why they're lingering. And of course a nexus such as Echo Point—and this house—adds a few factors."

"Well, that's clear."

She laughed. "I'm afraid you've entered a world with more questions than answers."

"What about the bad stuff?"

"There's time to worry about that later," she said, clearly shutting down that subject. And as Coby waited for us at the bottom of the stairs, I couldn't exactly press her for more.

"Hey," I said, smiling at the sight of him.

"How are you feeling?" he asked. He'd changed out of his uniform into a T-shirt and jeans and had slung a black messenger bag over one shoulder.

"Um . . ." How to explain?

"There's tea in the kitchen," Martha said, "I'll be in the study."

I watched her disappear, then turned to Coby. "Do guys actually drink tea?"

He grinned. "I've been known to imbibe."

"Well, then let's go crazy."

In the kitchen, there was an urn full of steaming water and a tray with cups, assorted bags of tea, and some pale cookies that were buttery and amazing. I briefly wondered if everything had been laid out by Martha or one of the ghosts. I hoped Martha, because

I wasn't sure I could deal with a ghost popping in at any moment.

I glanced shiftily around and Coby asked, "Is something wrong?"

"No!"

"Do I make you nervous?"

I smiled. "No, just the opposite. You are normal and real and that's exactly what I need right now."

"Normal and real." He sipped his tea. "A girl with low expectations."

"Believe me," I said, sitting beside him in the breakfast nook, "that's not as easy as it sounds."

Then we tried to outdo each other with stories about all the weird people we'd known. I mentioned the girl who drew spiderwebs on her face, but he won with a tale of a guy who wore surgical gloves to school. I figured seeing ghosts would top a guy who changed his latex gloves after every class, but before I could tell him, he unzipped his pack.

"I brought your homework. Want to do Trig together?"

See? Normal and real. "I'd love to," I said.

The sky darkened as we finished our assignment and Coby packed up his things. "I'd better get going. My mom is rigid about family meals."

"That sounds nice," I said, wistfully, as we walked through the halls.

"Oh, I forgot . . . about your family. I didn't mean to—"

"Don't apologize," I said, at the front door. "My family

isn't your fault." I hadn't explained about my parents and Max going missing, but he knew Bennett was my guardian, so it was obvious I didn't have the happy home life he did. "Thanks, Coby. I needed a friend today."

I went upstairs to finish the homework he'd brought me. It was a relief to bury myself in assignments and not think about Bennett, Martha, or so-called ghostkeeping.

An hour later Martha was at my door again, this time calling me to dinner. I followed her downstairs, my mind still filled with unanswered questions.

"Um . . . I don't mean to be rude, but who exactly are you?" I asked.

She smiled kindly. "I was Bennett's nanny and his sister's, before him. Then of course Olivia moved to California and Bennett started college. But I've always stayed with the Sterns between jobs, acting as temporary house-keeper."

"His parents live in France?"

"Mm, ever since . . . well, the Sterns always travel a great deal. Like your parents."

"You know my parents?"

"In passing, yes. It's a small community."

Did she mean the antiquities community? Bennett's parents had done some business with mine—purchases for their museum.

"And Martha is a big gossip," Bennett said affection-ately from the bottom of the stairs. He wore a white button-down, jeans, and brown suede shoes. With his tousled hair and self-confident ease, he reminded me of the Rake. A younger, happier version. "Dinner's ready," he said.

Even in cashmere, I felt underdressed following Bennett and Martha into the dining room. Maybe because I was barefoot. And maybe because the table now boasted a new floral centerpiece and sterling candelabras filled with beeswax candles. Evidently, I'd been eating with the daily china and silver, because tonight's settings were even more ornate.

I almost took my accustomed place at the head of the table, but Bennett pulled out the chair across from Martha, and I sat there instead.

"I'd forgotten what a beautiful table Celeste sets," Martha said.

"So you're a ghostkeeper, too," I said. It made sense, of course. "A summoner?"

"Martha is a compeller," Bennett told me.

"A compeller? What's that?"

"Bennett, business at the dinner table?" Martha said repressively.

"Sorry," he said, flashing me a look.

I grinned as I put my napkin in my lap, then watched Celeste and the ghost boy, Nicholas, arrive with chafing dishes. Celeste served us roasted birds, like miniature turkeys, with boiled potatoes and gravy.

"The cook," I said. "Is he French?"

"Anatole, yes, he and Celeste both," Martha said. "He's

not exactly, well... *au courant* with his recipes. I lost twenty pounds when I left this job."

"That's okay," I said, not wanting to hurt his feelings, because he could be hovering anywhere. "Everything's so delicious."

As Nicholas set the peas on the table, I cut into my bird, and inadvertently nudged him with my elbow. I gasped at the contact.

"What is it?" Bennett asked, his eyes bright with concern.

"I—I felt him!" It seemed rude to jab him again, so I offered my hand to Nicholas. He grinned, took my hand, and made a little bow. His skin felt cold, and my hand looked bright pink next to his pallor. You wouldn't notice in daylight, but in the candlelight he glowed very faintly. He and Celeste both. I wondered if they could dial it up a notch, like the man in the brown suit had when I'd needed light in the dark corridor.

My hand holding Nicholas's began to tingle and ache. When he dropped it, my fingertips were pale.

"That happens," Bennett said, watching me. "We can't touch them for very long. Ghostkeepers can't."

"And the more powerful the ghostkeeper," Martha said, "the more pronounced the effect. I've seen hands that never came back. Like frostbite."

"Nicholas," Bennett said, and reached out to the boy. The urchin scampered over and wrapped his hands around Bennett's. When he withdrew his hand from Nicholas's grasp, he wiggled his fingers in the candlelight. They were barely pale, and he'd held Nicholas's hand much longer than I had.

"But that means—," I said.

"Ghostkeeping runs strong in my family," Bennett told me. "I've dispelled ghosts who've lingered too long, who've mixed with less wholesome things. I'm not *un*powerful."

I looked at my own hand again, an unsettled feeling in my stomach. It meant that I was more powerful than Bennett. How could that be? I knew next to nothing about ghostkeeping.

Martha must've noticed my discomfort. "I called the school and explained you were sick," she told me. "It was awfully nice of that boy, Coby, to drop by with your homework. He's quite fond of you, Emma."

Thank you, Martha. Now Bennett's going to think I'm involved with Coby. "We're not—I mean, we just met."

"Sometimes one simply knows," Martha said.

"Yeah." I refused to look at Bennett. "Sometimes you just know."

Utterly uninterested, Bennett said, "Pass the peas? I'm starving."

We kept the ghost talk on hold until dessert. It helped that Celeste and Nicholas had silently dematerialized after serving. Their abrupt disappearance didn't seem to faze Martha or Bennett, but I wasn't sure how I'd get used to it.

Anatole brought in dessert himself, tall fluted glasses filled with a pale frothiness.

"Is this a vanilla milk shake?" I asked. "I love milk shakes!"

Anatole frowned and his ruddy cheeks grew redder.

"Um, yogurt?"

Anatole twirled his mustache fiercely. Oh dear.

"It's syllabub, dear," Martha said.

"Syllabub! Of course. I love syllabub." Which, despite the fact that I'd never heard of it before, turned out to be true. Apparently it consists of cream, lemon juice, sugar, and . . . brandy. Lots of brandy. When I finished, I licked my spoon clean and giggled.

Maybe because of the poof, I'd never experimented much with drugs or alcohol. I was afraid to lose control of myself. So learning that Bennett, Martha, and I were a secret sect of ghostkeepers, combined with an entire brandy-soaked syllabub, knocked my socks off.

"I'm going to name my first child Syllabub," I announced. I almost said "Syllabub Stern," but managed to restrain myself. "Or Rex, if it's a boy."

"Oh, dear," Martha said. "I'd forgotten the brandy."

I giggled again.

Bennett frowned at his glass. "In the dessert?" he said, in disbelief.

"Well, pardon me, college boy!" I said. "I'm not downing kegs at toga parties every weekend."

"Right. That's exactly how I spend my weekends."

"You're too grumpy for Greek parties," I informed him. "Catapultam habeo. Caput tuum saxum immane mittam!"*

"Sentio aliquos togatos contra me conspirare,"** Bennett said.

I sighed at his perfect pronunciation. All this, and Latin, too? Syllabub Stern actually had a nice ring.

"Bennett, have a little sympathy." Martha sighed. "Take her for a walk."

He stood and pulled me from my chair.

I clung to him happily, the brandy having stripped away my inhibitions. I *looooved* him. Maybe I'd tell him on our walk.

---

* I have a catapult. I will fling an enormous rock at your head.

** I think people in togas are plotting against me.

15

We strolled quietly past the front gates and—thank God—the cool air dissipated my buzz. At least a little. We walked through the narrow streets of the village. A sporty BMW prowled past, and somewhere in the distance two dogs barked at each other. A fresh breeze came from the harbor, and I remembered something that was eating at me. Back in the rose garden, Bennett had talked about missing pieces and I had some of my own.

"So it's always been real? Even as a kid, when I saw all those people no one else could?"

"They're not alive, but yeah, they're real. And there's nothing wrong with you, Emma. You're not crazy, you're not broken—you're exceptional."

I only wished my parents agreed. "When did you first start seeing them?"

"I was four—at least the first time I remember. Olivia summoned him. She was only eight, and playing around, but she summoned this huge guy—this tough old sailor.

He'd probably been lost at sea, but to me he looked like a pirate. I closed my eyes and willed him to disappear. My parents came running just as I dispelled him. I felt a sort of . . . *shove*, from inside, and he vanished."

I frowned. That's just what I'd felt among the encroaching shadows in the village, before they dissolved. But I was a summoner, not a dispeller . . .

"That's when they knew I had the gift," he continued. "It runs in families. They explained everything to me that day—as much as a four-year-old could understand."

"I guess my parents didn't know. That's why they sent me to the hospital."

Instead of responding, Bennett led me silently down a crooked little wooden staircase, then turned left toward the marina. We passed the boats in the harbor and walked to the end of the breakwater and stared at the sea.

The Atlantic felt so different from the Pacific. It was darker, rougher and less forgiving. The sea swallowed the few rocks Bennett tossed into the waves.

"Do you know why they named you Emma?" he asked.

I cocked my head, surprised by the question. "After some relative I never met."

"You never met her because she died over two hundred years ago. Emma Vaile. She was a legend. The greatest ghostkeeper in the New World."

"I saw her—in a painting at Thatcher."

"She lived there."

"That was her *house*? Not bad." And it explained a lot. "But why am I reliving her memories?"

"I don't know. Some ghostkeepers can recall the memories of the dead by holding things they owned, but you're definitely a summoner. You proved that this afternoon." A wave crashed against the breakwater. "But nothing's ever simple."

"Yeah, I'm getting that." More softly, I said, "I look just like her."

"Like the first Emma?" He glanced at me.

"Yeah, it was weird."

"Well, you're her great-great-great-granddaughter, or something." He watched me in the moonlight. "They say she was beautiful."

I let out a breath. "Maybe not *exactly* like her."

Bennett smiled and hurled another rock into the water. We stood there silently, as I mustered the courage to ask the questions I was afraid I didn't want answered.

Finally, I said, "So I'm descended from one of the earliest ghostkeepers, and all this runs in families."

Bennett nodded, looking relieved that it was out in the open.

"So, my family is like yours and my parents are . . . Oh God. *Both* of them?"

"Just your dad, now. He's a reader—he senses psychic impressions, reads memories in the belongings of the dead. There's a lot of information to be mined there—and a lot of wealth. He knows exactly how old something is and whether it's a fake or not." A wave rippled down the shore, and Bennett fell silent for a moment. "Your mom wasn't very strong; she needed what we call a 'focus' to magnify her power. Like repeating a mantra or—I don't know—a lucky charm or incantation. She lost her talent years ago. That happens, when—"

"Wait. What about *Max*?"

A sad smile crossed his face. "He's a badass compeller."

The chill ocean wind seeped into my bones. "How could they be—it's like I don't know them at all."

"Emma, that's not true. They're still your family."

"No. They're strangers to me. How could they keep me in the dark all this time? I thought I was losing my mind." I swallowed the bitter taste in my mouth. "They threw me in a mental ward. I was *seven*. They drugged me and—"

Bennett put his arm around me and it wasn't romantic, but I was comforted.

"Why?" I asked him. "Why would they do that?"

"I don't know. They had your ability wiped, or at least suppressed, until now. They must've had a reason. That's the piece of your past that we're missing."

I watched the ceaseless flow of waves, the old wounds fresh in my mind. Was there a reason they'd closed doors on me, so I wouldn't overhear what they'd taught Max? At least this explained their favoritism toward him—why they'd traveled with him and shared their obsession with death: the antiquities and funeral urns and books on necromancy.

"You call us ghostkeepers," I said, "but are we really necromancers?"

"No. No one can raise the dead to life."

"So there are rules?"

"There are limits," he said. "And there's always a price."

"What does that mean?"

He shrugged. "Most ghosts are like Celeste and Anatole, but some ghosts get twisted. They seek to hurt and destroy. We call them ghasts. They're dangerous, so we handle them, keep them where they belong. That's what we do, that's why we're called ghostkeepers."

I nodded, but I wasn't really listening—I was obsessing over my parents. They lived this secret life, never showing me who they really were. They hadn't just ignored me, they'd taken steps to *exclude* me.

"Let's go back," I said, needing to move, to burn off some of the emotion. Bennett walked beside me, giving me the silence I needed.

I didn't speak again until we'd passed through the museum gates, and were at the front door. "Why? Why would they name me after a famous ghostkeeper and not tell me who we were?"

"I'm named for a relative, too," he said.

"Bennett Stern?"

"Yeah." Bennett opened the front door. "Emma Vaile was a widow. He was her lover."

16

After I showered the next morning, I found a new uniform in the wardrobe. I put it on and examined myself in the mirror. Well, it fit. The skirt was a frumpy knee length and the blouse was shapeless. I guess Bennett took my "school slut" joke to heart.

Maybe he'd been jealous.

I left my tie unknotted and headed downstairs. When I stepped into the kitchen, Martha looked up from the table, where she sat with papers spread all around her.

"Morning," I said. "Um, is Bennett awake? I need help with my tie."

"Come here, dear. Happy to help."

"Oh! That's okay, thanks. Bennett's got this special knot I'm learning."

Her eyes twinkled. "The one that requires him doing it for you?"

"No!" I said, glancing at the door to check Bennett hadn't overheard.

"He's already back at school. He lost a week, fetching you from California and investigating . . . his other research. He'll be busy for a while."

"A while," I said despondently, flopping into a seat.

"A while," she repeated firmly, as though she disapproved of my interest.

She taught me a knot—not an Oriental—and I watched Anatole flit about, preparing my lunch. Cutting the crusts from sandwiches and tossing tangerine segments into a fruit salad.

Then he turned to me and said, *Ma chère, what may I bring you this matin?*

Except I didn't hear him with my ears, but inside my head. I goggled at him for a moment, then thought back: *You talk!*

But of course—and so have I always. He stroked his luxuriant mustache. *But you, now you've started to listen. Your ability grows with each passing day. What may I bring you?*

Is there any oatmeal? I could kill a bowl of oatmeal.

Ze porridge? Oui. But there is no slaughtering involved.

I smiled. *Cool.*

He frowned. *You prefer ze porridge cold?*

Uh, no, I said. *Hot, please.*

Good, good. I worked in ze town home of a viscount and his wife—I will not call her ze viscountess—she refused any dish warmer than tepid. Fah! He took a heavy-bottomed saucepan from the rack. *Also, she ate custard two meals a day. Those days tried a man's soul, to see my talents wasted.*

That must've been difficult, I said, suppressing a giggle.

Oui, a terrible waste. He bustled about, setting oatmeal and a little bowl of brown sugar on the counter. But then he got an odd look on his face and paused. The liveliness faded from his eyes as he opened the fridge and removed a carton of eggs. Instead of making oatmeal, he cracked eggs into a cast-iron skillet.

"Did you just compel him to make eggs? I asked him to make oatmeal."

Martha cross-checked her list. "Oh, he can't hear you."

"Um. He asked what I wanted. And then he started to make oatmeal, before you compelled him to make eggs."

Her attention snapped to me. "What?"

"Eggs are good. I don't need oatmeal."

"No, Emma. I mean you can *communicate* with him?"

"You can't?" I asked.

She shook her head. "I can merely compel him."

"But what if he doesn't want to make eggs?" I asked, glancing at the stove where Anatole was unhappily flipping eggs. "What if he wants to make oatmeal or huevos rancheros?"

Martha furrowed her brow. "A compeller compels, Emma. And while I like and respect Anatole . . . the dead serve the living, not the other way around. We aren't concerned with their desires."

Well, maybe we should be. But I kept that little tidbit to myself. Martha had only been kind to me and I didn't understand the philosophies and ethics of ghost-keeping. Yet.

"It's a rare gift, communicating with ghosts," she said. "Odd that Bennett thought you were a summoner."

"I think because I kind of did. Summon them, I mean. In the garden."

"Nobody has more than a single power. Perhaps you just . . . *asked* them to come near? And they were already present?"

"I suppose," I said. "Yeah, that makes sense."

Because what did I know about ghostkeeping? And as Anatole handed me my eggs, he definitely understood my *Merci.*

You're welcome, chère. Do not worry about Martha. She's an old friend, and means well.

I only had a chance to finish a few bites of egg before the church bells on the corner struck eight. I grabbed my backpack and gave Martha a kiss good-bye, which seemed to please her. I smiled at Anatole as he handed me my lunch and headed outside.

I ran into Sara in the apple orchard, and she said, "Coby likes you."

I'm not that girl who pretends she doesn't know that a guy is into her for more than just friendship, so I didn't bother denying it. Still, I didn't know *why* he liked me. With Sara's long chestnut hair, raspy voice, and electric blue wool coat, if I were Coby, I'd like *her.*

"Does he always like the new girl?" I asked.

Maybe that was just his MO. Or maybe he cycled through the girl geeks. There'd been a guy like that at my old school—and a new awkward dweebette each week, dressed in a turtleneck to cover the hickeys.

"Does he seem like that kinda guy?" she asked, a little sharply. "Because he's not."

"I just don't know why he'd like me."

"He's the quarterback, Emma. He's smart, he's cute, he can like anyone he wants."

I remembered they'd grown up together, and now she was acting like a protective sister. Maybe I should've told her I wasn't interested in Coby, but that seemed like a conversation I should have with him first. Besides, maybe I *was* interested. I wasn't sure of anything at the moment.

Sara suddenly took a step back and eyed my new uniform. "What happened? You used to look so cute. Easy, but cute."

"Bennett noticed," I said.

"Bennett Stern?"

"Yeah."

"Hot," she crooned. "I've seen him at Harry's parties. What's your relationship again?"

"Um, he's my guardian? My parents are traveling overseas." Which didn't exactly explain everything, but wasn't a total lie, either.

"Harry says you like him." She fluffed her hair as we walked up the school steps, and managed to look even more perfect. "That is so twisted romance novely."

I pulled on the ends of my own hair, trying to get it to grow. "If Harry gossiped any more, he'd be a girl." I thought of the ghosts. "Anyway, it's more of a horror film than a romance novel."

She paused at the school door. "Because of your clothes? Where's your phone? I'll give you the number of my tailor."

I knew her clothes fit too well to be off the rack. But I wasn't about to flash her the purple dinosaur. "I forgot to recharge it. Text me later?"

Harry caught us in the front hallway. He looked me up and down and said, "Goody Vaile, you seem to be missing your bonnet."

The day went downhill from there.

The man in the brown suit greeted me with a bow in Trigonometry.

I rolled my eyes. *Go away.*

Ah! Now she talks.

Thanks for disappearing on me in the attic, I said. *That wasn't scary or anything.*

I'm a ghost, Miss Vaile. Grant me my little moods.

I ignored him as Mr. Sakolsky passed out a pop quiz. *If you're going to stick around, at least help with my quiz. What's the answer to number two?*

No idea. I taught American history in this room, back when Thatcher maintained higher standards. Before they let girls in.

I shot him an evil look—which Coby thought was aimed at him, and appeared wounded.

"I hate quizzes," I mouthed.

"Emma," Mr. Sakolsky said. "No whispering."

I put my head down and began working on the problems, but ghost-man distracted me. *Don't you have better things to do?* I asked.

I could haunt the staff lounge.

Please do.

But he didn't. He loomed beside me, making concentration impossible. So I finally asked, *You taught here?*

Best years of my life.

How did you die, anyway? Is that rude to ask?

He shook his head. *I loved everything about Thatcher: the teaching, the students, the campus. I poured my soul into my work. And when I felt a heart attack coming on, in that corner right there*—he pointed to where Mr. Sakolsky was sitting at his desk—*I didn't want to go. I wasn't ready. I fought death every step of the way.*

And you won.

With a wry smile, he said, *This isn't life. I lost, but I remained in this form. I've regretted it ever since.*

I heard his voice in my head, the deep timbre, the old-fashioned posh accent. I sympathized with him, but was I supposed to be helping ghosts? I had no idea. So I finished one of the trig problems instead and circled my answer.

You could send me back, couldn't you? he said.

Back where?

To my body. I'm buried across town. Dispel me.

That'd be like killing you. I could never! Plus, I don't know how.

I was totally freaked out by the idea. Dispelling was the only thing about Bennett I wasn't sure I liked.

I'm already dead. I'm bored. It wasn't bad when they were still teaching history in this room, but I despise *trigonometry. You could help me. I'm ready now.*

I finished my quiz. *The answer is no. Now go away.* I shooed at him with my hands. He looked completely miffed and dematerialized.

Coby looked at me, wondering why I was waving at him.

"Fly," I mouthed.

At lunchtime, I walked with Coby and Sara toward the cafeteria. Coby teased me about acing the Trig quiz as Sara deflected the attention of two sophomore boys who'd clearly dared each other to talk to her.

As we turned the corner, a janitor loomed in front of me, mopping the floor. I yelped and sidestepped, and Coby laughed. "Emma! Drunk again?"

"What? I didn't want to"—to stumble into the ghostly janitor nobody else saw?—"to start drinking so early, but I needed to numb myself from the pain of fencing." I laughed nervously.

The janitor tipped his cap to me as we continued past, and I noticed a few more ghosts in the crowded hallways. It was like now that *I* knew I was a ghost-keeper, so did all the ghosts. I'd already been heckled by two idiot ghost boys during Fencing, who appeared shortly after I started sparring with Kylee, the twig-armed girl.

Watch out, one of them told me, *you're getting beaten by a girl.*

A weak girl, the other one said.

"Fleche!" the coach called. "No, no—the hit lands before the rear foot touches the floor."

Kylee slipped past my guard.

Oh! Clumsy, clumsy.

Go away! I dropped into en garde position and shooed them, just like I had the man in the brown suit. The look on their faces was similar to that of Anatole's when Martha had compelled him to make eggs. Was it possible I'd compelled them away?

"Emma Vaile," the coach said. "What on earth are you doing? We're fencing, not fanning ourselves. I know you're new, but please concentrate."

Easier said than done. Carrying on a conversation in the dining room proved a challenge, with all the ghosts vying for my attention. I needed to ask Martha how I could tune them out. In the meantime, a combination of asking nicely and, when that didn't work, *pushing* them away with my mind seemed to do the trick. And somehow I got through World Literature and Western Civ without making a fool of myself.

Still, I was completely fed up with the entire ghostly world by the time I got home. Unfortunately, Martha had other ideas. I'd hardly changed out of my uniform before she set me to work on my ghostkeeping skills.

She shepherded me into the ballroom, where the three resident ghosts stood against the wall, looking peeved.

What's going on? I asked Celeste.

She's on a—how do you say it? A rampage, mademoiselle! With ze cleaning and ze sorting and ze rummaging through old boxes . . .

Martha consulted one of her lists from this morning. "We've a great deal to cover today, Emma."

And me, she had scouring pots and pans, Anatole said. *Moi!*

"First introduce yourself," Martha told me. "By the end of the evening, they should know your name."

You are Miss Emma, of course we know, Celeste said. *She must think we are ze idiots.*

And tell her I am a cook, not a scullery maid! This ridiculous woman!

"Is Anatole saying something?"

"Um, yes—he says they know my name."

"Why is Celeste rolling her eyes?" Martha asked.

"She, erm—she says I'm Miss Emma."

How about you? I asked Nicholas. *How are you doing?*

Spent all day rootin' around in the chimneys, mum. Do you know how many chimneys there are in this house?

"Their accents are funny," I told Martha. "Sort of off, like their clothing."

No offense, I told the ghosts.

Fah, do we care? Anatole said. *I am only relieved to have someone who understands us again.*

Oui, said Celeste. *It has been too long.*

"Communicators often say that," Martha said. "I think our preconceptions affect how we see them—and hear them. We project our expectations on them."

Tell her I need a new chimney brush, said Nicholas. *And more toys. I've seen what the children bring when they come . . .*

Celeste tsked. *You need less time playing and more time on ze chores.*

Aw, Celeste!

Ze boots do not shine themselves!

Oh, is that why my boots look so good? I asked. *Thanks!*

"What are they saying?" Martha said. "Do you understand anything?"

I started translating, and Martha nodded slowly. "So I guess they know your name." She told me to quiz them about their lives, and I related what I learned.

Nicholas had died of consumption (Martha had to explain that was tuberculosis, he hadn't actually been consumed by anyone). He'd vowed to take care of his little sister, whom he'd promised he'd never leave. He lingered for her.

Celeste had fallen in love with the son in a neighboring house, who got her pregnant, then put her out on the street, where she had died of exposure. Her child had not survived.

Jerk, I said.

Oui!

Anatole had succumbed to bad eggs. Literally, food poisoning.

After an hour, my mind blurred with exhaustion. I

began to have trouble communicating with the ghosts and they with me. It was as though I'd been conversing in a foreign language and started forgetting the translation. I was ready for a break.

Martha ended the lessons and we went to the kitchen for tea. I noticed her getting that intense look on her face that meant she was about to compel Anatole to start the kettle. His mustache bristled with offense.

"I'll make the tea," I said, and told Anatole he could start on dinner. I took a teapot and two cups with saucers from the cabinet and turned to ask Martha what kind of tea she'd like.

She was staring thoughtfully at me. "You're not like other ghostkeepers, Emma. I don't know if it's because you weren't raised knowing your talent, or it's just who you are."

I thought about that. My powers grew stronger every day. Martha wanted to help me, but I wasn't sure where I was headed. Maybe that's what made me different. I didn't take the ghosts for granted. And I didn't know what my purpose in all this was. Martha and Bennett seemed sure of their roles; I didn't know if I'd ever be.

"Emma," she said softly, taking my hand. "Sometimes this path is so difficult and I know you've been hurt— badly hurt—by your family. I'm sure they had their reasons . . . but you have reasons, too. To be angry, wary of all that's going on. It must be hard for you to trust me, or even yourself."

I nodded through a thin veil of tears. Why does it hurt

more sometimes to have someone understand you, to sympathize, than to soldier on as though nothing's wrong?

"I promise, Emma, I will never leave you without telling you why. And as long as I'm here, I'm going to help you be the best Emma Vaile you can be."

"You mean the best ghostkeeper?"

"No. I mean the best Emma."

I guess that was really my problem: I didn't know who I wanted to be or how ghostkeeping was going to fit into my life. Was I suddenly supposed to make a career out of this? Or was it just a really awkward hobby?

Martha seemed set on forcing me to confront issues I wasn't ready to deal with. So I murmured something noncommittal and slipped away.

I'd let her compel Anatole to make her tea when the kettle whistled.

I wasn't ready to start my homework, but I wanted to stay in the sanctuary of the house. I was afraid if I ventured into town I'd see those scary shadows again. So I wandered around aimlessly. First, I paced the library. Then I knocked the pool balls around in the billiard room until I felt a familiar tingle. It was probably Nicholas, looking for a game to play, but I didn't want to face even him, not right now.

I went into what I decided must be Mr. Stern's office. I'd already discovered Mrs. Stern's upstairs. It was elegant and feminine, with beige walls and white woodwork, botanical prints and a spotless white desk. This one looked more lived-in, decorated in shades of blue and brown. Bookcases lined the walls, and I recognized many of the titles from my father's shelves. I wondered if Bennett had read them all, just like Max.

Maybe it was time that I did, as well. So I took one from the shelf and flipped to the first page and read a sentence and put the book back. Too boring for words.

I sat at the desk and considered turning on the iMac, but that felt like an invasion of privacy. Instead, I spun in the chair. Feeling . . . I don't know. At home. I'd never met Bennett's father, but I liked his office. Comfortable and uncluttered—with a botanical print that matched one in his wife's office, which I found sweet.

I liked the big globe on a wooden stand and the pictures of Bennett and his sister on the bookshelf. I even liked the pair of swords displayed crosswise on the opposite wall: thicker than our fencing foils, with slight curves and vicious-looking edges.

I stood and crossed to the swords, feeling the telltale pinpricks in my limbs that meant something ghostly was about to happen. But this time, I didn't just let it happen. I pushed forward and embraced it. I lifted one of the swords from the wall and fell into that tremendous *whoosh* that transported me back in time.

The world spun into a blur, then slowed—slower and slower until the rose garden outside formed around me. It was suddenly summer, the roses alive with color and scent, and my heart beat quickly in my chest.

No. In Emma's chest—the original Emma. No corset this time, the dress was loose and light, designed for motion. The sword hilt fit perfectly in my palm, exquisitely well-balanced. The man facing me was quick and dark. Despite his coloring, he reminded me for a moment of Bennett. Then his features resolved into those of the Rake.

He held the matching sword aloft, mocking me with his smile. And I felt—*she* felt—a jumble of emotions—passion and longing and sorrow—as I lunged forward.

We engaged blades and the Rake fell back. Triumph rose within me. Until with a twist of his wrist he knocked the sword from my hand. Yet for some reason, his expression looked like surrender as the tingling started again and—

Whoosh.

I was back to myself, standing in the center of the office, the sword lying on the floor at my feet. I grabbed the hilt and crossed the hall to the ballroom. The Rake—the ghost of the Rake—watched me from the piano, and I moved toward him. He looked different than in Emma's memory, the lines in his face etched deeper, his eyes more guarded. I couldn't figure out what he was doing here. Neither Bennett nor Martha had ever mentioned him. Was he purposely hiding from them?

His eyes flicked to the sword in my hand, then to my face. He raised a finger, telling me to stay still, then he circled behind me, his gaze intent, measuring me with his eyes.

I'm Emma. I watched myself in the reflection of one of

the windows. I stood alone. *Now you're supposed to tell me your name.*

There was a chill in my right hand, which held the sword. I looked down and saw his hand superimposed on mine. I looked at his face, and he shook his head, nodding to our intertwined hands, moving his thumb and forefinger.

Showing me how to grip the sword?

That's starting to hurt, I told him.

He withdrew his hand. I flexed mine until the blood returned, then changed my grip on the hilt. It was completely different from how I'd been taught at school, and for the first time the sword felt comfortable in my hand.

Oh, I said.

He gestured for me to continue.

I dropped into en garde position, feet shoulder-width apart, front foot straight and back foot sideways, my right arm loose and my left sticking out at shoulder height like a chicken wing. Then I bent my knees and tried to relax, like Coach told us.

The Rake narrowed his eyes, then flicked his wrist at me. His hand caught the flat of the blade and sent it twisting from my grip, clattering across the room.

You hold the blade, he said, *like a girl—*

So you do *talk!*

When I have something to say. His voice sounded low and hoarse in my mind, like he hadn't used it in ages.

You ghosts are so sexist. I'll have you know that women fight in armies now and—and that Resident Evil chick kicks ass.

En garde, he said.

I dropped back into position.

Caress the hilt with your thumb. Feel the warmth of the metal. The smith who forged that sword knew something of love.

I wriggled my thumb around, feeling ridiculous. Where exactly was the love supposed to be?

He sighed again. *Come.*

I lunged at him, and he swatted the sword with the back of his hand.

Would you at least use your sword?! I said.

I will teach you how to . . . kick ass, Emma Vaile. He curled his fingers at me, waving me toward him. *Again.*

I lunged and lunged until my quadriceps and calves burned. The entire right side of my body throbbed with a deep ache. Then he made me start over, holding the sword in my left hand.

Curt and demanding, the nameless rake gave me a total workout. If only I could videotape a ghost, we'd make millions selling the exercise routine.

Finally, he said, *That's enough. You learn quickly.*

I collapsed on a bench, sweaty and aching. *Why am I doing this?*

To stay alive.

God save me from overdramatic ghosts. *You taught her, too. The first Emma?*

His dark eyes turned darker. *Yes.*

To help her stay alive? I asked, setting the sword beside me.

No, he said. *To betray her.*

When I raised my head, he was gone.

17

I was quiet through dinner, letting Martha carry most of the conversation about cataloging items Celeste had found in the attic. Then she pushed a Game Boy across the table toward me.

"Don't think I'll be adding this to my list," she said.

It must have belonged to Bennett. I hadn't seen one in ages and couldn't resist flipping it on. It came to life with a distinctly digital noise that clashed with the elegance of the dining room.

"Emma, not at the table."

"Sorry." I slipped it under my napkin, after confirming Tetris had loaded.

Martha kept the evening light, telling funny stories of the crazy kids she'd known—and their crazier parents. I wondered how life would've been different if I'd grown up with her.

I didn't say much, but headed upstairs refreshed. I

finished my homework, checked my messages, then fell into bed, exhausted despite the early hour.

Just as I was dozing off, I heard a *tack, tack, tack.*

I mumbled, "Celeste?"

Tack. Tack.

"G'way, I'm sleeping."

Pock!

What the hell? I sat up and looked for the ghost responsible. Nobody around. Then a shower of pebbles—or marbles—bounced off my window.

Nicholas! I summoned him.

Evenin', mum, he said, hovering just inside the doorway.

Would you not call me "mum"?

Sorry, mum, he said. *Need them boots of yours polished?*

No, I need sleep. Stop knocking your marbles against the window or—

And another shower of gravel hit the windowpane.

Not me, mum.

Nicholas, I'm not old enough to be a mum or ma'am or whatever it is you're saying. Call me Emma. I crossed to the window. *And sorry for blaming you.*

I pushed aside the curtains, and saw the old maple trees stretching toward the sky. The manicured lawn rolled gently toward the stone fence and streaks of silver clouds glowed in the moonlight.

Then I saw him, and my heart almost stopped: Coby standing under my window, glowing faintly.

Dead. The ghost of Coby. I heard an anguished sound,

and realized it came from my own throat. I threw open the window as Coby stepped from the moonlight and stopped glowing.

"You're alive!" I called to him.

He laughed two stories below me, in the gravel of the drive. "You're not like other girls, are you?" he called up. "I never know what you're gonna say."

"Me either," I told him. "What are you *doing* down there?"

"Trouble with my Trig homework. What's the answer to five?"

"You lost your phone?"

"Your cell's never on."

"One second."

I ducked back inside, and found Nicholas offering me my backpack. *You've got a suitor, mum.*

He's not a suitor! I said, grabbing my pack.

I poked my head outside and called out the answer.

"Maybe I didn't come about the homework." He glanced up shyly.

Nicholas hopped onto the windowsill beside me. *Celeste says they won't buy the cow if they get the cream for free.*

I silenced him with a glare, and said to Coby, "So why did you come?"

"Halloween's next weekend," Coby said. "You want to go to Harry's party with me?"

With all the ghosts in my life, I didn't really feel up to a Halloween party, so I'd ignored Harry's Evite. Yet I did want to be a normal girl who went out with her friends on the weekend. And the one who said yes to the cute guy who'd come all the way across town to flirt with her by moonlight.

So I did. Say yes, I mean, and we made plans for Saturday night.

I watched Coby slink across the lawn, back toward the gate, telling myself I didn't really wish he'd been Bennett. When I closed the window, Nicholas shot me an arch look.

I decided to distract him from romantic advice.

Have you ever played Tetris? I asked.

He shook his head, his eyes big.

I pulled out the Game Boy Martha had given me. *You are gonna love this.*

We played past midnight, snuggling—though at a slight distance, to prevent frostbite—on my bed. Nicholas glowed with excitement. Literally. He glowed. And you'd expect ghostly laughter to sound hollow and chilly, but his burbles of childish delight radiated warmth.

When finally I fell asleep, the last thing I heard was, *Nobody ever done nothing like that for me before, mum. Not ever.*

"What are you going to wear?" Sara asked the next day as we headed for fencing class.

"Um, you know—jacket, mask, glove. The regular."

"Emma, focus!" She shook her head in disgust, and her

chestnut hair fell in lustrous waves around her shoulders. I found it hard to like her sometimes. "For the Halloween party," she said.

"Oh. Well, not my uniform." I'd dressed in full-on frumpy regalia again. Yeah, I looked awful, but it was more comfortable than the minuscule outfit. And the Thatcher ghosts made me jumpy enough without fidgeting with my clothing all day. "Back in San Francisco, I could get away with the slutty uniform. Public school kids find uniforms hilarious. Plus guys have those Catholic school-girl fantasies . . . except Coby—he's only into nurses, right?"

Her face closed. "Were you surprised he asked you to Harry's party?"

I shrugged. I'd been so distracted by all the craziness, I hadn't really thought it through.

"You know this is a *date*, right?" Sara said. "A guy doesn't visit a *friend* by moonlight to ask her to a party."

"I guess." Yeah. Obviously it was a date.

"So you like him?" she asked.

"Yeah." Of course I liked him. He was cool, smart, cute, and reliable. The only problem was, I liked him for all those perfectly good reasons, but I liked *Bennett* for no reason at all. I was torn between them. Coby was probably a better match for me and, unlike Bennett, he actually expressed some interest. But somehow that didn't stamp out all my feelings for Bennett and it was *big* that I could talk to Bennett about ghosts. If Coby and I got together for real, I didn't know how I would keep my ghostkeeping skills from him.

"Promise you won't hurt him," Sara said.

I almost laughed. The idea that I wouldn't be the dumpee in this relationship was ridiculous. I mean I was literally a freak. "I promise," I said, mock solemnly. "Now what should I wear?"

"Well, since we're in costume all week, I like to wear normal clothes on the weekend. I'm just going to dress up and wear a mask. I suggest you do the same."

"Oh, thank God," I said, as we descended the winding staircase to the gym. "I hate Halloween parties. You choose between a bulbous pumpkin, hideous witch, or slutty police girl in a garter belt. Embarrassing whichever direction you go."

"Actually, last year I was a slutty witch."

"Really?" I said. "I was a hideous police girl."

She laughed as we entered the locker room. "Do you want to borrow something? I've got extra masks."

We removed our uniforms, and even Sara's underwear was lacy and chic.

"Yes, please," I said.

Inside the gym, I saluted Kylee, the nearsighted ninety-pounder, and we dropped into en garde position. This time, however, I used the grip the Rake had taught me, and managed to swat her foil across the room.

I glanced toward the two jock ghosts in the stands.

No witty repartee today? I said. *No insults?*

Your uniform's on backward, the skinny one said.

I glanced down. *No, it's not.*

Made you look!

Grrrr!

Kylee returned with her foil, and we engaged again—and I disarmed her immediately.

Then Coach called, "Halt!" We stopped, and she checked my grip and asked, "What is this?"

Dizzy with triumph, I said, "I know, right?"

"I've never seen anyone hold a blade that way."

I shrugged modestly. "Just felt more comfortable."

"And you believe we're learning *comfort* here?"

Uh-oh.

"Fencing is a martial art—emphasis on *art*. We're learning balance, poise, proportion, discipline. And honor. Think about that, Miss Vaile."

She went on and on, until in the end I held the foil the proper way. And Kylee beat me like a rug.

The dark-haired ghost jock must have somehow seen an episode of *The Simpsons*, because he made a perfect Nelson impression as I slunk back to the locker room.

Ha-ha.

At lunch, my date with Coby was the elephant in the cafeteria. The news had spread like wildfire and everyone seemed to be treating us like we were a couple. Especially Harry, which was really annoying. Thankfully, Coby didn't act like we were dating. I don't know what I would've done if he'd put his arm around me.

Then in Western Civ, the teacher said, "In lieu of a

midterm, you'll be writing a paper on a family heirloom. You can choose—"

Brittle Britta raised her hand. "What if you, like, don't have any heirlooms?"

"Perhaps if you let me finish my sentence, Britta?"

"I mean, *I* have heirlooms, the whole *estate* is an heirloom—but I'm thinking of those less fortunate students who can't, like, even afford tuition."

She glanced archly at a few kids in the back of the classroom. The autumn light streamed in through the long-paned windows and fell across the oaken tables. The two ghost jocks from Fencing materialized in back, leaning against one of the walnut bookcases.

What are you two doing out of your cage? I asked.

We like pretty girl, the dark-haired one said with a Neanderthal impression.

They meant Britta. *Too bad her personality doesn't match her looks,* I said.

Personalities are overrated, the other one said.

What is she on about anyway? I asked.

Financial aid students, the dark one said, disdainfully. *A few students a year are accepted on scholarship.*

A thought struck me. Who was paying my tuition? My parents probably didn't even know I was here. Were Bennett's parents footing the bill?

The teacher cleared his throat. "As I was saying, you can choose any item. An old photo, a used car—if the oldest thing in your family is your mother's wedding ring, do a history of wedding bands."

"Maybe like their dad's La-Z-Boy?" Britta sneered.

"Industrial design," Mr. Jones said, "is a fascinating subject."

"How about, like, architecture?" I said, widening my eyes in an imitation of Britta. "Then I could, like, write about my entire estate."

A few kids laughed and Britta hissed, "What've *you* got? You're just freeloading off the Sterns."

That struck a nerve. "I've got my ponies," I continued, "and, like, sometimes Mummy and Daddy buy me a friend."

At that, Britta burst into tears and called me a bitch.

Then the light-haired ghost boy reached out and pinched Britta. Which would've been funny if I didn't get blamed. And if I hadn't sort of felt she was right, that I had been a bitch. Did I really have to stoop to her level?

Mr. Jones made me apologize and I got my first detention and demerits at Thatcher. I couldn't help feeling manipulated by the ghost jocks. They snickered in the corner, as though they'd planned this all along.

I wanted the darker one to pinch the other one, see how he liked it. I willed him to do it.

And he did. I watched as he reached over and goosed him on the bottom.

Ow! Why'd you do that? The light-haired ghost punched him in the arm.

He winced and said, *I don't know. I think* she *made me do it.*

They turned bitter faces toward me.

Was it possible? Had I *compelled* him? Only one way to find out. I willed the light one to slap his own butt and the dark one to pat his head and rub his tummy.

They did it! Their eyes bulged at me in indignation. I almost burst out laughing, but remembered myself just in time. I didn't want a second round of detention.

Oh my God! I could compel ghosts! I wondered if I could make them disappear, too. Not dispel them, just compel them to go away. I *pushed* at them with my mind, willing them to just leave, like when you will your number to be picked for a lottery. Only that never works and this did. It didn't take much effort as I watched their furious faces fade into the ether, while they continued to whack themselves silly.

The class bell rang, but I remained at my desk, my heart beating faster. I almost wanted to summon the ghosts back, to see if I could. But I knew I didn't need to. They'd come if I beckoned.

Mr. Jones noticed me and told me I couldn't talk him out of detention. Then said he knew I wasn't living with my family, so if I wanted a different assignment . . .

My family. Full of ghostkeepers. But did any of them have powers like mine? Able to summon, compel, *and* communicate with ghosts? I pulled the amulet I'd found in my mother's jewelry box from inside my shirt. If I were home in San Francisco, there'd be loads of heirlooms to choose from, like Nefertiti's head. But this was the closest thing I had. I rubbed the cool jade spirals. Somehow I felt that researching the origin of the amulet would give me a clue to my parents' lives. Maybe even into their secrets.

"No, I'm good," I said.

Sadly, my punishment didn't end with detention. After I explained what had happened with the ghost jocks at school, Martha decided it was unsafe for me to roam the streets without learning more control.

"You have to admit, it's kinda cool I can do all that," I said with a grin.

"Into the ballroom, missy," she said repressively.

I don't know why, but I couldn't say no to her. Maybe because my mother wasn't exactly motherly and Martha was like a sweet grandma who always offered wise, loving words and cookies warm from the oven (even if she compelled someone else to bake them). Plus, she'd been Bennett's nanny, and I was certain she held the secret to figuring him out.

It was all so *Karate Kid*—minus the headband—as I practiced in the middle of the ballroom. Martha drilled me in summoning, communicating, and, despite my reluctance, compelling. It was one thing, getting even with the ghost jocks, but I was uncomfortable compelling Nicholas, who'd offered himself as a test subject. It was easier to just ask him to do things. But I did learn how to dampen my reaction to ghosts and to protect myself from the frostbite of physical contact—which were useful. After an hour and a half, Martha suggested a hot chocolate break.

We sat in the kitchen, and she said, "The Knell isn't going to believe this. Believe *you*."

"Who's Nell?"

"The Knell, with a *K*. They're the . . . the CIA of the ghostkeeping world."

"You mean they eavesdrop on our phone calls?"

"They track the identities of ghosts—their appearances and abilities. And their crimes."

"Crimes? Like ghasts, you mean?"

Martha sipped her cocoa. "Mm. When they hear what you can do, they'll want to recruit you."

"Recruit me? I'm still in high school."

"You're uniquely talented, Emma. Communicating is rare enough, but you . . ."

"Can do all of it." Summon, communicate, and compel.

She nodded. "As far as we know. You haven't dispelled yet."

"And I'm not about to try." I was willing to do a lot for Martha, but not that.

She'd urged me to practice on a strange ghost I'd summoned, but I couldn't be as blasé about ghosts as she and Bennett were. They treated them like second-class citizens, but they were still people, right? I mean, dead people were people, too.

I wouldn't dispel any of them without good cause. Or even *with* good cause. The man in the brown suit wanted me to dispel him, but I couldn't bring myself to do it.

We practiced for another hour before Martha again brought up the Knell.

"I don't want to meet them," I said. "I've got enough problems." I was barely surviving Thatcher and missing my parents. I didn't want to get involved in fighting off ghasts or whatever they did. I only wanted to be with the house ghosts.

"But you already have," Martha said. "Bennett is a member."

"Are you?"

She got a distant look on her face. "Not anymore."

I would've questioned her further, but Anatole rang the bell for dinner. As Martha refused to talk business at meals, I had to leave it for another time. But my mind was racing with questions. Why hadn't Bennett told me he was working for the Knell? Why had Martha quit? And what did they know about my parents?

It seemed the more I settled in Echo Point, into being a ghostkeeper, the more I realized how little I knew.

18

The rest of the week followed the same routine. School, ghostkeeper training with Martha, then sneaking into the ballroom for more abuse from the Rake after homework and dinner. The Rake didn't say five words to me all week, but I kept going back, despite his surliness. There was something about his presence that comforted me, perhaps the echoes of the original Emma's memories.

So life was going pretty okay in Echo Point. Ghostkeeping felt more natural all the time. At least Nicholas no longer danced like a marionette when I compelled him. I'd done as Bennett asked and made friends at school—actual humans—and was even acing Trig, despite the lack of help from the man in the brown suit. Turned out his name was Edmund. Well, he'd always be the man in the brown suit to me.

Then in class on Friday, Harry paused during a rant in

Latin about my dowdy uniform and switched to English: "SILF at three o'clock."

"Would you stop with that?" I said. "You're like ten years too late with it."

Lately, he'd been using the ILF part of MILF to describe anything he liked: pizza was PILF, Coke was CILF, and *S* obviously stood for "student."

"Et tu es a taedium sus,"* I said, though I couldn't help but glance at the door.

And there stood Natalie.

Yes, that Natalie. Slim as ever, dark and beautiful with her flowing hair and fitted uniform.

My stomach dropped, and I felt my world crash around me. Natalie would instantly be best friends with Sara. Coby would ask her to the Halloween party. And Harry would start being snide to me. Well, snid*er*.

And I'd go back to being the girl with no friends.

"What's *she* doing here?" I said.

"You know her?"

"Yeah, she's more like a BILF."

"Good," Harry said. "You can introduce me."

"Since when do you need an introduction? And I'm not talking to her."

Even if she stood right at the edge of my desk. "Hey," she said. "Long time no see."

"Not long enough." Okay, so I broke already. I'd never

---

* And you are a disgusting pig.

been good at the silent treatment. Just ask Max. If you could find him.

"Yeah, I was hoping we could talk about that," Natalie said.

Harry cocked his head. "Talk about what?"

"Not now," I told Natalie. "Or Gossip Girl here will repeat it to everyone."

"Don't believe a word she says," Harry told Natalie, standing politely to greet her.

"Yeah, *I'm* the liar," I muttered.

He ignored me and took her offered hand. "I'm Harrison. Very pleased to meet you. You knew the frumpy one in San Francisco?"

"We partied together," she said. "Briefly."

Instead of saying something biting and perfect, I just goggled at her. I couldn't believe this was happening. Natalie showing up was like some recurring nightmare, worse than anything the ghosts had thrown at me. What could she possibly be doing here? Besides torturing me.

She and Harry flirted outrageously until class started. She probably thought I had a crush on him like Jared. Well, she was welcome to him. Coby, too. Just as long as she never met Bennett, everything would be fine.

After Mr. Z introduced the new student, Natalie mentioned that we knew each other, so he paired us for the weekly dialogue.

"Don't hate me," she said in Latin.

"You're horrible. Why shouldn't I hate you?"

"Quoniam tu es non bonus proculi exosus,"* she said.

I didn't know what to say to that. "How come you speak so well? You didn't take Latin in San Francisco."

"I'm beyond what they offered." She eyed me archly. "We're always advanced at Latin, hadn't you noticed?"

"We who?"

"Phasmatis custodies."

Custodians of phantasms? Oh God. Ghostkeepers.

She saw my expression and nodded. "We're good at dead things—including dead languages."

"No way." No way that backstabbing, Jared-kissing Natalie from San Francisco was a ghostkeeper. "You're lying. Again."

"I never lied, I—"

"You said you were my friend. And now you're saying you're a ghostkeeper—" Except how much could I reveal about that? The more Martha talked about the Knell, the more they sounded like the Mafia. "Not that I have any idea what you're talking about."

"Fine." She frowned in concentration, and a befuddled old man wearing nothing but long johns appeared beside us. She wrinkled her nose. "Where are all the cute ghosts when you want them?"

"You didn't just . . ."

She raised one brow. "I did."

Thank you, I told the old ghost. *Sorry to, um, interrupt.* I shooed him back to wherever he came from, poor old guy.

---

* Because you're not good at hating.

"Where'd he go?" Natalie asked.

I executed a flawed but recognizable Gallic shrug. Martha wasn't the only one who'd been practicing.

"You got that from Celeste, didn't you?" she asked.

She knew Celeste? Did she know Bennett? Who the hell was she? My sharp intake of breath caught the attention of Mr. Z.

"Is everything all right here, ladies?" he asked.

"Fine," Natalie said.

"I was shocked," I said, "by her correct usage of the dative case."

"Excellent," he said, and strolled past Harry, who in the nick of time stopped trying to translate MILF into Latin.

Natalie and I had three classes together, including Fencing. Which was great. Now she and Sara would have some quality time together and become best friends. Both beautiful, both freakishly self-confident and, well, let's just say I was happy I'd always been nice to Kylee. After Natalie and Sara met, we'd have plenty of time together.

To delay the inevitable, I tried rushing Sara out of the locker room. But Natalie, of course, didn't let me. She chatted with me like we were friends, then introduced herself to Sara.

Despite my worries, they were not a match made in heaven. Sara turned on the frost—that polite rich-girl chill she did so well. I didn't know why she did it, but I loved her for it.

Of course, class itself wasn't great. First, Natalie looked tons better in her fencing costume than I did. Then Coach paired the two "new girls" after the drills, called "Play!" and Natalie kicked my ass.

I was tempted more than once to ignore the rules, change my grip, and see what I could *really* do. The Rake had drilled me in switching hands in the middle of a fight and slashing at the femoral artery. Or the eyes. Or wrist.

But instead, I took an honorable beating. At least the jock boy ghosts hadn't appeared.

At lunch, Harry asked Natalie to sit with us, and flirted outrageously, completely infatuated. She called him Harrison, making him her slave forever.

After lunch, Coby walked me to Advanced Biology. "So what's the story?"

"With Harry? Hormones."

"With you and Natalie."

"Oh. No story really." Then I realized this was Coby—I trusted him. "We were friends, or at least I thought we were. She encouraged me to have a party—because my parents are gone, you know? Then when the cops came, she told them I was living alone, plus I'm pretty sure she called them in the first place. So I spent the night in a halfway house and ended up here."

"So she's evil."

"Incarnate."

Coby half smiled. "On the other hand . . ."

"If you say she's hot, I'll bite you."

". . . If it weren't for her, you'd still be in San Francisco. And I kind of like that you're here."

"Oh," I said.

He laughed. "You're welcome."

I liked that he got my awkward randomness. We stopped outside the classroom door and I said, "I'll see you tomorrow night." And suddenly, I was looking forward to it.

I obsessed about Natalie all through fifth and sixth period and then found her waiting at my locker when school was over. Thatcher's lockers were all housed in lounges; apparently there was a lot of negotiating and jockeying each year for the best spots. You had to be voted in. Thankfully, I'd missed all that and was assigned to the "Lame Lounge" with the other nerds. Though, I did yearn for the club chairs, fireplace, and potted palms.

Guess who was given a locker next to mine? I would've left her there, but I needed my books.

"Go away," I said, twirling the combo on my locker.

"I can't," she said. "I need you to forgive me."

"Fine." I grabbed my backpack. "I accept your apology. *Now* will you go away?"

"No," she said. "I want to explain. Will you at least listen?"

I headed out of the lounge and down the front steps of the school without answering, walking quickly to outpace her.

She trotted beside me toward the gates. "Please."

"Stop following me."

"I didn't want to do it, Emma."

I blinked back tears. I couldn't believe she was here—and a ghostkeeper. As if she'd devoted her life to ruining mine. Kids streamed through the gates and I noticed Harry heading in our direction. If he saw this, he'd turn our argument into gossip about a catfight.

"C'mon then," I said.

We walked a block in silence, before shuffling through a drift of fallen leaves. "Just say it, Natalie. How can you explain what you did?"

"You never would've left San Francisco if we'd just asked," she said.

"'We' who?"

"The Knell," she said.

"The Knell?" I stopped walking. "So you work with Bennett?"

She bit her lower lip. "He didn't tell you."

"Let me get this straight." I started walking again, faster this time, my growing anger causing me to pick up speed. "The Knell sent you to pretend to be my friend and then ruin my life so Bennett could drag me to Echo Point."

"The friendship part wasn't pretend."

"I'd hate to see what you do to people you *don't* like. Why not just tell me who you were and what you wanted?"

"Hi, we're ghostkeepers!" she said chirpily. "We see dead people—and so do you! Wanna fly across the country and live in a haunted house with us?" She followed me up the driveway to the museum. "We weren't sure how much you knew. I kept dropping hints, hoping you'd open up, but you never did. Bennett thought—"

"That I was only pretending."

She nodded. "And your parents . . . I don't know. Emma, the Knell's like the army, and I'm just a private. They give the orders, I salute. Like Fencing class, except nobody yells 'Play.'"

I refused to smile. "Are you even sixteen? Or are you some kind of ghostkeeper narc, infiltrating my school to get close to me?"

"I'm sixteen," she said, and for a moment her confidence faltered. "I just never finish a school year in one place."

We climbed the stairs, and I turned to Natalie before opening the door. "Just tell me one thing. Whose idea was that? Knowing I'd be so desperate after a night in a half-way house, I'd go anywhere? You or Bennett?"

"You're not going to like the answer," she said.

My stomach soured. "It was Bennett."

"The Knell—"

"What about Jared?" I took a breath. "Did Bennett tell you to hook up with him?"

She frowned. "No. He was cute."

I shook my head. Just when I was getting used to living with ghosts, Natalie came back to haunt me.

"I understand why you're mad at Bennett," she said. "But he was only trying to do what's right."

"Then why does it feel so wrong?" I said.

19

The door opened and Martha said, "Are you girls coming inside?"

"Martha!" Natalie squealed, rushing into her open arms and clinging tight.

"Sweetheart," Martha said, stroking Natalie's hair. "Let me look at you."

"I missed you," Natalie said. "It's been so long."

"I looked after Natalie when her powers emerged," Martha explained.

"Better and better," I mumbled.

Martha disengaged from Natalie and swept us into the foyer. I stood there stiffly, watching them get reacquainted. Martha told Natalie how well she looked, Natalie asked Martha if she'd finished making her lists. Natalie looked her age for once, and as happy as I'd ever seen her.

Until Martha noticed me watching. "You haven't made up, then?" she asked.

I shook my head.

Martha touched Natalie's cheek. "Then I don't think you should stay."

"But I haven't seen you in so long." Natalie looked crestfallen. "I wanted to stay here, with you . . ."

"I'm sorry, Natalie, I have to think of Emma now."

I stared at her in shock. Had Martha just chosen me over Natalie?

Natalie nodded, her face resigned. "I'll ask the Finches if I can stay awhile longer. I'm in their apartment over the garage."

"When Emma's ready, you'll come back," Martha told her. "Until then, I think that's best."

Natalie flashed a brittle smile and left, her head high. For a moment, Martha and I stood there silently. Then I threw myself into her arms.

"Thank you," I said, and began to weep.

We sat on the grand staircase, Martha cradling me until the tears stopped flowing.

"Why?" I asked, wiping my face on my sleeve. "Why did you choose me over Natalie?"

"Because what they did to you in San Francisco was wrong. And because you need me more."

That evening after dinner, I passed Bennett's dad's study, then turned back, thinking of the swords on the wall. I needed to sweat, to lose myself in exertion.

I took down a sword and whipped it back and forth on my way to the ballroom. The moment my hand closed on the hilt, I felt calmer, more focused. At least *this* was something I could control. I didn't even have to summon the Rake, he appeared the moment he heard me step into the room.

He grinned wickedly and pointed his sword at my heart. *En garde.*

Oh, yeah? I drew an *E* in the air.

What was that?

An E *for Emma, like* Z *for Zorro.*

Who?

You've got to start watching more DVDs.

And I lunged at him. I attacked so aggressively that the Rake warned against losing my temper. Of course, he also cocked an eyebrow in approval when I flicked the sword point at his face, then twirled to kick him in the knee. We practiced for an hour. He stopped me every ten minutes or so to correct my stance or show me a new move, but I saw the approval in his eyes. By the time we were finished, I was drenched in sweat. He still looked like a ghost.

We relaxed together in the white linen chairs at the far end of the room.

You've never told me your name, I said.

You know my name.

Bennett. The original Bennett.

You may call me Stern, he said, humor in his eyes.

Of course, it suits you, I said. *Why are you hiding from everyone but me?*

For a long moment, he looked out the window. *Some*

ghosts haunt a place, and some are drawn to an emotion. I'm pledged to her, *and you're the closest thing. So I am not drawn to the others—only you.*

Because you loved her so much?

No, Emma, he said, very softly. *Because I killed her.*

The terrible truth of his words shone in his eyes.

But you loved her. How could you? I asked.

Everyone who knew Emma loved her . . . with a few exceptions. A group of men in town thought she was too opinionated, too rich, too strong willed. And a witch.

Goose bumps raised on my arms at his tone. Echo Point was twenty minutes from Salem. They took witchcraft seriously around here, even if she had lived a hundred years later. I remembered the torture device I'd seen at Redd's Pond.

He nodded at my expression. *Yes. And in truth, she did consort with the dead, didn't she? More completely than any ghostkeeper since. Still, she was too well loved for their rumors to do much harm.*

So what did they do?

They hired me. He started to pace, his voice still loud in my mind even when he stood across the room. *They found me at a low ebb.*

Hired you for what?

To seduce her. To ruin her.

And you agreed?

A crooked smile. *They offered a fortune as a reward. I'd gambled and lost quite a bit.*

You seduced her.

No. I fell in love. I told her everything—even that I still intended to seduce her. I expected her to send me away, but she'd fallen in love as well. His voice faded, and as he stood staring through the window, he faded away, as well.

Wait! I want to know . . . I didn't summon him back. When he was ready to tell me why he killed her, he would.

The next morning, I taught Nicholas how to throw the football I'd found in Bennett's attic. I'd only ventured into his domain to help Martha discover whether it needed cleaning. It's not like I poked around in his private stuff and didn't find anything of interest.

Anyway, Nicholas mastered a wobbly spiral, then started asking about Xbox. I don't know where he heard about these things. Fortunately, Celeste commandeered him for dusting, so I headed to the kitchen and stuffed my face with fresh éclairs Anatole had made. I really needed to buy him a South Beach Diet cookbook before I turned into a beluga.

Then Sara phoned. "When are you coming over?" she asked.

"Um," I said.

"You didn't forget, did you? I want to make sure you're decent for your date with Coby."

Yikes, the Halloween party. I had forgotten, but didn't want to hurt Sara's feelings. "I didn't forget, I just didn't want to bug you."

"No problem. The party's at eight. I'll see you at six."

Sara lived on the opposite side of the harbor, in a neighborhood called the Neck because it sorta stuck out by itself. Well, and because calling it that distinguished it from the rest of the village. I'd quickly learned at school that if you lived on the Neck, you had even more money than the regular wealthy people in Echo Point. Anyway, it was too far to walk, so Sara came and got me in her BMW.

She gossiped in her raspy voice the whole way to her house about kids at school and it suddenly made a lot more sense why she and Harry were buds. It was a relief to think about something other than Natalie, ghostkeeping, and Bennett. I still didn't know what I was going to say next time I saw him.

She turned into a cobbled drive, and I was surprised to find a cute little cottage—until I realized that was just the garage. Sara lived in a mansion. Her house sprawled atop a rocky bluff, and she occupied her own suite with a bedroom, sitting room, bathroom—and, of course, ocean views.

Did I mention the walk-in closet? I was in heaven, sorting through racks of designer wonders. Her body was mini, but I'd worn my own vintage Levis that I figured I could dress up and—score!—we wore the same size shoe.

Only problem was, with all these options, how could I decide?

Sara stepped past me and pulled out a satin cap-sleeve top in the most gorgeous shade of magenta. "This," she said. "And . . . these." She grabbed a pair of jade green leather sandals with a three-inch heel.

Oh, I guess that's how I'd decide.

I had trouble squeezing into the top, but Sara insisted that was a good thing. And I never would've chosen the green shoes, but they worked perfectly.

Sara examined me. "Earrings." She handed me a pair of silver hoops. "Now a mask."

She scoped the closet for her collection and presented a selection of three: one a muted gold, one canary yellow with feathers, and the third electric blue. She held them to my face, then wrinkled her nose. "They're all wrong."

"I should've just gone as the slutty schoolgirl."

"But how would they know you were in costume?" She smiled wickedly.

"Hey!"

"I'll do it with makeup. It'll look cool. Trust me."

I had some issues with trust, but I followed her into the bathroom and sat on her sink, while she wetted and blew out my hair. Then she applied makeup until I couldn't take it anymore and said, "If you're painting me like a clown . . ."

She swiped her mascara wand twice more. "You can look now."

I turned to the mirror and almost didn't recognize myself. My hair was perfect—it actually looked longer. And wearing a blouse you'd see in the pages of *Elle*, I finally felt ready for my close-up. Well, maybe for the masquerade issue, with a pale purple eye mask across my temples, accentuated here and there with artistically placed sequins. Amazingly cool.

The only problem was, it wasn't me in the mirror. It was someone else. A girl who lived in a huge mansion, dressed for fancy balls, and thought ghosts looked like Casper the Friendly.

But I didn't tell Sara that. Instead I said, "Wow. Thanks. Don't take this the wrong way, but you're a lot nicer than you look."

Sara smiled. "It's my secret weapon."

The doorbell rang and Sara squealed. "That's him! He's going to think you look so hot."

I felt a glow of pleasure, imagining Bennett on the other side of the door. Then I remembered that "him" was Coby . . . and I hated Bennett, anyway.

I followed Sara to the front door—close on her heels so I wouldn't get lost. We found Coby charming Sara's mom, dressed in tight jeans, a ripped T-shirt, black leather cuffs, and silver chains. His eyes were ringed in guyliner.

"Rock star," I said. "Very nice."

He smiled. "You look . . ."

"It was all Sara's doing!" I interrupted, feeling awkward in high heels and satin, like I'd gone to all this trouble to impress him. Why had I let Sara talk me into this?

Sara tried to press one of her pastel coats on me, but I grumpily shrugged into my black wool peacoat.

"You haven't sufficiently admired my artwork," Sara said, gesturing to my face.

"I like the mask," Coby said. "And the little sparkly things."

"Sparkly things." I loved guys sometimes.

Sara took a bow. "Thank you."

"Do you want a ride?" Coby asked.

"I'm not dressed yet," she said. "I'll be there in a half hour."

"What's she going as?" Coby asked, as he opened the door of his dad's Lexus SUV for me. "You?"

"Why do you say that?" I asked.

"Because you're dressed like her, so I thought maybe . . ."

I laughed. "I think she's going as herself, too, so there'll be two Saras tonight. I don't know how you'll tell us apart."

He smiled a secret smile, as he started the car. "Oh, I'll know."

Hmm. Maybe I liked him more than I realized.

Harry's house was *insane*. It made Sara's house look like the servants' quarters. It was like one of those spreads in *Architectural Digest* that makes you think, *people can't possibly live like that.* All Roman columns and marble floors, perched atop a jutting cliff.

"What's Harry's dad do again?" I asked Coby as we wandered through the ornately decorated rooms.

"His mom invented recyclable plastic bags."

"Oh. Sweet!"

"Yeah. I keep telling my mom to get on the ball."

I smiled. "What does she do?"

"Social worker."

I giggled.

The whole school had been invited, even the geeks, which was cool. They were the only ones willing to wear silly costumes.

"What are you?" I asked a guy from Trig, wrapped in a mass of pink foam speckled with little dots.

"An amoeba."

"Excellent."

"Wanna pet my pseudopod?" he asked. Then he blushed and giggled and oozed away.

I glanced at Coby.

He shrugged. "You're irresistible to the single celled."

We chatted with a few kids, and I noticed a number of evil looks from girls, probably because I came with Coby. And not one, but three of them asked me if I was wearing Sara's top and shoes. Coby finally dragged me away, saying we needed to find Harry.

We found him in the kitchen, wearing a plaid cape and smoking a pipe. Sherlock Holmes was the perfect costume for his eccentric brilliance and his lanky build. Instead of manning the pump of one of the kegs, he was operating a gigantic red espresso machine.

Perched atop the counter next to him was a slutty white snow bunny. She wore ski goggles, skintight ski pants and a top that revealed a complete lack of body fat. Yet she still had all the right curves and cleavage.

Natalie.

"Emma!" she said. "You look beautiful."

"She does," Harry agreed, after eyeing me critically. "She's a FILF. I thought she was Sara for a moment."

"The highest compliment," Natalie said, with an edge in her voice.

"A second-rate Sara's better than a first-rate anything else," Harry said seriously.

Okay, the Sara comments were getting old. I just hoped I didn't run into Britta. I wasn't in the mood for her sneers.

"I need a beer," I told Coby, and he led me across the kitchen. "How come Harry's doing shots of espresso?"

"He doesn't drink."

"Really? I pegged him as a gin-martini man."

"Close. Vodka martinis. But not anymore."

"What do you mean?"

"Rehab, last year."

"Whoa. At fifteen?"

"Yeah. He was a mess."

I remembered Harry's venomous comments about some "blackout drunk." He must've been talking about himself. "And now he . . ."

"Only gets jacked up on espresso." Coby nodded back toward the espresso maker. "There's Sara. She does it with him."

Sara looked spectacular in a formfitting shiny gun-metal dress and the bright blue mask.

"Hmm. Maybe I should try that."

"You really want to hang out with Harry after six espressos?"

I snickered. "He must get wild."

"And Sara's voice gets all high," he said.

"No way!"

"It starts to crack like a pubescent boy's."

I laughed and helped Coby fill a couple of cups. We drank and danced—Coby a little stiffly, which made me like him even more. All that grace and power on the football field, yet he was still slightly self-conscious while dancing. Gangly Harry, on the other hand, danced like a dream—to the obvious lust of half the girls, even though he only had eyes for Natalie.

When Coby and I returned to the kitchen to catch our breath, we found Harry and Sara at the espresso machine again. With Natalie.

"You know," I said. "I think I'm going to just look at the view."

"I'll come with," Natalie said.

"Great," I murmured.

Coby offered to come, but I could tell he wanted to hang with Sara and Harry, so I let Natalie follow me outside alone.

I wore my peacoat and Natalie slipped into a white puffer shrug that matched her costume. The air was cool and the full moon glistened on the waves. And on the pool. And hot tub. And cabanas. And the manicured gardens leading to the cliff's edge. The mansion glowed behind us, like a swanky resort.

"Nice house, huh?" Natalie said.

"Can you believe he lives here?" I said.

She shook her head in amazement. "I can't believe *anyone* lives here."

"C'mon—tell me you weren't raised like this."

"Not quite," she said. "Our helipad's bigger."

I didn't answer, not entirely sure if she was joking, and we followed a stone path toward the cliff. I hadn't forgiven her, but we'd been friends, and I found it all too easy to be comfortable around her again.

We stopped and looked over the harbor. "I wonder which yacht is his?" I asked.

"That biggest one," Natalie said. "He made a point of telling me."

"So Harry does have some insecurities," I said.

"Mmm. Still, a nice boat," she said. "So, Coby's cute. Have you slept with him yet?"

"What? No!"

"Oh my God. You've never—" She giggled and bit her lip. "Sorry! Want to hear about my first time?"

"Not particularly."

"How about my other first time?" she asked. "The first time I summoned a ghost." There was a wicked glint in her eyes. "Can you feel them?"

Yes, I could feel them. The area was rife with ghosts; my spine tingled and silent echoes sounded in my mind. But I was happy to ignore them.

Not Natalie. She closed her eyes and I could tell she was getting ready to summon.

"Natalie, don't," I protested. "Not here. Not now."

"Relax. It'll be fun," she said, her eyes still shut. She stood rigidly and quietly and I felt her calling forth a spiritual presence. I expected an old sailor or maybe a long-dead gardener, but that's not what appeared before us. This was something entirely different.

I smelled and felt the cold salt wind as it rose from the ocean and heard the waves rippling against the rocks below. The soft glow of the house fell into the darkness over the cliffs, as a thread of spectral fog thickened in the air and crept toward us. This was what Natalie had summoned. I'd never seen anything like it before and judging from Natalie's expression, neither had she.

As we watched, the fog morphed into a shape that looked nothing like other ghosts I'd seen. It had a skeletal, malformed body and wore tattered clothing. Except that it wasn't clothing. It was skin. Its bones were joined in the wrong places somehow, making it look more insect than human.

We watched it drift past us, trailing an inky fog behind it. It slunk toward the house, closer to the kids hanging under the cabana.

I shivered at the malicious chill. "What *is* that?" I whispered.

"I—I don't know."

"Is it a ghast?"

"No." Her eyes shone with panic. "At least, I've never seen one like that."

"Well, make it go away!"

"I can't! I'm a summoner, not a dispeller. I can't make it go away."

The thing had two black holes instead of eyes and the dark sockets honed in on the kids at the cabana.

"Oh God," Natalie breathed. "Do something, Emma, please."

"Me? I don't even know—"

And I stopped, hearing a discordant voice: *Food—flesh. Crack the skin and feed. Feed.*

"It's going to eat them," I told her.

"Ghosts don't eat people," she said desperately. "Wraiths, though. Wraiths might eat people. But there's no way I summoned a wraith. I couldn't even begin to—"

"Get ready," I said, because I had to do something.

She swallowed. "For what?"

Hey! I yelled at it. *Yeah, over here, you black death freak show.*

It paused and pivoted toward us. *Feed, feed. Taste the marrow.*

Yeah, I said. *I'm talking to you, Bernice.*

"What are you telling it?" Natalie asked. "What are you saying?"

"I'm calling it Bernice."

"What? Why?"

"No idea." It creaked toward us, away from the other kids. "But it worked."

"What's the plan?" She grabbed my hand. "What's the plan, Emma?"

Crack the bones. Feed the flesh. It drifted closer. *Drink the soul. Feed.*

"Um," I said. "How fast can you run?"

"Watch me." She pulled me with her. "Come on!"

"I'm staying here." If I ran, it'd only turn back to those kids. "You go."

She started to say something, but I couldn't hear her as the ghost—or whatever—was upon us. It engulfed me. Whiplash welts rose on my skin under my clothes, but the raw emotion of that thing beating in my brain felt even worse. I sensed its endless craving, an insatiable need to feed. Its desperate hunger and pitiless hatred resolved into one thought: *Neos . . . Neos . . . Neos.*

That word sparked me into action. It was what I'd heard curling in smoke from the urns outside my father's office and when the shadows had haunted me in the village— somehow this was all connected.

Instead of trying to dispel it, I lashed out with my thoughts: *There's nothing for you here. Go back. Now!*

In response, I felt my breath crushed from me. A terrible constriction, and I opened my mouth to scream but couldn't make a sound.

Go! I shouted in my mind.

Neossss. Feed.

It was going to kill me. And when it was done with me, it'd move on to Natalie and the other kids. If I didn't stop it, no one would.

I focused, despite the ghost howling for my blood. I wrapped myself around that vile thing, like diving into a sewer, and drew whatever bleak spark animated my ghostkeeping ability deep into my heart. The power radiated within me and I realized I could control it. The ghost thrashed and tore at me, smoky tendrils leaving frozen white stripes on my skin, as I refused to release it.

Go, I said again. And this time, I showed the thing a glimpse of my power.

The ghost faltered.

And I struck again. I *shoved* with all my might, battering at it with the light that flowed through my veins and out my fingertips. At least, that's what it felt like. Martha said it was different for all ghostkeepers, but my dispelling power felt like lightning coursing through my body and out of my hands, even if the bolts weren't actually visible.

But at the height of my attack, I shifted. I couldn't dispel it. Not even this abomination; it felt too much like murder. Instead I compelled it. *Go. Touch nothing. Harm nobody. Go.*

I lost myself in the struggle, my will against the ghost's, until my world shrank to a tiny point and my awareness vanished into a single command: *Go.*

Then a new sensation came: warmth and light and softness. I jerked in surprise and found Natalie holding me upright, saying my name.

I blinked at her. We were alone. It had gone. The kids still hung around the fire at the cabana. Only seconds had passed.

"Emma!" She rubbed my shoulder. "Are you okay?"

"Barely," I exhaled. "Yeah. Yeah, I'm . . . oddly fine."

"You didn't look fine. You were white as a—" She stopped, about to say "ghost," and we both laughed, shakily.

"Why did you stay?" I asked.

"I wasn't about to leave you again," she said. "Besides, you were all waving your arms around."

"What?"

"I didn't want the other kids to talk."

"I was not waving my arms around!"

"Occupational hazard," she said.

We both fell silent, looking out at the ocean. What else was out there, lurking in the realm between life and death? How had Natalie summoned such a horror?

"Okay, we've gotta figure out what that was," she said. "And where it came from. I'll warn the Knell, and maybe you can . . . um, tell me where you got your hair cut?"

"Huh?" I said.

"Hey." Coby was suddenly behind me. "You still out here?"

"Girl talk," Natalie said.

"I saw you from the house." He looked at me. "What were you doing with your hands?"

"Told you," Natalie said.

"I was pretending to shove Natalie off the cliff."

She snorted. "I kind of deserved it."

"Harry's looking for you," Coby told her.

She grinned with slow satisfaction. "Yeah, he wants me to teach him all the dirty phrases I know in Latin. You know a few, don't you, Emma?"

"What? No!"

Her laughter didn't sound at all diabolical as she slunk back toward the house, flipping open her cell.

I sighed. "She is my nemesis."

"When your nemesis is a ski bunny," Coby said, "you need to get out more."

I laughed. "Yeah, my life is so boring." If only he knew.

"Do you want to get out of here?" he said gently in my ear.

My body shimmered from his breath. "Yes, please."

"We'll walk to Echo Point."

"The Neck's not in Echo Point?"

"No, I mean the actual point—the place the town's named after."

He put an arm around me and I snuggled closer. Coby was real. Coby was safe.

Was he going to try and kiss me when we got up to the point? Would I let him? Yes. Because what kind of girl turns down kisses from a guy like Coby?

Plus he had nothing to do with ghosts and I loved that about him.

And I liked his guyliner.

We strolled through the grounds to a cliffside path that wound from Harry's property past his neighbors' mansions toward Echo Point. The sky was clear and the moon full. It was a perfect night for kissing under the stars— even if you were still shaken from dealing with a supposed wraith.

The path suddenly jutted out to a point and there was

a bench for taking in the remarkable view. A set of rickety wooden steps led to a small beach below.

"Want to walk on the beach?" Coby asked.

A sudden suspicion hit me. "Did Harry tell you I like long walks on the beach?"

He laughed. "Doesn't everyone?"

"Oh. No, I'm happy here."

And I was. Forget about Bennett, Natalie, and hungry ghosts. Standing here I could just be myself, Emma, with a cute guy who looked like he wanted to kiss me.

He leaned closer and touched one of the silver hoops Sara lent me. "You don't usually wear jewelry."

I thought about the amulet I tucked away beneath my shirt. Maybe I'd let him see that later. "Not much."

"And I like your hair this way," he said. "And your mask is . . . sexy."

I placed my palm on his chest, feeling that tingly moment when you want a guy to kiss you, but aren't sure what it's going to be like. His chest was warm and hard under his jacket and I tingled some more.

Tingled too much.

Something was wrong.

There was a ghost nearby. I glanced past Coby, dread forming in my stomach. I recognized this malicious tingling. Not just a ghost, but that soul-sucking wraith that Natalie had summoned.

"What?" Coby asked, seeing my expression.

"I don't know. I think—" I glanced down at the beach.

"I think someone's down there." I looked closer, and caught a blur of motion in the evening gloom.

Coby leaned back into me. "Don't worry, he can't see us."

"No," I said, pulling away. "I think he's in trouble."

"He's fine. Just practicing tai chi or something."

My breath caught. "It's Bennett!" He was alone on the beach, trying to fight off that wraith. "Stay here. Please?"

I didn't wait for him to answer. Instead, I kicked off my heels and ran.

Down the stairs, across the sand. I heard Coby calling my name from the cliffs, but didn't stop. I kept my eyes on Bennett and the writhing mass of shadow he was trying to dispel. Before I reached him, the ghost curled into a roiling ball and rushed him, a mist of supernatural darkness spreading like a bat's wings around him.

"Bennett!" I called.

"Emma—" He didn't turn toward me; he focused on keeping the thing from his throat. "What are you *doing* here?"

Oh, just hanging out on the cliffs, about to make out with a guy.

"Go!" he said. "You can't be here—"

The thing drove him to one knee, reeking a cold malevolence. I stood behind Bennett and *pushed* with him. The wraith turned into a vortex and sucked my attack into itself. Okay, what the hell? I got that this wasn't a normal ghost. Your average ghost was a slacker, standing around, looking semi-normal (though a little pale), and maybe moving stuff now and then. They didn't have flesh hanging from their bones and curl themselves into death balls of ghostly essence.

"It's a wraith, isn't it?" I tried to communicate with it, but couldn't penetrate its nebulous shell. "That's what Natalie thought—"

Bennett growled. "Emma, now isn't the time. I need you to help me."

"I compelled it earlier, maybe—"

"That's why it came back stronger." He fought to his feet, forcing the thing toward the ocean. "Stop playing, Emma, and dispel the thing."

"I can't!"

"Then leave," he said through clenched teeth.

The ghost hovered a moment over the sea, then curled into itself, an ever-shifting mass, blasting toward Bennett. He sidestepped, but the thing veered impossibly fast and a storm of plasma erupted through his torso.

He collapsed to the sandy beach and lay there unmoving. Oh God. Bennett! I knelt beside him. "Please," I whispered. "Wake up."

He stirred, but didn't wake, and I heard Coby calling my name from the cliff. I froze in fear as the ghost started curling into itself again. I closed my eyes and focused, feeling the tendrils of energy and spirit that connected me to the wraith. I used every trick Martha had taught me to compel the thing away once and for all.

But it had gotten too strong.

"Dispel it," Bennett murmured, his voice weak.

I shook my head. I couldn't even remember how.

The ghost pulsed. Once. Twice.

Then erupted. Not at me. At Bennett again.

I shoved my hands into the thickest coil of its blackness and ignored the biting cold as I *blasted* with those invisible bolts that felt like lightning shooting through my body.

Its back arched and its mouth opened in a silent scream. There was a flash of light and the darkness recoiled. I loosed blast after blast until nothing remained of the ghost but a long smudge on the sand, like an oil slick.

"Kill it," Bennett whispered.

"It's done."

He sighed and I barely heard him say, "Or it'll come back stronger."

The oil slick thickened and grew in the sand. It took the form of a child, a little blond girl who looked a bit like me at that age. She crawled toward Bennett, her black eyes intent and hungry. He lay there unmoving as I tugged at him, and the girl reached for him, inky tendrils spiraling from her fingernails.

She whispered that word that frightened me every time I heard it: *Neos. Neos. Neos.* She grabbed Bennett and started digging into him with those ghostly death claws and I lost it.

I killed her, okay?

A little blond girl, who writhed in agony and stared at me in terror, as I shot endless bolts into her and ended her life.

Bennett pulled himself into a seated position, watching

shreds of the wraith's darkness shimmer and fade on the sand, like cockroaches scurrying from the light.

I didn't know what I felt. I'd killed something—something evil. But still, it had lived, before I snuffed it out. As I watched Bennett rise and brush the sand from his pants, a sudden suspicion hit me. "You set me up. You—you wanted me to kill it. So you pretended you couldn't fight it off, just so I'd have to."

"Natalie called me," he said. "And I didn't believe her. But that thing was a wraith, which means someone is raising them, feeding them. We need to—"

"We?" I said. "There is no 'we.' After what you did in San Francisco? You're a liar. You sent Natalie to get me tossed into a halfway house. And now you have me killing—" I blinked back sudden tears. "I trusted you, Bennett."

He ran a hand over his face. "I'm sorry. I—"

"Whoa!" Coby called, trotting toward us from the stairs. "Did you see that lightning?"

The whole thing had happened in mere minutes, yet I'd never be the same again. Coby stopped beside us and looked at me carefully. I don't know what he saw, but he offered to take me home.

"I'll take her," Bennett said. "I think as her guardian, I should—"

Something inside of me snapped. "Shut up!"

I grabbed Coby's hand and led him toward the stairs. "Let's go."

. . .

Coby led me back along the cliff's path, around the side of Harry's house to his car. He knew I didn't want to say good night to anyone. Then he drove me home. Five minutes of silence in the car, with me feeling like a murderer— even if it was justified.

Then I sighed. "You know the best thing about you?"

"My screen pass?"

I giggled. "I don't even know what that is. Football?"

"Uh-huh. I'll also accept my keen intellect, my perfect attendance record, or how cool I look as a rock star."

I smiled at him. "Your mascara's starting to run."

He swiped at it, only making things worse.

"What I like best about you, is that you always . . . know. When I need quiet, you're quiet. When I need a friend, you're there."

Coby kept his eyes on the road. "Do you wish Bennett drove you back?"

"No," I said.

"I like you, Emma." He half shrugged. "But if you just want to be friends . . ."

We turned into my neighborhood before I answered. "I don't know what I want. I don't want to make any promises. But I also don't want you to go away."

"You're not with Bennett?" he asked. "The two of you fight like there's something—"

"There's nothing between me and Bennett." I half laughed. "Nothing but ghosts of the past." And I wanted it to be true, I wanted to stop caring about him.

"Good." He parked in the maple-lined drive. "Will you go to Homecoming with me?"

Homecoming? I wasn't expecting that.

"Coby, I went to Harry's party with you, and ended up on the beach arguing with my idiot guardian. There are girls who are, you know . . . prettier, and more eager to please. Don't you want—"

"I want you to say yes," he told me.

Homecoming with the high school quarterback. A normal girl, on a date with the cutest guy in school. I so wanted to be that girl—and only that girl—and forget all about the one who killed ghosts.

So I said yes.

And he leaned across the seat and kissed me.

20

A shadow fell across the car and Bennett tapped on the door.

We jumped apart and I cracked the window. "Go away!"

"We need to talk."

I turned to Coby. "I'm sorry. Maybe if Bennett catches the Ebola virus, we'll have a real date sometime."

He started to answer, but I kissed him again. Not so gently, this time.

"Or maybe he'll go on exchange to India," I said, stepping from the car. "That'd work, too."

I could hear Coby laughing as he drove away.

I stood in the drive, next to a glowering Bennett. "I think they still have the plague in India."

"Are you finished?" he said. "We need to talk."

"No, Bennett, what you need to do," I said, "is *listen*."

"I know," he said, as we headed inside. "You must have a lot to say to me."

Huh? Not what I'd expected. I'd been gearing up for a fight. "Um. Where's Martha?"

"I'm here, dear." She stepped from the kitchen, wrapped in a cashmere robe, holding a book. "Did you have a nice time?"

"I killed a ghost," I blurted, and fell into her arms.

"Oh, Emma . . ."

"I didn't want to." I sniffled. "Bennett tricked me."

"You can't kill ghosts," he protested. "They're already dead. And I didn't trick—"

"Bennett," Martha said, "she's had a scare."

He looked so contrite at this that I almost forgave him everything. Almost. Instead, I poured out my feelings to Martha. She comforted me, understanding that it wasn't only the dispelling that upset me.

Truth was, now there was no going back, no denying that I was part of this world—a world made of fear and wraiths and lies. I could pretend that I was a normal girl, with parties and friends and a date to the school dance. But it wasn't the real me. The real me could slay a ghost. So I wasn't only crying for that dead ghost on the beach, I was crying for myself. For the girl I no longer was.

When my tears softened into sniffling, Bennett set a cup of tea in front of me. Not just any tea. Chai. A red-eye chai.

"How did you know?"

He shrugged as I silently gulped the chai. When I set the empty cup on the table, Martha said, "Emma, you and Bennett do need to talk. Go for a walk. I'll be here when you get back."

As always, I was unable to displease Martha. I pulled off Sara's heels, dusting the floor with sand, put on my boots, and wrapped a silver gray scarf around my neck. I stomped to the front door and glared back at Bennett, who was shrugging into his jacket.

Before we left, I noticed Nicholas watching us through the stair railing on the second floor. His pale face looked worried, his eyes grave. I gave him a little wave, but he just stared. Had he heard me say I'd killed a ghost? Could he smell the dispelling power still on me? Finally, he waved back, tentatively.

Like he was scared of me.

I couldn't take it. I shoved outside and Bennett and I walked down the driveway in silence. It was after midnight and the evening had turned cloudy, fading jack-o'-lanterns and old streetlamps providing the only illumination in the wispy fog. I had to admit that it spooked me. There was no telling what might turn up in this atmosphere.

"I'm never doing that again," I said.

"Kissing a guy?" Bennett asked. "I find that hard to believe."

"What is wrong with you?" I asked. "You're not a normal person."

"No, Emma, I'm not. And neither are you."

I stopped walking. This wasn't what I wanted to hear. I should've been home in bed, analyzing my feelings for Coby—worrying about why I still lusted after Bennett. He'd stopped too close to me, his coat unzipped. I wanted to slide inside it, feel his warmth, smell his skin, and brush my hands through his wavy brown hair.

"You manipulated me, Bennett, and ruined my life in San Francisco to get me here."

"Yeah," he said. "I'm sorry, Emma. Look at me. Please."

I bit my lip and blinked up at him. The night cast shadows on his face, making him look older and harder—more like the Rake.

"I didn't want to hurt you," he said. "I never want to hurt you. I've worked for the Knell, since . . . well always. I've sworn my life to ghostkeeping, to protecting the innocent from ghosts that might harm them. I can't break that promise."

"Even when you think they're wrong?"

"It's like being a cop, Emma. You don't want every guy out there making his own laws. You expect cops to uphold the law, even when they disagree."

I swallowed. "So, if the Knell told you to do that to me again, you would?"

"And hate myself again."

It wasn't the answer I wanted to hear, but I didn't turn away. I couldn't let go of whatever it was that connected us: our ghostkeeping skills, our shared family history. Or maybe just that I never felt more alive, more right, than when I was with him.

"I thought that wraith was going to kill you," I said.

"Would you have minded?"

"Yes." I sighed into him. "I would've minded. Too much."

I saw his pulse thumping in the open neck of his shirt. I pressed my thumb against it and laid my other palm against his chest. He looked down at me and reached around to run his fingers in between my scarf and the back of my neck. This was the moment. The second kiss in one night.

The kiss I really wanted.

The kiss that didn't happen.

Because Bennett pulled up my scarf and stepped away.

I stood there, shaky and confused. I'd really thought it was finally going to happen. How could I have been so wrong? Then I noticed the ghosts. Three women, dressed in Colonial garb, watching me and Bennett.

"Did you summon them?" he asked.

"No," I said. "I don't think so."

"You're not sure?"

"Um . . ." Was it possible that my feelings for Bennett somehow drew them forth? Were my tingles all mixed up? "Sometimes they just appear, right?"

Bennett took a deep breath. "Emma, I need to know what's going on with you."

Really? Well, I think I'm in love with you when I should like Coby, especially since I still hate you for using Natalie to ruin my life and drag me here under false pretenses. And you *still* don't want to kiss me.

"I mean about your talents," he said, reading something in my face. "You summon, you communicate. Now we know you dispel."

"Lucky me."

"You're like the original Emma, aren't you? You can do it all."

"Martha hasn't told you?"

He shook his head. "She doesn't say much about you. She doesn't even keep the Knell fully informed."

"Because I can trust *her*. You're going to tell them I killed that wraith, aren't you?"

"I already reported in."

I shook my head in disbelief, a sick feeling in my stomach. Already? He hadn't even talked to me first? He automatically told them everything. Oh God, maybe he told them I was fixated with him, too. That I wanted him to kiss me. What if they were using him to manipulate me more?

"Yeah?" I said. "Where do I report in about you?"

"What would you report?" he asked. "That I do my job?"

"Oh. Right. That's all I am to you," I said. "A job."

"That's not what I—"

"No, I get it now. I'm just one of your duties, right? A job that has to be done."

"Emma, the Knell is—"

I told him where he could stick the Knell, and ran back to the house.

I wanted to go straight to bed, but stopped first in Bennett's dad's study. I scanned the shelves until I found the book I was looking for. It was leather bound and felt ancient and heavy in my hands as I carried it upstairs.

I could see a crack of light under Martha's door as I passed her room. I considered knocking and letting her solve all my problems. But I needed to be alone, to figure out how I felt about everything before I got any advice from her.

My plan was short-lived as I discovered Nicholas stoking the fire in my room and Celeste turning down the bed.

It is true? Celeste asked. *You can dispel us?*

Yes.

Nicholas glanced at her furtively. *Told you so.*

I knelt beside him. *I promise you—I promise you both—I will never hurt you.*

He nodded, biting his thumbnail.

You don't ever need to be afraid of me.

Celeste laid out my pajamas on the bed. *You are like her then.*

Who?

The first Miss Vaile.

You knew her? I asked.

Memory is a hazy thing in the Beyond, Celeste said. *But we know of her.*

They say she cared for the ghosts, too. Nicholas ducked his head shyly.

That she was very kind, Celeste said. *Like you.*

Reassured, Nicholas faded out while Celeste helped me off with my clothes and into my pajamas. *Good night, Emma, sweet dreams.*

Tucked under the covers, I thought about Coby. He was the perfect guy. I liked that he'd kissed me. And I liked kissing him back, even if I'd only done it to prove something to Bennett. I wanted to fall asleep while fantasizing about Homecoming—what I'd wear, what *he'd* wear, where we'd go to dinner. Imagining slow dancing in the school gym, or considering it was Thatcher, probably the swanky yacht club.

But I couldn't stop thinking about Bennett.

We'd fought again; we always fought. Why did I like him *soooo* much? Especially when he treated me like some bratty younger sister. Why couldn't he just like me back? It would make life so much easier.

I willed myself to forget about him. Because he was so wrong for me. He was older and clearly I wasn't his type and besides, he'd never put me first before the Knell. And I wanted that—to come first in somebody's life. Isn't that what we all want?

I fingered the tooled leather cover of the book I'd brought to bed with me. I knew what I didn't want: this life, the life of a ghostkeeper. I'd never wanted any of this. Especially now that I'd killed one of them.

That's why I'd gotten the book from Mr. Stern's study. To find out about wraiths. To convince myself that what I'd done tonight wasn't wrong. There was no title on the cover, but I knew what it contained because my own father had a matching copy in his office. The pages were yellowed with age and filled with illustrations and information about ghouls and ghasts and ghosts and wraiths. Max used to scare me with this book when we were kids. Tell me everything in it was real and they were all coming to get me.

I'd thought he'd only been torturing me.

I leafed through the pages, wanting to absorb it all. Because one thing was clear—I'd been chosen for this life. And there was no turning back.

21

On Monday, two girls I didn't know cornered me in the hall outside Trig and congratulated me.

"Thanks," I said. "Um. For what?"

"You're going to Homecoming with"—synchronized squeals—"Coby Anders!"

How did they know already? Coby kept a pretty low profile, and— I saw Harry down the hall, a crooked grin on his face. I smiled at the girls and nodded, and flipped him the finger when they weren't looking. His laughter floated down the hallway toward us.

I glared at him, then slipped into the classroom and sat beside Coby.

"I might have to beat up Harry," I told him.

"Well, watch his elbows—they're sharp like javelins."

Mr. Sakolsky called the class to order, but I barely paid attention, my thoughts stuck in a constant loop of Bennett and Coby, ghosts and wraiths.

I managed to get all the practice problems right anyway.

You're getting smarter, the man in the brown suit—Edmund, as he kept reminding me—said. He'd materialized halfway through class.

I'm seventeen years old, I think my intelligence level is already well established. You should see my PSATs.

Then why are you so easily achieving perfect scores in math?

I looked at him. *Why are you unable to change clothes?*

He flicked an imaginary piece of lint off his lapel. *Why would I want to? And you haven't answered my question.*

Because I don't know, I said. *How smart does that make me?*

I believe it's the school, he mused.

An exceptional private education?

He snorted. *You're not the first ghostkeeper student I've seen. Something about this school, the Beyond being closer at hand . . . they all changed. Smarter, stronger, more focused than before.*

I straightened in my chair. That'd be killer. Maybe I'd get into Berkeley after all. I'd already moved all the way across country—my parents could no longer balk at across the Bay. I frowned. That is, if I ever saw them again.

Coby tossed a note onto my desk.

A note!? Edmund tsked. *Believe me,* he *is not getting any smarter. He can't afford to be passing notes.*

Oh, go away, I said, and fluttered my hands to compel him to leave.

You may be getting stronger, but you're not getting any nicer, Edmund said before fading.

I inwardly sighed, because I agreed with him. Then I checked that Sakolsky wasn't looking and unfolded the note.

Pay attention. I'm not going to have to help you with your homework again, am I?

I answered:

Ha! Text me tonight and I'll give you the answers.

I tossed the note back and noticed a few girls looking between me and Coby. Probably imagining romantic liaisons. Let them dream—maybe Coby and I wouldn't last past Homecoming, but at least I had him through Trig.

I couldn't face the cafeteria at lunchtime, so I ate my chicken sandwich in the computer lab. I needed to work on my research project for Western Civ. One of the benefits of a superexpensive private school is access to state-of-the-art databases. I removed my necklace, and scanned the amulet. Kinda blurry. I scanned the image a few more times, then did a graphics search.

Ten thousand crappy matches, including a Victorian brooch on eBay with a pearl border, a glassy green jade bamboo charm, and a jade filigree Edwardian ring. None of which looked anything like my mother's pendant.

After half an hour, my eyes blurred. I narrowed the

search and kept scrolling. Forget the design, I'd just focus on the history of jade trading.

I started to close the search window when I saw it. The exact design.

Seventeen hits of the image on some true-crime Web site. I clicked before I realized what the pictures showed. The crime scene of a murder.

A mutilated woman. Shapes carved into her skin—shapes that echoed the design of the jade amulet. And branded into the floor beside her body, an exact match to my mother's necklace.

I read the page in blank horror. The woman, name withheld, was killed at home. In San Francisco, only a mile from my house.

"Oh God." I covered my mouth with my hand.

The Curlicue Killer. Not an urban myth, a brutal murder.

I felt a sickening sense of foreboding in the pit of my stomach. What was my mother doing with the symbol found burned into the floor of a ritualistic murder?

I needed to learn more about the amulet. But who could I trust?

After two more classes, I stumbled outside to head home, and remembered Periwinkle Antiques on Charles Street in Boston. The same day I'd found that death mask, I'd found the paperwork about Max's internship. And anyone who knew Max would help his little sister, right?

Well, maybe. Still, I didn't have a better idea.

Except how was I going to get to Boston? Echo Point was fifteen miles north with no T service. I stopped just outside the front gates, wondering about calling a cab, when Sara approached.

"You look lost," she said.

"You have no idea."

She laughed. "Your name is Emma. You live in a museum. Do you need directions?"

"Let's go shopping," I said.

She peered at me. "If you're teasing, I hate you."

"No, no. I'm serious. I need to steal your style."

Her eyes lit up. "When? Saturday?"

"What are you doing right now?" I asked. "Let's go to Boston."

"Yay!" She dragged me to her BMW, which she unlocked with a satisfyingly expensive noise. "Where do you want to start?"

"Charles Street?" I suggested.

"Oh. I was thinking Neiman Marcus."

"Well, I need to make one stop there," I said. "Say hi to a friend of the family. If you don't mind."

"No, that's cool." She steered the car through the village toward the highway. "But you have to spill—where'd you and Coby go after the party?"

I bit my lip. This is exactly why I'd been avoiding her all day. "Didn't you ask Coby?"

She wrinkled her nose. "He won't say. He didn't even tell Harry. Except about Homecoming. God, he's so perfect it makes me sick."

"It does kind of make him hard to live up to," I said.

"He's just completely nice with that freak of nature beautiful face. And his body . . ." She gave a little shiver. "If he was an ass, girls would still lust after him, but he's not, you know?" She sighed. "He's always there for you. I mean, you can trust him, right?"

She fell silent, looking slightly embarrassed.

"Were you ever . . . you're not into him, are you?"

She drove in silence for a moment. "Always," she admitted. "Since the day I met him."

"*Sara!* Why didn't you tell me? You know I'd never have gone out with him!"

"Yeah, because *I* love Coby, he should never date."

"But you helped me dress up!"

She cocked her head. "He likes you, and I want him to be happy. You can't help it, can you? Who you like. And you can't force them to like you back."

"No, you can't," I said, thinking of Bennett. "But how can he not like you? *Look* at you!"

"He loves me," she said, her voice wavering slightly, "like a sister."

"Oh, Sara."

She shook herself. "Stop. I'm a walking pity party. I don't want sympathy. I want *gossip*."

So I told her we'd just gone to the Point, and onto the beach, where we found my insanely jealous guardian stalking me. I didn't tell her about the kiss in the car. Then we traded boyfriend stories—hers were far more numerous than mine—until we got into Boston.

"What about Harry?" I asked. They seemed to get along great, better even than her and Coby. I wondered if she liked him, too.

"He's not a bad kisser," she said.

"You've kissed him?!"

"Once or twice. All that caffeine makes me kind of . . . you know."

"Oh my God, you're a coffee slut!" I teased her.

She giggled. "We're here. What's the address?"

I took in the neighborhood around us. We drove down a narrow lane with cute shops on either side. I didn't want Sara to tag along, but I wasn't sure how to tell her to just let me out.

"Why don't we meet back here in half an hour?" I said. "You don't want to get stuck listening to my great-aunt talking about her bowels."

That did the trick. I waved good-bye to Sara, and headed down the sidewalk, looking for Periwinkle Antiques. In two minutes, I stopped outside a little hole-in-the-wall shop, not nearly so grand as my parents'. It was closed.

No, not just closed. Out of business. With a For Lease sign in the window.

I put my hand against the glass and peered inside. Empty. I ran my fingers over the window, sensing the faint remnant of some ghostly presence.

My spine began to tingle and I turned to find a woman suddenly beside me. She was a tall blonde, dressed in an original Diane von Furstenberg wrap dress from the seventies, with an incredibly large collar and ridiculously loud pattern. She wore brown suede platform sandals, and I tried not to shudder at her suntan panty hose.

Poor Mr. Periwinkle, she said.

What happened? I asked. *Is he dead?*

Very much so.

I need to talk to him. Maybe I can summon him.

I should think not! she said. *You ghostkeepers cannot return.*

He was a ghostkeeper?!

Until the day he died. Murdered, right there—in the middle of his shop.

Murdered? Who killed him?

A ripple passed through her, and she shook her head.

I can compel you to tell me.

Please don't, she said, trembling with fear. *Please.*

I swallowed. *Did you ever meet his intern, Max? Max Vaile?*

Oh, yes—he was here that night. Despite being a ghost, she managed to pale. *Poor Mr. Periwinkle. So much pain. Such a long time dying.*

Who killed him?

She shook her head. *There's a spare key to the side door inside the frog in the alley.*

I reached within myself to gather the force to compel her, but she looked at me with such terror, I couldn't continue. Still trembling, she started fading away. But before she disappeared entirely, her lips formed a word: *Neos.*

That word again. What did it mean?

Fine. I'd try the side door.

Around the building, a narrow arch extended over a tidy brick-lined alleyway. I passed a bank of electric meters and a fire escape, and next to a stack of recycle bins found a little ceramic frog. In its mouth was a key.

"Great."

I slipped the key in the lock and went inside the shop, a little surprised there was no alarm. It looked just as empty from the inside. Three rooms with nothing in them. The showroom had built-in cabinets with empty shelves and a looming chandelier and burnished hardwood floor.

Was I supposed to conduct some arcane ghostkeeping rite to find an answer? The air smelled of old wood and dust—and I felt a shiver of dread.

Not a tingle, like a ghost. Just a sudden premonition.

I crossed the room, searching the floorboards. Then stopped suddenly, goose bumps on my arms.

The symbol from the jade amulet was branded into the floor. I clutched my chest. *My* mother's jade amulet. There were a dozen stains splattered around it—bloodstains, from designs carved in flesh.

I felt myself pulled to the floor. I reached toward the branded wood and ran my fingers around the rough, charred edges and *whoosh—*

Pain. Mr. Periwinkle's memories. His agony and terror, and a hellish place beyond pain and fear, a place of hopelessness and torment. And beyond that, worse. Something had been torn from Mr. Periwinkle, but what? His soul?

The agony turned unendurable, and—

I tore my fingers from the brand, my harsh breath echoing in the empty storefront. And I remembered another empty storefront, from ten years ago, and fear broke over me like a wave.

I fled.

I slammed into the passenger seat of Sara's car, trembling.

"What's wrong?"

"Someone was murdered."

"What? Who? Your great-aunt?"

I shook my head. "No, a—a neighbor."

"Whoa! Did you know him?"

"No. My brother did."

Oh God. My brother. The first murder happened a mile from my house, the design from my mother's necklace carved into some poor woman. And now this—also linked so closely to Max. The ghost even said she'd seen him here the night of the murder. But ghosts, they weren't good with time.

I needed Max. I needed to know what happened. They were all gone, like they were on the run, with no way to contact them. My whole family had disappeared.

Except me.

Me, they'd left behind.

"Wow," Sara said. "Are you okay?"

"I'm kinda freaked."

"Let's just go home."

"Do you mind? I dragged you all the way here."

"Sweetie, you're a mess. I'm taking you home."

We drove back to Echo Point in silence, as I tried not to relive every moment of Mr. Periwinkle's murder.

"Thanks, Sara," I said, when we pulled into the drive. "Thanks for being a friend."

She smiled. "You know, I'm glad you moved here. You make everything . . . interesting."

I half laughed. "I could use a little *less* interesting."

"You're supposed to say that you're glad, too!"

I hugged her good-bye. "I am."

Not only for my new friends, but because I was getting closer to the truth. About who I was, about Max and my parents. The only question left: did I really want to know?

22

I found Martha in the kitchen, compelling Anatole to make dinner.

"There's a dead ghostkeeper!" I blurted.

"What?" She clanked her cup into the saucer. "Who?"

Maybe that wasn't the best way to tell her. "Mr. Periwinkle—he owned an antique shop in Boston. Someone killed him."

"Oh. Yes, I know." Martha stared off into the distance. "Francis. He was a dear friend."

I scooted next to her in the breakfast nook. "I'm so sorry. But I—do you know who killed him?"

"The Knell is investigating. Bennett's working on that." She furrowed her brow. "What were you doing there?"

"My brother Max interned for him. I thought maybe . . ." I found myself reluctant to say too much. "Maybe he'd heard from him."

Martha smoothed her linen napkin. "Did you hear anything else? About how he died?"

I nodded. "I saw the bloodstains."

"And . . . ?"

How could I reveal what I'd seen without implicating my family? Between my brother's internship and my mother's jewelry, I was even afraid of my own suspicions. But this was Martha. I could tell her. "There was some kind of design burned into the floor."

Martha took a deep, shuddering breath. "Francis wasn't the first victim. That mark on the floor—remember I told you some ghostkeepers need a focus? The Knell believes that mark is someone's talisman."

"Whose is it?" I asked, dreading the answer.

"*Was,*" she said. "They stopped practicing a long time ago. It doesn't make any sense."

She hadn't answered my question, but I was afraid to ask again. Instead I said, "Where are my parents? That's what doesn't make any sense. Why don't they contact me?"

"The Knell can't find them."

"The Knell," I said. "They didn't bring me to Echo Point just because there's so much power here, did they? They're not only curious about what I can do—they suspect my family's involved with these murders."

"Maybe they wanted you here to protect you."

Or maybe they knew I wore my mother's talisman around my neck. Or were using me to bait a trap.

"I can protect myself," I said, and stomped away.

. . .

The next morning, I woke with a new resolve. Forget the Knell—I'd do my own investigating. So in fencing class I managed to pair up with Natalie, to ask what she knew about the murders.

She beat the crap out of me. With the proper fencing posture, and all the rules, I'd finally improved to the level of average, but Natalie was superb. I resisted the impulse to fight dirty, and managed to surprise her with a riposte. But as she was in the middle of a remise—another immediate attack—I didn't get far.

I glanced at the two ghost jocks who, as usual, mocked me from the bleachers.

"They think you're hot," I told Natalie.

She didn't deign to look at them. "What's it like, communicating with them? Ben and I have always wondered."

She called him Ben? I frowned then yelped as she scored another point. Why was she always catching me off guard? Had she called him Ben just to throw me?

"It's better than talking to someone who keeps jabbing me with a foil," I said.

She grinned. "En garde!"

After a few passes, I started digging for information. "So you and Bennett both work for the Knell. How'd you start with that?"

"Did he tell you how we met?"

"Should he have?"

"I grew up in a fundamentalist sect in Texas." She easily parried a wild thrust. "You know that polygamous group they raided?"

I nodded, trying to keep my back arm at the proper angle.

"It was like that, without the polygamy. Though if our minister had suggested it, I'm sure my parents would've agreed. Hell, if he'd suggested *cyanide*, they would've agreed."

"So they aren't ghostkeepers?"

"My mom was," she said. "My dad convinced her that ghostkeeping was the devil's work. So my mother stopped practicing and tried to 'cure' herself." Natalie shuddered. "Then I started showing tendencies . . ."

We stopped fencing and I bit my lip at her expression, forgetting all about interrogating her.

She stared into the distance. "They beat me, they starved me. They locked me in the basement. And when nothing worked, they tried exorcism."

I shivered. "What does that mean?"

"They found more inspired ways to hurt me." She shook her head, like she was banishing the memories. "I didn't break, though. I never broke. I like it, Emma. I like summoning ghosts. It's who I am."

"Yeah," I said. "Me, too." And I realized it was true, despite everything.

"Then once, the minister tried to choke the devil out of me. That's when my mom finally called the Knell. They sent Bennett."

"Oh my God. Natalie, why didn't you tell me?"

She half smiled. "It's not something you bring up over lunch. I just—I wanted you to know why I'd do anything for the Knell, anything for Bennett. He saved my life."

So Bennett really did fulfill my knight-in-shining-armor fantasy. Just not for me.

"We're not here to gossip," Coach snapped, crossing the gym toward us. "Natalie, *you* should know better. I'm afraid I've almost given up on you, Emma."

"Maybe I can't fence," I told her. "But I do know how to use a sword."

Which was exactly the wrong thing to say.

Coach saluted me. Her impressive calves bulged as she curled her back arm and drove me across the gym. Her style was much more intent and controlled than the Rake, who'd seemed to pay about as much attention as someone brushing their teeth. I think that helped me, actually, because it had caused my own style to be similar.

So I switched my grip and easily batted her away. She redoubled her attack, quick and controlled, and I lazily parried every strike. I felt a grin rise on my face—the Rake's grin, infuriating and smug, but I couldn't help myself. For once, I felt in control. For once, I was simply *better* than my opponent.

When she began to flag, I saw an opening . . . and I didn't take it. I was afraid I'd learned the Rake's lessons too well. He'd never shown me how to score points, only how to draw blood. I resisted the urge to switch hands, break her ankle with a kick, and drive my foil into her throat.

Instead, I dropped my guard and let her through. "Touché," I said.

Then I spent the rest of the class period getting scolded, with my head bowed to hide my smile.

"What the hell was *that*?" Sara asked, back in the locker room.

"Oh . . . well," I said, "I've been practicing at home."

23

I spent the weekend in lockdown mode. Coby and Sara tried to get me to go out, but I pretended I was sick and texted them bi-daily updates on my condition for verisimilitude—one of the few PSAT words I had gotten right.

I filled my hours with research in the museum's archival room and told Martha I was doing homework, which wasn't a complete lie. I still had to turn in my Western Civ paper on Monday. I surfed the net to find some hint of my parents' whereabouts, reading endless travel blogs, hoping to find mention of a couple of antiquities dealers. I checked auction sites looking for the kind of items they generally sold, trying to find some connection somewhere, but nothing resonated.

Next were the conspiracy sites. It was weird to see theories about ghostkeeping mixed with lore of vampires and extraterrestrials. It made me wonder if there really were bloodsucking aliens. Then again, most of the whack-jobs thought ghostkeepers controlled ghosts like families of mobsters, contracting them out for crime, so it was hard to give them any credence.

I couldn't find a single reference to the Knell, which was a disappointment. I'd grilled Martha over breakfast, but she'd remained vague, simply saying, "When you're ready, you'll meet them. You needn't worry until then."

But I was worried. Worried that they were after my parents or Max for killing ghostkeepers and there was no way for me to protect or even warn them.

Sunday afternoon, an e-mail dinged in my mailbox:

Hey Emma,

First off, I'm sorry I deserted you. I know I suck as a best friend.

The thing is . . . I see ghosts, too.

Yeah, I'm serious. That's why my mom worked for your parents, to be around people who understood. I never saw much until I fell for Max, and then I started seeing ghosts everywhere. And I freaked out. Max got all paranoid I'd steal his powers or something. Only I didn't want his powers OR mine.

Emma, I HATE seeing ghosts!!!!!!!!!!

I despise that heebie-jeebie feeling you get when they show up——and have you ever touched one? It's like insta-frostbite. I just hate them!

Anyway, that's why Max dumped me and why I dumped you. My mom explained to me about ghostkeeping running in families. You know that's what you are by now, right? You're a ghostkeeper. If not, get help.

So I thought you had been like Max all along and had never told me. I'm glad you weren't keeping it from me, but I don't want to see ghosts anymore, Emma. I don't know how you're dealing. I'm sorry, I just don't want anything to do with it.

Sooo . . . this sucks. I want to be there for you, but I can't. Not even by e-mail.

I know I'm a terrible person.

Love always and forever . . . just from afar.

Abby

I spent the rest of the day going through the five stages of grief.

Denial: she couldn't really be a ghostkeeper.

Anger: how dare she not like ghosts? Natalie loved being a ghostkeeper so much she wouldn't let her family exorcise it out of her.

Bargaining: I'd never bring up ghostkeeping in Abby's presence, then she'd still want to be friends with me.

Depression: I'd never see her again—never even talk to her. Abandoned by my parents, my brother, and my best friend. Forever.

I never quite worked my way into Acceptance.

Sunday night, I finished my paper. There wasn't a single reference to ghostkeeping, talismans, or murders.

Or best friends who desert you. Not that it was relevant.

. . .

Monday morning, I found Martha drinking her tea in the solarium. It was more of a greenhouse, really, with small citrus trees growing in blue and white Chinese pots and orchids blooming on red lacquered tables. It was warm and smelled faintly of dampness and earth. I sat beside her on the wicker settee with sage green pillows.

There was a second cup on the tea tray and I helped myself.

"Is everything ready for winter?" I knew she'd been helping the ghosts clean and prepare.

"We're close. A few more rooms. The house needed some love." Her eyes shone with affection. "Some life."

She thought that I'd brought life to the museum. But that wasn't how I felt, since I was constantly shrouded in the trappings of death.

"Will we have to shut off this room?" The scent of the orange trees made me miss California. Even the trees and flowers would all be dead soon. I wasn't looking forward to it.

"No, the sun and a heater keep it warm. And Anatole uses the fruit." She set down her teacup. "I was going through some drawers and I found something that will interest you."

"What?"

"It's a surprise. Bennett's coming to dinner, so let's wait until then."

"Okay." I hadn't talked to him since our last fight. I was nervous about seeing him.

"Will you work on the menu with Anatole? So convenient that you can talk with him." She gave me a few dish ideas, then said, "And how are *you*, my dear?"

"Well," I said. "I've been thinking. I can't do this alone. I need to know all the secrets you're keeping—you and Bennett."

Martha took a long sip of tea, then said, "You're right. We've been trying to protect you, but we're only endangering you. I've spoken with Bennett—that's one reason he's coming. We'll talk before dinner."

"No more secrets?"

"Well, the Knell always has *some*. We all have some—even you."

I managed not to touch the jade necklace under my shirt. "All I want to know is how my family is involved. Who killed those ghostkeepers and why? What's the story with wraiths? What does 'Neos' mean? Why didn't—"

"Wait." Martha's gaze sharpened on me. "Neos?"

I nodded. "Yeah. I think *all* the wraiths kind of . . . chanted that. The ones back in San Francisco, the ones here."

"All the wraiths? How many have you seen?"

I tallied in my head all the times I'd heard that name: the ashes in my father's urns, the shadows in the village and that monstrous thing I killed. "Three? I don't really know if that's what they are, though."

"Neos," she said, thoughtfully. "I'll look into that while you're at school. Should I invite Natalie to dinner?"

"Um . . ." Natalie and I were coming to terms, but I needed Martha and Bennett to myself tonight.

"If you let her, Emma, Natalie will be a real friend to you."

"Oh, Martha." I hugged her before leaving for school. "All I need is you."

I waited at Thatcher's front gates until Harry and Sara showed up. Coby had already gotten to school at the crack of dawn for football practice. Every waking moment he wasn't in class, he was on the gridiron—that's the football field. See what you learn when you're almost kinda the quarterback's sorta girlfriend?

On the way through the orchard, Harry recited an ode to Natalie's butt. Seriously. In *terza rima*, he told us, with rhyming couplets. Neither Sara nor I had a clue what that meant. Except that he liked her butt. We got that part in triplicate.

By the time we reached the front doors, I started getting suspicious. Harry's infatuation with Natalie was so completely over the top, I didn't quite believe it anymore. Like maybe he was just trying to make Sara jealous or something. Especially when Natalie showed up for Latin, looking like she was made to wear a school uniform, and Harry didn't blink an eye.

The mysteries of Harry's mind were beyond me I decided, as I sat down in Trigonometry. Coby arrived to class looking flushed and windswept, and half the girls simultaneously sighed.

He really was perfect. If only he were perfect for *me*.

After Trig, I sat on the bench during Fencing, still in trouble. The idiot ghost-boys kept me distracted with their running commentary. Mostly about the girls in class.

Would you stop? I finally told them.

Hey, there weren't girls here when we were alive, one said.

The other nodded. *That's right. Cut us some slack. This is a novelty.*

You've been dead for like thirty years! How long can girls stay a novelty?

Shall we tell her? one asked the other.

Tell me what? I wasn't sure I wanted to hear.

Our advice from the Beyond, one of them intoned. *Do not die a virgin.*

I laughed, and the whole class turned to me. Coach was not pleased.

For lunch, I met Harry and Sara in the bleachers outside, where we shared the picnic Anatole had packed. We watched Coby practicing plays, throwing perfect spirals through the crisp autumn air. I would've enjoyed myself more if I hadn't seen Sara's face, shining with admiration as her eyes tracked him. How evil was I, kind of dating the guy she loved?

When she raced off for class, I asked Harry, "Do you ever wonder if you're kind of a jerk?"

"All the time," he said.

"No, I don't mean *you.* I mean . . . What do I mean?"

"You mean you," he said. "Do I ever think that *you* are a jerk."

"Yeah."

"You're not a jerk, Emma," he said, kindly. "Maybe a cretin, or a nitwit."

I shoved him. "Oh, shut up."

"'Ode to a Cretin.' I'll get right on that."

"You're such a comfort to me," I told him, and trudged off to Western Civ.

Our essays were supposed to be fifteen hundred words, which is like six double-spaced pages, but what Mr. Jones hadn't mentioned was that we were going to read them aloud in class.

After the first three boring presentations, I gave my own lackluster report, all about the history of jade. I hadn't wanted to put my necklace on display, so I plugged my memory stick into the class computer and referred to a fuzzy image on the overhead monitor. Eyes glazed from the front row to the back.

Except for one pair that didn't look away or even blink. Edmund, the man in the brown suit. He'd wandered in shortly after I'd started and watched intently.

When I finished, I stumbled to my chair next to Britta, who started presenting a paper on her father's one-of-a-kind vintage Mercedes-Benz. I ignored Edmund, who was standing in the back of the room, not in the mood for his banter, but he pressed his thoughts toward me.

I need to speak with you.

I'm busy listening to the history of Nazi capitalism.

That jade design, he said. *I've seen it before.*

I spun toward him, startling Britta, who complained

to Mr. Jones. "Is it too much to ask that Emma stop fidgeting while I speak?"

"Sorry," I murmured. God, she was such a drama queen. I kept my face forward and my eyes focused on her as I communicated with the ghost.

Where? I asked. *Where did you see it?* I watched Britta drone about the custom leather interior. *Who had it?*

He took a shaky breath. *I don't want to say his name. He is strong and growing stronger. He hears things and punishes those who—*

Neos?

He nodded quickly, eyes wide in his pale face. *He raises wraiths, I don't know how—he's . . .* Edmund shook his head. *I can't explain. Twisting things.*

Who is he? How can I find him?

He's one of you, Edmund said. *Or he* was. *I don't know any more than that.* He knelt beside my chair. *Do you really want to find him? He's killed before. Killed the living and the dead.*

Just tell me how, Edmund.

Then you'll dispel me?

No. I was never doing that again.

He stood abruptly, his face clouded. *I don't know how to find him. You should worry more about him finding you. Someone's been compelling spirits all morning, seeking information about him. He's on the hunt right now.*

But who would be—

Oh God. Martha.

My chair scraped across the floor as I stood. "I'm going to be sick," I said, and raced from the room.

24

I stumbled through the front doors of the museum. "Martha?"

No answer. I ran to the kitchen, but she wasn't in her usual spot in the breakfast nook. I called her name again, checking the porch, then her bedroom.

"Martha! Martha!" I galloped down the stairs. "Celeste, where is she? Anatole? Nicholas, come tell me what—"

I stopped, spotting the three of them at the end of the hall. Standing in a line, like when we'd first met, staring into the front parlor. They appeared duller somehow, grayer and dingier.

My throat clenched and I rushed past them to the open door. It was a large, ornate room with uncomfortable formal furnishings, so we hardly ever came in here. A clock ticked loudly on the mantel. The afternoon sunlight, dappled by falling leaves outside, shone across the far wall.

The wide-planked wooden floor was painted white,

and in the middle Martha lay on her back, legs and arms spread in an *X*. I screamed when I saw her.

Her skin was pale and cool. I shook her and called her name—even though I knew. She was dead. Martha was dead. I couldn't catch my breath, I couldn't stop crying.

"Martha, no," I said, sobbing. "No, no—please."

Anatole? Celeste? What happened?

But when I turned to the doorway, they were gone.

I knelt next to Martha's body, afraid to touch the blood seeping from her chest and forehead. Her features were etched with fear and blood dripped into her eyes. I took a shuddering breath and forced myself to examine her.

The wound in her head trailed down one temple, across her chin, down her neck to her chest in a snakelike pattern. Her white blouse, so properly buttoned when I left her this morning, had been torn open to reveal her chest. The starched linen was soaked in crimson blood from the designs cut into her skin.

She looked so undignified that I moved to pull her shirt closed, then realized I shouldn't touch anything before the police got here. I didn't know what to do. I needed to call someone, but couldn't move.

On the floor beside her, I found the pattern burned into the wood. Same as the amulet I wore around my neck.

I sat beside her corpse until shadows filled the room. Finally, I took her cold, limp hand between both of mine, to say good-bye, and realized that her fist was slightly closed. Inside her fingers, I discovered a gold ring, like a simple wedding band, with a little tag on it: *Emma*.

I removed the tag and held the ring to the fading light of the afternoon sun—then started crying again. This was the keepsake she'd found while organizing. Her surprise. Martha had died alone, frightened, and in pain—with a gift for me clenched in her hand.

"Oh, Martha," I said. So sweet and good and giving.

Until someone brutally cut her life short. And I knew who.

The anger built inside of me and I summoned: *Neos*.

The house creaked with the wind. An ache crept into my chest, my skin itched and my stomach clenched. I felt a shifting of air behind me, but when I turned, there was nothing.

Emma Vaile. The voice came, slick and slithery, into my mind. *Do not call what you cannot control.*

I'm not going to control you, I'm going to dispel you.

Spectral laughter echoed. *You are going to writhe under my knife.*

Show yourself, then.

A patch of unnatural shadow slunk across the floor, and I shoved at it with my mind. The laughter grew louder.

I am not to be pushed around like any old ghost, he said.

What are you? A wraith?

I am the wraiths' master. I am Neos.

He appeared, with crow eyes and spidery fingers. There was a dagger in his left hand, the blade still wet with Martha's blood.

Have you seen my little white dog?

I stepped back. The ghost from the abandoned storefront. All those years ago. The ghost my mother saved me from. But where was my mother? Who would save me now?

My poor lost Snowball, all alone. Will you help me find her?

"For Martha," I whispered, and summoned my powers and lashed at him.

His form frayed and his edges feathered into dust. I struck harder—again and again—until he crumbled like a sandcastle.

Then swirled and re-formed, the same as before. Unhurt.

He laughed in triumph. *All these years in the fog, growing stronger. But never strong enough—not until* you *started coming into your power.*

No, I said, and lashed at him again.

Don't you see? I've tasted your blood. As your power grows, so does mine. And when I find that talisman, I will straddle the border between life and death.

Then he unwove himself into strips of darkness. Snakes of smoky blackness wrapped around me like a cocoon, winding tighter and darker.

I struggled to find the spark inside me and I blasted him with everything I had. He bound me tighter and his darkness swallowed my light. I felt myself fading and all I could think was, *Martha, I've failed you.*

As my consciousness ebbed away, I felt the ring that she'd set aside for me still clasped in my fist—her final gift.

I slipped it on my finger. And a rush of foreign memories and emotions sang in my mind. The ring throbbed with power and tightened on my finger. All at once, I disappeared.

I became a ghost.

Weightless and untouched, I fell through Neos's smoky snakes and stepped into the light of the front parlor. My body had become transparent and my mind flashed with foreign memories as I straightened.

Neos's surprise and anger boiled toward me, and I fled.

Like a ghost, I escaped through the walls. It would've been so cool—if I hadn't been so freaked out.

He screeched and followed close behind with his dagger. I twisted through the walls and ceilings, slid through the brick of the chimney, and spun with quicksilver weightlessness into the basement. Then I went up through the stone foundation to the rose garden.

Before Neos reached the garden, the Rake appeared. He engaged Neos as he was halfway out of the cellar door and fought him fiercely, his blade flashing against Neos's knife. But he was only a ghost, not a walking nightmare. He pierced Neos in the shoulder then fell back, desperately defending himself against Neos's snakes of shadow.

I reached out with my mind—if I couldn't dispel Neos, I'd compel him away. But his thoughts revolted me. They were disjointed and tortured, livid with madness. Wearing the ring seemed to make it worse; I couldn't compel him while overcome by his sick thoughts.

I removed the ring and Neos turned to me as the Rake vanished. I tried to force him away—I compelled with all my will—but his form, made of shadows and inky black-ness, simply faltered, then refocused.

Behind me, there was a crush of gravel. Bennett, arriving in his old Land Rover. He sped from the drive-way across the lawn toward us.

He leaped from the driver's seat and launched a spear of light at Neos. Martha had said everyone's power was different, but I couldn't believe I could actually see Ben-nett's. He advanced toward Neos, his face a mask of con-centration.

Watching him use his power was like watching the Rake with a sword: intense and masterful. But he was also unable to defeat Neos. At first they seemed evenly matched, but slowly Neos overwhelmed him.

I circled behind Neos, and loosed a blast of my own into his back. He screeched, and I poured everything into a ribbon of light, my own power no longer invisible, but an endless stream from my fingers into the blackness. Neos clawed at my light and Bennett leaped closer and thrust one hand inside Neos's chest.

His fist glowed with my power, and my ribbon of light swayed like a python. Slowly, slowly, Neos started to waver, then to fade.

Until he was gone.

We stood there a moment, stunned and breathless. Until I ran to Bennett and he hugged me fiercely.

"Thank God, Emma. Thank God you're all right."

He kissed the top of my head and held me. I'd lost Martha and fought some nightmare monster from the

Beyond . . . but finally, wrapped in Bennett's arms, I felt safe.

Bennett. It was Bennett who had saved me.

He kissed my temple, his lips moving closer to my mouth. "Emma," he whispered. "I've wanted to tell you for so long—"

I couldn't let him finish. "Martha's inside," I interrupted. "She's dead."

When the police finally left, I wandered into the kitchen and collapsed into the breakfast nook. A notebook sat open beside the teapot. Martha had just begun another list. The tears started again.

Anatole appeared and quietly took the notebook away, then coddled me with cookies and tea while Celeste wrapped a blanket around my shoulders.

What is he? I asked.

*We do not know. An abomination. We just—*Celeste blew a puff of air—*fled into ze Beyond when we felt ze wickedness.*

I wish we'd been braver, Anatole said.

Oui. For your sake, Celeste agreed. *And for Martha.*

I glanced at their distraught faces. She might have been bossy, but they'd loved Martha in their way.

There's nothing you could've done, I told them.

But what about me? I'd given her Neos's name. This was all my fault.

. . .

Hours later, Bennett found me sitting at the piano in the ballroom. I'd left the lights off, preferring the darkening gloom and the few candles flickering in a silver candelabra on top of the piano.

I missed everyone so much. My parents, to tell me everything would be okay. Max, who made me crazy but was always my brother. I loved my new friends, but still ached for the intimacy I'd shared with Abby. I just couldn't pinpoint where I'd gone wrong. If only I could go back, make a better choice. Somehow stop Martha's death. At least keep my family from disappearing.

"We're going to get frost tonight," Bennett said, sitting down next to me at the piano.

"I've never seen real snow. Martha told me it's magical the first time."

Bennett smiled sadly, then played the opening phrases of Beethoven's *Moonlight Sonata*. My dad was totally into classical music and made me listen with him on Sunday mornings. I suddenly yearned to see him, to lie on the couch in his office and have him explain yet again why Mozart was so very brilliant.

"I didn't know you played," I said when he finished.

"Not very well. My sister—" He shook his head. "She played better than that when she was eight years old."

He sampled a few measures of something else, mournful and slow, then we sat in silence for a time.

"Why did you lie to the police?" I asked. "You told them you found the body."

"To protect you, Emma."

"Oh," I said in a little voice. He wanted to protect me. "Thank you." I plunked a few piano keys. "Except . . . what exactly do I need protecting from?"

He made an unhappy noise. "You're not going to like it."

"Martha's dead. The worst thing that could happen already did."

"You know that image next to—" His jaw clenched. "Next to Martha, on the floor?"

"Yeah." I swallowed. I still hadn't told him about the version of it I wore around my neck.

He glanced at me. "Did she tell you what it is?"

"Some ghostkeepers need a talisman to hone their power. She said the owner didn't practice anymore."

"Yeah, but did she tell you whose it was?"

"No."

He stood and ran his fingers through his hair. "Your mother's."

Yeah, I'd pretty much figured that out. "Bennett, just because someone's using my mom's amulet, doesn't mean— that's not evidence she's involved in the murders."

"It's not proof," he said, "but it *is* evidence. She's involved somehow."

"She's—someone else is using it."

"Emma, no one else could use it. Each focus is unique and individual."

"What about me?" I stood and walked across the parquet floor toward him. "Why did you bring me here, Bennett? Do you think I had anything to do with this?"

He hesitated a fraction of a second too long. "Emma,

you're the most powerful ghostkeeper I've ever seen, and now wraiths are appearing. And that thing today—what was that?"

"Neos."

"You know his name?" He ran a hand over his brow. "You haven't learned to control your abilities yet. Isn't it possible that you're summoning these things without meaning to?"

"No," I said in a small voice. But I thought of what Neos had told me. He'd tasted my blood and we were connected. I didn't tell Bennett about the ring. I wasn't sure what he'd do if he knew I could turn into a ghost. "I don't think my powers are out of control. I just think . . . I don't know what they all are yet."

He looked at me. "I want to believe you."

His lack of confidence stunned me. And made me furious. "Do you really think I'm capable of hurting—of *murdering*—Martha?"

"Of course not, but you keep demanding the truth, while you're keeping your own secrets." He grabbed my arms. "I'm not stupid, Emma."

I wrenched myself away and went to the windows to stare at the moonlight. I wasn't ready to explain about the ring or the talisman. How could I share anything more with Bennett when he didn't trust me? I didn't even know who I was talking to: Bennett or the Knell.

"Emma," he said from behind me, "tell me about Neos."

I shook my head. I'd told Martha about Neos, and gotten her killed.

"Ghostkeepers are dying. The killing's not gonna stop now."

I pressed a hand to my chest, feeling the jade through my sweater. I pictured my mother in her uniform of black T-shirt and pants and chunky jewelry, not a hair out of place in her blond bob. She couldn't be involved. She just couldn't.

As if sensing my thoughts, Bennett asked, gently, "Have you heard from Max?"

"No," I answered. "Not from any of them."

And I felt guilty. Because the truth was, I already missed Martha more than I missed them. I was left with nothing. "What am I going to do? What am I going to do without Martha?"

Bennett cleared his throat. "I'm leaving tonight. And you can't stay here."

"Don't leave."

"I have to. The Kne—"

"Don't say it!" I snapped.

"You can stay with the family who's hosting Natalie."

I made a strangled noise. "With Natalie." I turned back to the darkness in the window.

"Emma," he said. "Please."

"Fine. Whatever," I said. "I'll get my stuff."

Nicholas and Celeste were waiting for me when I got upstairs.

I'm leaving, I said.

No, you mustn't go, Celeste said. *You belong here, with us.*

I glanced at Nicholas who was cleaning the grate. He gave me his best starving-waif look and it was all just too much. Maybe Abby was right to hate ghosts. Had they ever done anything but cause me problems? I was ready to forget them all. Go back to San Francisco and live my boring, asocial, but normal, life.

I'm sorry, I mumbled and compelled them away.

I dug my suitcase from the floor of the wardrobe and shoved my meager clothing and necessities into it. The room was clean and the bed still made. I zipped my case and paused at the door, my hand on the polished nickel knob. It looked like I'd never been here.

I met Bennett, waiting in his jacket, at the bottom of the stairs. He grabbed for the suitcase.

"I've got it," I said, stepping toward the door. I didn't bother looking back.

At the Finches' house, I found Natalie in the front doorway, her hair pulled into a sloppy ponytail, which only served to highlight the shadows under her eyes from weeping.

The little flat over the three-car garage included a small living room and kitchen, two minuscule bedrooms, and a bathroom, where the tub was filled with steaming hot water that smelled of grapefruit.

"That's for you," Natalie said. "I thought you'd need a soak."

I stripped and sank into the tub, liking the scalding water on my skin. The aftershock of Martha's death was setting in and I was beginning to go numb.

After an hour, Natalie knocked on the door. The water had long gone cold.

"Emma," she called. "Are you all right?"

"Yeah," I croaked.

I unstopped the drain with my foot and rose from the tub, wrapped myself in the fluffy lavender towels and opened the door. In my bedroom, my suitcase was a mess. I already missed Celeste. Amazing how easily you could get used to a maid, even one of the ghostly persuasion. I finally settled for an old T-shirt and leggings and found Natalie bawling in the kitchenette.

"I'm sorry," she wailed. "She w-was a better m-mother than my mother was."

So I hugged her and started sobbing as well. We stood, wailing into each other's arms. Then the absurdity of it hit us at the same time and we both started to giggle.

Natalie wiped tears from her eyes. "God, what if they could see you at Thatcher? You'd no longer be the most popular girl in school."

"What?" I said. "I'm not that popular."

"Your best friends are Harry and Sara, and *Coby* is taking you to Homecoming."

"Oh." Back in San Francisco, I always fantasized that if I moved away, I'd become popular. Well, it had happened. "You'd think I'd enjoy it more."

Natalie shook her head and made another pot of tea

while I poked into cabinets until I found some almond cookies. Then we sat at the little table and maybe this wasn't the right moment, but I said it anyway, because I couldn't get it off my mind. "Natalie, I need to know about the Knell."

"We're not supposed to talk about it." She sipped her tea. "What do you want to know?"

"Well, does the government know about it?"

"Not officially. There are ghostkeepers everywhere: CIA, FBI, all the military branches. When they come across something ghost-related, they let us know."

"Is there an office somewhere?"

"Yeah, a few—it's more of a home office sort of thing. I don't actually know the details."

"Does Bennett?"

She shrugged. "I don't know if you've noticed, but he's not, like, chatty." She bit her lip. "He likes you, you know."

"No he doesn't."

"He doesn't want to," she said, "but he does."

Why didn't he want to like me? Because he thought my mother was a murderer, that's why. "He's not even *nice* to me."

"*Exactly,*" she said, as if that only confirmed her opinion.

"It doesn't matter," I said. "Nothing matters anymore but finding Martha's killer."

25

I threw myself into school. It was either that or obsess about Martha and Neos. I didn't summon ghosts and if one approached, I compelled it away. I didn't even give Edmund, the man in the brown suit, a chance; he flashed me his most offended look before fading away.

I absolutely banned Bennett from my thoughts—well, more or less—and immersed myself in normal life. I texted Sara catty comments about other girls (mostly Britta), perfected my secret smile and flirted with Coby—and Harry, of course, because he didn't know how to have any other interaction with a girl.

I even went Homecoming-dress shopping with Sara and watched her plunk down a cool nine hundred dollars on a bloodred velvet gown by a designer I'd never heard of at her beloved Neiman's. I couldn't find a dress, but used my dad's credit card to buy a pair of black satin peep-toe pumps on sale. Even Sara approved, despite the sticker shock—she was bowled over by how cheap they were.

And I really enjoyed being normal. Well, I enjoyed pretending to be normal. Pretending that I wasn't worried about wraiths looming from the darkness and that I didn't mourn Martha every time I woke. And pretending that I didn't wonder what Bennett had wanted to tell me for so long.

Then came Martha's funeral. Instead of going with Natalie as planned, I'd hung back until the last mourner, a dapper middle-aged man I didn't recognize, climbed into his car and left.

The cemetery was located in the oldest part of the village, next to a Congregational church built when Massachusetts was a colony. It was too small for a backhoe to fill the grave, so an old gravedigger had begun to shovel in the final dirt when I asked him to give me a minute. He wandered off to have a smoke as I stood at the edge, staring down at the oak coffin.

For a moment I hesitated—I'd gone through a Stephen King phase, and couldn't help thinking about *Pet Sematary*. Would Martha's ghost be just like she was, or wrong, like in *Pet Sematary*?

Then I shook my head. It didn't matter. I wanted her back.

I closed my eyes and summoned her. And nothing happened. There was no familiar tingling, no sense that she'd been waiting for me to summon her. I tried again and again to no avail.

She wasn't coming back.

I only wanted . . . I wiped tears from my eyes. I only

wanted to see her one more time. Okay, more than once. I thought she could live in the museum with Anatole and the rest. But once would've been enough. To tell her I was sorry and that I was going to find who did this to her. And dispel them for good.

The gravedigger was done with his smoke. He came back to Martha's grave and I walked away, trying to tune out the sound of the dirt hitting the casket.

When I got home, Natalie met me at the door. "You tried to summon her, didn't you?"

I nodded. "Didn't work."

"Ghostkeepers don't come back, Emma."

"Never?" I asked.

"Never," she said. "When we're dead, we're dead."

A few days later, Natalie and I were watching some MTV reality show rerun, when she said, "So are you going to dump Coby after Homecoming?"

"What?" I said. "We're hardly even going out." We had lunch together every day and hung out after school a few times, but he hadn't tried to kiss me again.

"Everyone else thinks you are." She shot me a look. "Including Coby."

"Am I going to find you kissing Coby behind the stadium at Homecoming? This has Jared written all over it."

"What is your problem?" Natalie asked.

"What's my problem?" Martha was dead, my family

was missing, the guy I liked didn't want to like me, and the guy who liked me I only liked as a friend. Plus some nightmare demon wanted to kill me, and my family might be responsible for the deaths of several ghost-keepers. "Where do I start?"

But before I could, there was a knock on the door.

"Oh, he's here." Natalie eyed me. "Are you going like that?"

"Like what? Who's here?" I was wearing a stained T-shirt and an old pair of ripped Sevens. My hair had finally started to grow out and consequently was driving me crazy, so I'd braided what I could with little rubber bands I'd found in a kitchen drawer. I was not prepared to see anyone.

"Didn't you get my e-mail about Bennett taking us to dinner?" Natalie asked.

Yeah, but I'd deleted it unread—she sent a dozen e-mails a day. Of course, I'd noticed she was wearing matchstick jeans, a flirty burgundy top, and leopard-print flats, but the possible reason hadn't registered.

She went downstairs to open the street door for him, while I stood frozen like a deer. I fingered my braids trying to decide which looked worse: leaving them in or the inevitable crimping from taking them out. There was a little mirror by the apartment front door, and catching sight of myself, I realized frizz was preferable.

I'd only gotten one braid unraveled when Bennett walked in. He looked gorgeous in a gray canvas motor-cycle jacket over a black T-shirt and jeans. He smiled, and for a moment I thought he was happy to see me, then noticed myself in the mirror again and realized he must be laughing at my hair.

"Emma's not ready," Natalie said.

"No?" Bennett said. "Looks ready to me."

I yanked the rest of the rubber bands from my head. "I'm not going."

"What? Why not?" Bennett asked. He looked at Natalie. "Did you forget to tell her?"

"No, I did not."

"I just can't." I grabbed my peacoat and shoved a black newsboy cap over my hateful hair. "Any news about Martha's killer?"

"That's one thing I wanted to talk about."

I slipped into my boots at the door. "Is that a yes?"

He shook his head. "It's a no. I'm sorry."

"Then I've gotta go."

"Emma," Natalie said, "don't be like that. We're going to the harbor for oysters. Come with us."

Bennett watched me intently, but said nothing.

"See you," I said, and shut the door behind me.

Tears welled in my eyes as I stumbled downstairs. When I got outside, I realized I had nowhere to go. So I walked, wandering around the village, past the harbor to Redd's Pond with its hateful dunking-chair contraption where they'd tortured witches. *What kind of town made that a tourist attraction?* I wondered, thinking about the original Emma. Then I went out to the Neck and back again, until I stopped because my feet hurt.

And I found myself outside the gates of the Stern House Museum.

I saw the outline of the house through the trees, the windows dark but the white columns of the grand facade still visible. I wondered how Anatole and Celeste and the Rake were doing. I'd promised Nicholas I'd find him another Game Boy cartridge, but had never delivered.

Why had I come this way? It only reminded me of Martha.

Maybe that's why I'd come. I needed to be reminded of Martha. I couldn't ignore what had happened.

I needed to stop pretending I was someone I wasn't.

While I stood on the sidewalk, lost in thought, the sky suddenly opened and rain poured down; lightning blazed and thunder roared. We never had this kind of storm in California. I shoved open the gates and ran down the drive to take shelter in the front portico of the museum.

I stood a moment, cold and wet. Inside, I could get Anatole to bring me hot tea, Celeste to run me a bath, and Nicholas had mad skills with a fireplace. But that would break my current no-ghost policy.

So I stood there, shivering. Then I laughed. "This is ridiculous!"

I closed my eyes and felt the familiar warm tingling that summoned a ghost. *Anatole, I need you. Please open the door. Celeste, I'm freezing! I could use some dry clothes. And a fire, Nicholas.*

I didn't bother compelling them—they were happier when asked.

A moment later Anatole opened the door and I punched in the code to the alarm that Bennett had taught me.

Ma chère. He smiled and twirled his mustache. *I am so pleased to see you.*

Anatole, I said. *If I could hug you, I would.*

Emma! Celeste ran down the stairs. *I mean, Miss Vaile! You are too wet. I've already started ze bath. Come upstairs. Nicholas is in ze den lighting ze fire.*

Are you hungry? Anatole asked.

Starved, I said. *What isn't a bother to make?*

Well, I suppose I could make something from ze spa cookbook?

I giggled. *Never! I don't know what I was thinking when I gave that to you.*

Well, then, he said, pleased. *There is a good cheese and some eggs. Yes, I think I perhaps will whip up an omelet.*

That would be divine, I said and let Celeste whisk me upstairs.

I climbed into the half-drawn bath, warmed my icicle feet under the faucet, and gingerly lay back against the still cool porcelain of the claw-foot tub. I closed my eyes. It was good to be home.

26

By the time the hot water ran out, I was sufficiently toasty. Wearing the terry-cloth robe Celeste left, I padded downstairs into the den. Nicholas had started a fire and Anatole had left a plate of fruit and crackers. As I nibbled a grape, Nicholas wandered in with the Game Boy.

I held out my palm. *Let me show you.*

I can't get past level 85, he complained.

Of Tetris? I asked. *Then you don't need my help.*

He grinned, for a moment looking like any normal preteen boy. Then Anatole shooed him away as he came in with my omelet and Nicholas disappeared in a puff of ghostliness. So much for normal.

I smelled fresh herbs and onion as Anatole placed the silver tray on a table by the fire. *He wasn't bothering me,* I told him, then forgot all about Nicholas as I dug into the omelet. *Heaven!*

Bon appétit, ma chère.

I finished the omelet and the grapes, enjoying the sound of rain against the windowpane. Maybe I shouldn't be here—without invitation, without Martha—but it's where I belonged.

I wandered into the hall and passed Mr. Stern's study. I thought of the swords and the Rake. My body missed our daily spars. Then a sudden concern hit me. What if he hadn't gotten away from Neos?

I ran into the ballroom and couldn't find him. I raced around the room, my bathrobe flapping around me, and—

He appeared, lounging on the piano bench.

I tightened the robe. *You're okay?*

I am indeed "okay," he said, mocking my slang. *And yourself?*

We didn't kill him.

I failed you. He gestured at his own ghostly presence. *This pathetic form. When I was alive, I ate wraiths for breakfast.*

No. You were perfect. Thank you.

Come along, he said.

He led me through the corridors to the door of the front parlor, where Martha had been killed. After eyeing me a moment, he walked through the wall into the room. I stood there staring at the closed door, unable to lift my hand to the knob.

I imagined I still smelled the charred wood, the tang of Martha's blood. I still felt the chill of seeing her lying there, dead beyond summoning. Natalie had said that when ghostkeepers died, we died forever. Our spirits couldn't linger. But if we could, I'd raise Martha and—what?

Fall into her arms? Ask her how to find Neos?

No. I'd beg her forgiveness. "Forgive me, Martha," I said, and opened the door.

I stepped inside and found the Rake standing where she'd lain. I crossed to him, trying to ignore the bloodstains underfoot.

You're not afraid? he asked.

I was terrified, but I'd be damned if I let it stop me. I walked a circuit around the room, trailing my finger along the back of the silk-covered couch. *When you were alive, you fought wraiths?*

And ghasts. Yes.

Then you were a ghostkeeper.

He bowed his head in agreement.

But you're here. You're a ghost. I thought when ghostkeepers died, they couldn't come back.

When I lived, I was a ghostkeeper. When I died, I wasn't. He stood beside the couch. *Come, sit.*

That meant he was in a formal mood—waiting for me to sit before he did, despite the fact that I ran around in a bathrobe.

The men who hired me, he said, *who accused Emma of witchcraft—they were not pleased when I fell in love with her, and even less so at our betrothal.*

A memory flashed in my mind. *You asked her in the gazebo outside of her house.*

Yes. We'd both been married before, but our spouses had died young. Not uncommon at that time. She had two children, I had one. You're descended from her son. His eyes softened at the memory. Then his expression changed. *Do you know what happens when a ghostkeeper kills himself?*

I shook my head.

He is lost. He lingers forever, severed from the Beyond—going slowly mad. Turning into an eternally twisted thing, a pitiable creature.

I swallowed. You'd think someone might've mentioned that.

The men who hired me caught me alone. They horsewhipped me within an inch of my life, then told Emma they'd nurse me back to health and do it again. And again. Down through the years. Unless she paid the price.

A feeling stirred in me—a fierce, bright anger, and an unbreakable iron will. It was Emma's memory. *They wanted her to kill herself.*

Yes. They gave her the poison. What do you think she did?

I knew what she'd done. *She drank.*

Sentencing herself to eternal torment, to save me a few years of pain.

What did you do?

I broke my bonds, he said. *And the first thing I did, as she lay dying, was gather her into my arms and plunge a dagger into her breast. I killed her.*

You saved her.

I killed her.

So she wouldn't linger forever!

But he wasn't listening. *Then I hunted them down. One by one. And killed them all.*

I didn't know what to say to that. I couldn't blame

him, yet it was still pretty gruesome. So we sat in silence for a time, listening to the rain, the darkening room lit only by the Rake's faint glow.

Finally, I said, *I have her ring.* I took the plain gold band from my robe. I'd been transferring it from pocket to pocket, never letting it out of my possession. I handed it to him. *Your engagement ring?*

He ran his thumb over the smooth gold. *She never wore it.*

But I remembered the moment I'd slipped on the ring, the rush of feeling. *She always carried it close,* I told him.

Truly?

Yes.

He handed me the ring. *Thank you. You could've been her daughter. Our daughter. I would've liked that.* And then he dematerialized.

I slipped the ring back into my pocket, thinking I would've liked that, too. I wished he hadn't gone. I wanted to know more about his relationship with the original Emma and what she was like.

Feeling restless, I wandered into Mr. Stern's study and pulled one of the swords from the wall. I hoped if I showed up in the ballroom, the Rake would reappear and spar with me.

But when I strolled across the hall, I found the living Bennett dripping all over the parquet floor. He stood there barefoot, his damp hair slicked back. His jeans were sodden and his T-shirt clung to his chest. If possible, he was even more gorgeous wet.

I swallowed and pulled my robe closer together. "What are you doing here?"

He half laughed. "*Me?* It's my house. I've been looking everywhere for you."

"Why?" I asked, suspiciously.

"Because I was worried about you," he said. "What are you doing with one of my dad's prized swords?"

I shrugged. "Practicing?"

There was a glint in Bennett's eyes. "Don't go anywhere." He stepped into the hall and came back a moment later with the other sword from his father's study.

"Oh, of course, you fence," I said.

"I went to Thatcher, didn't I?"

God, he must've been hot in his fencing whites.

"Here." He handed me the sword he'd brought in. "You've got the wrong one."

"What do you mean?"

"They were commissioned for a couple, for the first Bennett and Emma. You have the male companion," he said.

I frowned. "But they weren't married."

"Neither are we."

I was trying to make out what he meant by *that* when I gripped the sword. "Oh no."

I felt my body convulsing with memory and longing. My spine tingled and with that great whooshing sound the world spun away into the past.

The ballroom looked remarkably the same as I spun around, taking in the pianoforte, ivory walls, and heavy velvet curtains glowing in the light of the candle chande-liers. Something brushed my shoulders, and I realized my hair was longer, and I was wearing an intricately woven silk robe with dainty little slippers. The amulet from my mother had been left back in the present.

And Bennett stood beside me, dressed in tight-fitting buff-colored breeches and a white shirt with a high, starched collar. It appeared costumey, like all ghosts wore, but instead of an eighteenth-century gentleman, he looked more twenty-first-century rock star. And I was his biggest groupie.

"Are you seeing this?" I asked him.

He looked at me strangely. "Yes."

"What?"

"You're beautiful."

I felt myself blush. "I think—I think we're still in the ballroom, in our time. We're sort of seeing memories. *Their* memories—Emma and Bennett. So, that's why I look like this."

"That's one theory," he said. "Has this happened to you before?"

I nodded.

"With someone else?" he asked.

"No." For me, there was no one else.

Bennett glanced around the room, taking everything in. I expected him to scold or blame me for transporting him back in time. Instead he laughed and lowered him-self into a fighting stance. "Are you ready?" he asked.

I saluted him. "Can't touch this."

Bennett grinned as he returned the salute and we began. Back and forth, circling each other, probing and lunging, advancing and retreating. For the first time, I really understood fencing. It was a beautiful dance, executed with poise and flirtation.

Until I caught my arm in the robe. "Wait," I said, pulling away.

I shrugged out of the robe, and stood there in the delicate white silk shift, with lace straps and a skirt that flowed to my knees.

Bennett almost dropped his sword.

I smiled in satisfaction. Advantage in.

"If we're getting more comfortable . . ." He took off his shirt.

Advantage out.

And it was stupid. Yeah, we were just fooling around, but my teacher would've had a fit at our lack of protection. Bennett was better than good, so I wasn't worried about getting hurt. I, on the other hand, wasn't so great. I think he felt the same, and was taking it easy when I saw an opening and used a crossover technique the Rake had taught me to nick him on the chest.

"Oh God, I'm sorry!" I said.

Bennett wiped at the little speck of blood. "First blood," he said. "Where'd you learn that?"

I shrugged. "This guy I know."

"Teach me?" he said.

"Sure." I showed him the pass.

He mimicked me, uncharacteristically clumsy.

"No, no," I said. "Like this."

I stepped in front of him, my back to his bare chest. I felt the heat rising off his body, making me woozy as I grabbed his hand.

He pressed closer, our bare skin touching. "Oh, you mean like this . . ." He crossed his arm over mine, locking me in his embrace, and executed the move perfectly, with more style and flair than I'd shown.

"Um . . ." I could barely breathe.

He flipped my hair over my shoulder. "I miss your short hair."

"Why? I'm growing it out."

"Because I like the back of your neck," he whispered against it.

Goose pimples ran down my spine. I turned in his arms to face him, nothing between us but the thinnest silk.

"If only," he said, "we could stay here forever."

The air was electric with that pre-kiss knowingness. My head felt light and my skin warm. I dropped my sword and slipped my arms around him as he bent his head toward mine.

And we were back.

Back in real time. In the real ballroom, wearing our normal clothes. Well, if you considered a bathrobe normal.

He didn't kiss me.

The moment was over. He closed his eyes briefly and let out a long breath.

"I wish things were different," Bennett said. "That we'd met some other way. That you were just a normal girl and I . . . Why does everything have to be so complicated?"

"Does it?" I asked. "Stay here tonight. With me."

"I'm not sure that's a good idea," he said, his voice rough.

"I don't want to be alone. Please."

"You can't know how much I want to, but—"

"Bennett . . . I need you. You're the only one who understands all this. Who understands me." I couldn't let him pretend that there wasn't something between us. I held my hand to him. "Stay."

He took my hand and we stood there for a long moment, silent and intense, the air filled with longing. Then he led me upstairs.

Just inside the doorway of his attic bedroom, he stopped. "I don't know what to do."

"About what?" I asked.

He ran a finger along my collarbone, exposed by my open robe. "About you."

"Bennett," I whispered. "Do whatever you—"

"What's this?" he said, his voice suddenly sharp.

I blinked at his tone. "I—"

He pulled my mother's amulet from under my robe. "What the hell *is* this, Emma?"

I shook my head.

"Where'd you get it?" he demanded.

"In—in my mother's jewelry box."

"How long have you been wearing it?" He dropped

the amulet like it had scalded him. "The whole time. The whole time you were here. Why didn't you tell me?"

"Because I knew you'd overreact and think my mom's guilty. I had to protect her." Maybe she wasn't the best mom in the universe and I couldn't understand why she had sent me to the poof, but she was still my mom. Despite the incriminating evidence, I couldn't believe she was guilty. Even if she was, I'd wanted to know the truth before I turned over the amulet to Bennett or the Knell.

"Protect *her*?" Bennett said. "How about protecting yourself? Why do you think the Knell hasn't dragged you off? Because I gave them my word that you're not involved."

"I'm not—and neither is my family."

"Emma, you have no idea—this could be the key to the murders. Don't you want to find who killed Martha?"

"I know who killed Martha. It was Neos. Why don't you ever trust me?"

"Because you do things like *this*! You think I understand you, but I don't. I don't understand why you keep things from me. I don't understand all your power. And, God knows, I don't understand why I keep trying to protect you."

Then I started yelling, and he started yelling back. Loudly enough that Anatole, Celeste, and Nicholas came to investigate, shimmering into being in the hallway.

Finally, I said, "Get out."

"It's my house, Emma."

"I don't care," I said. "They're my ghosts. My family. You can't even talk to them." Which was a cruel thing to say.

He clenched his jaw. "Give me the amulet."

I clasped my hand over it. "No."

"Emma, there are ghostkeepers in the Knell who can read objects. They'll know what to do."

"Bennett, I'm one of those ghostkeepers. Don't you think *I* would know if there was anything to read?"

"Maybe." His look was suspicious.

"You don't think I'd tell you." I unclasped the gold chain and gave him the amulet. "Fine. Take it. I have nothing to hide."

27

I woke in a sweat, the dampness of my skin mingling with a fading mildew scent from a dream. A nightmare. I huddled under the covers, back in my old room at the museum.

I'd stood at the window last night, waiting for Bennett to leave after we'd fought. He didn't, not for an hour. An hour in which I'd paced the room, wondering what he was doing and whether he'd come back to apologize.

He hadn't.

I'd watched from the window as he'd climbed into his ancient Land Rover and pulled away. He hadn't even glanced up at my room. I'd thrown myself onto the bed and wept.

Then I'd closed my eyes and fallen into the dream:

I walked through a graveyard at dawn, the sun still trapped below the horizon. There was the crunch of gravel echoing in the stillness as I passed ancient gravestones with etched names that were faded and indecipherable.

Then I reached the tomb.

It was carved of granite, with black iron gates and grotesque statues in a semicircle around the front. A thousand whispers spoke my name, and I shivered in terror.

Then a portly man with a baseball cap walked past me. I'd never seen him before, but his eyes shone with the same terror I felt. His motions were confused and jerky and *compelled*. But he wasn't a ghost.

He stopped at the gates and bony fingers reached through the iron bars to pluck at him. Withered skin dangled from the hands like tattered clothes on a line. A rotted corpse pulled him close and licked at him with its desiccated tongue. I felt the man's revulsion and fear and pain. Then his surrender.

It was a wraith. With wet, sharp teeth it bit into the portly man's neck—its tongue working inside his skin—probing and scraping. It suddenly pulled back and between its skeletal teeth, I saw my mother's jade amulet, and heard a howl of triumph and—

I woke in a sweat, surrounded by the scent of mildew.

I shivered again under the covers, but firmly told myself to get it together. There were enough *real* nightmares in my life that I couldn't start worrying about the ones I dreamed.

I glanced at the clock on the bedside table. Ugh, it was too late to go to Natalie's for my uniform. At least I still had the slutty outfit hanging in the wardrobe.

I pulled off the T-shirt I'd slept in and slipped into the uniform. Downstairs, I found Anatole in the kitchen, stirring raspberries into a steaming bowl of oatmeal, while Celeste set the table.

Morning, I said.

They exchanged a glance. *Did you feel that, last night?* Anatole asked, stroking his mustache.

Like a spider, Celeste said, *running down your spine.*

I shook my head. *I was kinda distracted. I had a nightmare.* I told them what I remembered.

That may not have been entirely a dream, Anatole said.

A chill struck me and I ran to the phone and dialed Bennett. For once, he answered. "Emma," he said, "you're okay?"

"I'm fine. Did something happen last night after you left?"

"I gave your mother's talisman to a reader."

"What did he look like? Did he wear a baseball cap?"

"How did you—"

"I dreamed about him. A wraith—"

"He's dead, Emma."

"*What?*"

"The amulet's gone."

"Oh God. Neos," I said. "He told me he needed it. Why would he need it?"

"I wish I knew." A horn honked on his side of the line. "I've gotta go."

"Bennett, wait. I'm sorry. I should have given you my mother's amulet before. Maybe if I hadn't held on to it, that guy . . . or I should've—"

"It's okay, Emma. Everything's going to be all right.

Stay there. Go to school and stick close to Natalie. And stay out of trouble, both of you."

So I went to school. The walk was a long three blocks. I felt responsible for everything: the fights with Bennett, the death of Martha and the other ghostkeeper. And now Neos had the amulet. What would he do with it? I stopped in the middle of the block, overwhelmed by it all. Sometimes this endless roller coaster exhausted me. So, of course, the ride wasn't over.

Sara's little BMW darted to the curb in front of me. "C'mon!" she said.

"I'm pretty sure I can walk from here." There was only a half block to go. Then I saw Harry in the passenger seat and Natalie in back. "What's up?"

"We've got the day off," Sara said.

"It's not a holiday."

"It's a Harry-day," Harry called. "Get in!"

I wasn't in the mood for whatever they had planned, but Bennett had told me to stick close to Natalie, and by trouble, I think he meant with ghosts, so I crammed myself in beside her. "Am I going to regret this?"

"Don't worry," Sara said. "Once a year, Harry arranges an unofficial day off."

"They tell me it's basically a school tradition," Natalie told me.

"Where's Coby?" I asked. "Football again?"

"Always." Sara sighed.

"So where are we going?" I saw a gleam in Harry's eyes. "And why do you look so pleased?"

Natalie laughed. "He thinks we're going skinny-dipping. He's got a heated indoor pool."

"Wait," he said. "We're not?"

"Harry," Sara said, patting him fondly on the knee. "Look at you. Now look at me, Natalie, and Emma. Do you think that's gonna happen anywhere outside your dreams?"

I tried not to hurt his feelings by snickering.

"We're going to Sara's house," Natalie said. "To raid her closet for Homecoming."

Harry groaned, but when we got there he stationed himself in an oversized chair outside Sara's walk-in closet, probably hoping for a peep show. He passed judgment on everything we tried.

"That one," he told Natalie after three dresses. "Stop. You're done."

"This?" She ran her hands down the short black sheath. "It's too plain."

She looked flawless in it.

"It'll please your date," Harry said.

"Well, then"—she gave him a secret smile—"I've found my dress."

Harry was her date.

Here's what he said about my five choices:

1) "No."
2) "Please, no. I beg of you."
3) "That dress is an offense against God and man."

4) "You look like a boy."

5) "Poor Coby."

"Be nice," Sara called from inside the closet. "Emma's beautiful."

"I never said she wasn't beautiful," Harry said. "She just looks awful in your clothing."

I threw a shoe at him.

Sara strutted out of the closet in her new dress and I noticed Harry's expression. Maybe he was remembering the times they'd fooled around.

"You, on the other hand, wear them quite nicely," he said.

"You're going to make your dates—both of them—very happy," I said. She'd grudgingly allowed the two sophomore boys who'd been crushing on her to escort her.

"Who gets the first dance?" Natalie asked.

"I thought they could sandwich me," Sara quipped.

Then Harry complained of hunger, so we went into the village for sushi, and on to his house for a swim. *With* swimsuits we'd borrowed from Sara.

Coby showed up at one, looking sexy and spent from a lunch-hour practice. Bennett drew me irresistibly, like a moth to flame, but in terms of pure gorgeousness, Coby was in a league of his own. He stripped to his trunks, then dove into the pool. We all watched as he broke the surface and climbed from the water, his muscles slick and wet, his green eyes glowing in the half light of the glass ceiling.

I heard Natalie and Sara both sigh, and Harry murmur that it almost made him want to go gay.

Coby stretched out on a chaise beside me and asked, "So you still sorry you moved here?"

I thought about that and everything it meant. Being with Bennett, becoming a ghostkeeper, Martha's brief presence in my life, and the ghosts. Always the ghosts.

"No. I'm not sorry," I said. "It's where I'm meant to be."

"I'm sick of practice," he said. "Feels like I haven't seen you in a week."

"You've got the whole school counting on you." Then I noticed Sara staring at us from across the pool. I bit my lip. "Can I ask you a weird question?"

He rose onto his elbows. "Sure."

"How come you and Sara never . . . ?"

"We did," he said, looking away.

"*What*? I meant how come you never *dated*, not how come you never—"

"Oh. Damn." He looked completely abashed. "It was only 'cause we'd been friends forever." He lowered his voice, not wanting her to overhear. "Sara said we should lose our virginity together, because, you know, why not with your best friend? But then . . ."

"What?"

He glanced at Sara. "I don't know. She kind of withdrew."

I nodded, fiddling with my towel. She was in love with him, the idiot. She couldn't handle being only friends after that—at least not for a while.

"Anyway," he said, taking my hand. "If I was with Sara I couldn't take *you* to Homecoming tomorrow."

I squeezed his hand, and made a vow. After Homecoming, I was getting Coby and Sara together. No matter what it took.

Saturday morning, while helping Celeste clean the side parlor, I told her about my Homecoming predicament. *None of Sara's dresses worked. And the dance is tonight.* I'd spent a sleepless night back at Natalie's feeling guilty about Coby and worrying about why I hadn't heard from Bennett.

Have you looked in ze attic? Celeste asked, dusting the blue and white ginger jars.

What will I find in the attic? One of Bennett's old suits? I recalled Harry's "You look like a boy" comment. A men's suit wasn't going to help.

Non, I would not put you in men's clothing. She didn't quite arch her eyebrows at my jeans and T-shirt. *In ze attic are dresses—even some from my mistress, Bennett's great-grand-mère.*

You think that'd be okay, to borrow something?

Celeste shrugged elegantly. *What else is to be done with them?*

Ten minutes later, we knelt over an open cedar chest in the attic. Inside were layers of tissue paper enshrouding blouses and skirts and several dresses. Celeste pulled out each item and let me inspect it before gently rewrapping and laying it to rest again. When I brightened at a white beaded flapper dress, Celeste said simply, *Non, not for you.*

At least she was kinder than Harry, but I'd almost given up hope, when we found The Dress.

This is ze one, Celeste said.

She carried the dress to the window so we could examine it in the light. A satin gown, formal without being fussy, and the color reminded me of, well . . . ghosts. In the shadows the fabric looked gray, but in the light a shimmer of blue appeared.

I love it, I said.

Celeste held it against my skin. *Perfect,* she said. *Try it on.*

I took off my jeans and T-shirt and stood before her.

No brassiere, she said.

I hoped Bennett didn't show up. I kept my back to Celeste as she slipped the dress over my shoulders, and I shivered as the satin touched my skin. The neckline was high and the back open to the waist, and the skirt grazed the floor. For once, I guess it was good I didn't really need a bra.

As I smoothed the skirt, there was a slight *whoosh* as I flashed on memories from Bennett's great-great-grandmother. But they didn't overwhelm me. They were like snapshots of her dancing and dining in this dress. She had been happy.

I turned and found Celeste with a finger pressed to her mouth, gazing thoughtfully at me.

What? That bad? The fabric felt exquisite and the color

for some reason satisfied me. Like even though I could only admit it to a few, I was letting the world know what I saw.

Turn, Celeste said briskly.

I turned. There was no mirror, so I was relying on her judgment.

Again, she said. *Oui. Very good. Take it off.*

I slipped from the gown and she sailed from the attic before I finished dressing, trailing satin behind her.

Celeste? I called after her.

I will find you in your room, mademoiselle, late afternoon. You will have showered.

Great, now I was getting hygiene advice from a nineteenth-century French ghost. But I just said, *Right. See you then.*

I spent the afternoon with Anatole in the kitchen, first listening to his philosophy on cheese soufflé, then watching him make gingerbread dough, which Nicholas and I rolled out, cut into little men, baked, and decorated. In a fit of panic over Bennett and Coby, I bit the heads off a couple.

At four, fresh from the shower, I slipped the original Emma's gold band onto my now-empty chain from my mother, then found Celeste in my bedroom. She'd set up a dressing table with a mirror, and motioned for me to sit.

First ze makeup, she said, gesturing to the MAC and Chanel spread before her.

Is this Bennett's mom's makeup? I asked.

Oui. Your own supply is . . . pfft.

Thinking of my lip balm and mascara, I couldn't really argue. She faced me away from the mirror so I couldn't see what she was doing and promised to keep it simple.

Hair, she said, when she'd finished powder-puffing my face.

If I'd had my watch, I would've been checking the time obsessively. First, Coby was picking me up for a pre-Homecoming cocktail party at Harry's, then the game started at 7:00. I was looking forward to cheering in the tiers while wearing my gown, an ancient Thatcher tradition, then we'd head to the catered ball at the Echo Point Country Club after the game. These private schoolers really knew how to do it up. At my old school we shuffled to a DJ in the school gym. We were lucky if we got streamers.

I twitched in my seat as Celeste fiddled with my hair. Whatever she was doing involved a surplus of pins and braids. What was I going to do if she made me look like some nineteenth-century lass missing her bustle? And how exactly would I tell her? She might be dead, but she still had feelings.

Celeste made a small hum and smiled. *Finis. But do not look. Let us put the dress on you first.*

When she took the dress from the wardrobe, I almost didn't recognize it. The stormy blue color I loved was the same, but she'd lowered the neckline, nipped in the waist, and trimmed the arms so they revealed more shoulder. As I slipped into the dress and my new black satin peep-toes,

I wondered how I'd explain to Bennett's family what I'd done to their heirloom. Then I forgot all about it as Celeste turned me toward the mirror. The effect was magical.

Boysenberry lipstick, heavy mascara, and the faintest of blush. The dress was perfectly suited to my figure. You couldn't even tell that I'd eaten half a soufflé and maimed a bunch of gingerbread men. She'd transformed my blond strands into something totally current to go with the retro dress.

I turned to hug her, then remembered she'd burn my skin, which wouldn't really help my look. *Thank you, thank you! Now I won't feel like the Wal-Mart special at Barneys.*

I have no idea what that means, but I'm glad you are happy.

I'm not just happy, I'm thrilled. I gave a little spin. I wished my mother could see me. *I wish Martha was here.*

Oui. She would say you are a beautiful angel.

She'd tell me all about her own school dances. I bet she— I stopped, hearing footsteps downstairs in the front hall. *He's early!*

I galloped to the top of the grand stairway, then remembered the gown and slowed. Halfway down, I saw *him*. Bennett. Watching me, one hand on the banister— simply standing there, as I walked down the stairs, my gown trailing after me. I paused and met his gaze. Neither of us smiled, neither of us spoke. Then I descended to where he waited, and he took my hand. I thought he was going to kiss the back of it.

Instead, his eyes never leaving mine, he kissed my palm.

Heat rose in my face. I'd never felt anything so intimate, and for a moment I didn't care about anything—nothing but standing here right now with Bennett. The doorbell rang, and I looked over his shoulder. "That's him."

Bennett nodded and disappeared down the hallway. I stood irresolute. There was so much left unsaid.

The doorbell rang again and I remembered Coby. This was his night, the high school quarterback's big game. I couldn't disappoint him—he deserved better than that. I opened the door and he smiled, looking spectacular in his dark gray slim-fitting suit.

"You look amazing," he told me.

"Thank you."

"I brought you something." With a charmingly shy expression, Coby held out a box. "You don't have to wear it. Sara said you're not really a corsage kind of girl."

Nestled inside was a thin bracelet of tiny white flowers sewn to black satin ribbon. "I love it," I said, and held it out so he could tie it to my wrist.

"I wasn't sure what color your dress was, so I got black and white." He squinted at me. "What color is that, exactly?"

"The color of ghosts," I said faintly.

He smiled. "That's what I like about you. No other girl will be wearing the color of ghosts tonight."

"No," I said. "No, they won't."

We headed outside, into the cool air. For a moment, my entire body tingled with the incipient presence of a ghost, as if the veil had parted fully and the Beyond encroached on our world. The feeling was so strong that I stumbled a little, and Coby steadied me with a steely hand on my elbow.

I longed to go back inside, to the safety of Bennett's arms, but I couldn't disappoint Coby.

I touched Emma's gold ring for luck. I still wondered whether or not I should have given Bennett the amulet. It had been safe around my neck. Was I responsible for Neos getting it? Had my newfound powers somehow summoned him? Were all those deaths my fault?

So many questions I couldn't answer.

But they'd have to wait. I followed Coby to the car. Tonight I just needed to pretend everything was normal and go to the high school dance with the cutest boy in school.

Not such a bad fate.

28

Coby helped me into the passenger seat like a true gentleman—or a guy afraid his date would tumble off her heels again.

"I don't wear heels that much," I told him.

He started his dad's Lexus.

"Or gowns." I tried not to think about Bennett's look when I'd descended the staircase.

Coby concentrated on driving, and a silence fell. Not one of the comfortable ones.

"Maybe we should go to that tailgate party instead of Harry's," I finally said.

Coby didn't answer, watching the road. I examined his face in the light of the dashboard. Did he regret asking me? Maybe it was my dress—he wasn't into vintage. Or his parents were going to be at Harry's, and he was worried about me meeting them.

Or maybe he knew I was in love with someone else.

I vowed to be an exemplary date. He was the high school quarterback and my friend. For God's sake, he deserved a satisfactory Homecoming. Then I noticed he wasn't driving in the direction I expected him to. "We are going to Harry's, right?"

Coby didn't answer. He just kept driving.

"On the Neck, I mean."

He turned right, away from the Neck, as a faint drizzle started to fall from gray clouds.

"Coby," I said, a little sharper. "Where are we going?"

"A surprise," he said, his voice tight, like he was nervous.

"Oh, good," I said, trying to feel the school spirit. "I hope it's not a parade, though—I hate parades. I mean, I don't *hate* them. But it is raining and—"

He pulled into a parking lot. "Here."

"Here where?" I asked, trying to see under the rapidly darkening sky.

He stepped out and made his way around to my side of the car.

I cracked my door. "Maybe I'll just stay here. My shoes—"

Coby wrenched the door open and dragged me from the car.

"Ow!" I said, stumbling in the mud. "What is up with you?"

He dragged me through the squishy parking lot and my satin peep-toes were immediately ruined, not to mention the hem of my ghost dress.

"Coby, what's wrong? Where are we?"

He grunted and pulled me along toward a black

mass of water, and I realized where we were. Redd's Pond.

Martha told me kids skated here when the water froze over, which sounded romantic, like a winter wonderland. Tonight the water smelled of pond scum mingling with mildewed earth, and the water looked sluggish and black. And I felt a tingle of *wrongness*. A wraith.

No. Worse.

Neos.

I tried digging my heels in the ground, but my heels were satin and the ground was wet and slick. I stumbled along in Coby's painful grip. "Coby, listen to me. We have to get out of here. There's something out here, that shouldn't be—" I realized that telling him ghost stories wouldn't change his mind, so I made a play for his sense of chivalry. "I'm scared, Coby. Take me home."

"Home," he whispered, as the tingle in my spine grew even stronger. There was something totally wrong with him.

I punched him in the arm. "Coby! What are you *on*?"

He pulled me closer to the pond, where the grim wooden contraption—the ducking chair—loomed in the gray drizzle. The feel of wraiths pricked my skin and the stench of evil clogged the air.

"Coby, I'm serious," I told him. "We have to leave!"

"Not going anywhere."

Coby was a football player in perfect condition, eighty pounds heavier and a foot taller than me—yet I knew I could get away. The Rake hadn't taught me to waltz, after all. My only problem was I didn't know if I could get away without crippling Coby. Whatever was going on, he didn't deserve *that*.

"Coby," I said, my voice calm. "We need to leave *now*."

"You're going nowhere," he said, a little stronger.

So I stopped resisting, and let him drag me while I dug inside myself and channeled my ghostkeeping ability. I reached into the night, trying to find the source of the wrongness.

It only took a moment—and I recoiled.

Neos stood next to me.

Wearing Coby's skin.

Looking at Coby with his beautiful eyes and his quick smile—but sensing the roiling evil inside—I felt myself sway for a moment, overwhelmed. How could I not have known? I'd been so distracted by my feelings for Bennett, I'd ignored what had been sitting beside me.

Then I punched him in the throat.

But I didn't follow through hard enough to crush his windpipe—I couldn't endanger Coby like that. Not that he was in much danger. Neos laughed inside of him and socked me in the stomach with inhuman strength.

I folded over, breathless and in pain, as he whispered in my ear, "Do your worst. Hurt your friend—kill him. I'll throw him aside like a used suit. Maybe I'll wear *you* next."

"I'm going to kill you," I gasped.

"I'm already dead."

I forgot my training, everything Martha had taught

me. And freaked. I pounded his chest, screaming. "Get out! Get out of him."

"Well, I *do* owe you." He inhaled deeply, nostrils quivering. "If not for you, I'd never have learned how to step through the veil into a living body."

He dragged me along the water's edge, and I didn't put up a fight. I needed to focus. I felt his arm digging into my skin, the bushes scratching my legs, and wet mud worming into my shoes. Summoning the sparks inside, I *shoved* power at him and felt all my force swallowed by his darkness.

"Maybe this," he said, "will motivate you." With his free hand, he pulled out the silver blade that he'd cut me with as a child. The blade that had killed Martha. "She begged when she died. She begged for you to help her."

The world flashed red and the power inside of me burned brighter with fury, condensing and tightening to a single point. My body erupted with the might of all my hatred. But it was compelling power I shot at him, afraid that if I tried to dispel him, I'd hurt Coby. It was still a tremendous force—one aimed at driving him away.

He stumbled and his grip on my arm tightened until his fingernails punctured my skin. I poured everything into him, wrapped him with bands of light and skewered him with javelins, but something protected him. Some force deflected all my attacks.

Spent, I slumped in exhaustion.

Neos looked down at me in triumph. "You are too weak."

When he spoke, something glinted on his tongue. My

mother's jade amulet, her talisman, embedded somehow in his mouth. Her focus animated Coby and protected Neos.

A sound I didn't recognize came from my throat, full of anguish and horror. My body went lax and my mind blank, as Neos dragged me onto the platform of the ducking chair. The chains had been shattered and the mechanism was free. Part of me believed that if I went along with him, I wouldn't get hurt.

That part of me was very wrong.

He strapped me to the heavy wooden chair, the stiff leather biting into my wrists. Neos pulled on a rope and the chair swayed and I rose into the air. I screamed as the beam overhead swung me toward the center of Redd's Pond.

My fear overwhelmed me. More than fear. Panic, terror, a mindless horror—I realized my own fear was magnified by sitting in the chair. I felt the memories of other women who'd been strapped here, I flashed on the leering faces of their accusers. I couldn't separate their terror from my own.

Until the chair fell into the icy pond.

The shock spiked through me. I couldn't think, couldn't see. The water was pitch-black, and the skirt of my beautiful ghostly dress ballooned around me. I blinked frantically in the murk, my hands clenching and my lungs burning. I kicked, trying to find solid ground, to push myself upward, but my peep-toe shoes only sank into the pond slime.

Finally, the chair rose and broke the surface. My body shuddered and my teeth chattered uncontrollably. I couldn't decide which was worse—the freezing water or the chill night air. "Wh-wh-what do y-you—"

"What do I want?" Neos said, his voice strong, as though he'd learned to control Coby's body perfectly now. "Power."

"F-from me?" I asked, to keep him talking, to keep him from drowning me.

"Look at me. A ghost, mastering the flesh of the living." He smiled horribly, no trace of Coby left in his expression. "Have they told you that possession is a myth? That no ghost can possess the living? Well, they were right—until me."

I trembled in the rain and wind of the growing storm.

"I've taken physical form, but you . . . You took spectral form. You turned into a ghost. How did you do it?"

The ring! I felt it, dangling on my necklace, but strapped to the chair, I couldn't reach it.

"Tell me how, and I'll kill you quickly instead of agonizingly slow."

There was no truth in him. He'd kill me like all the rest of the ghostkeepers. I'd writhe in agony as he carved designs into my skin.

"No," I croaked.

Neos let the rope slide through his fingers and I dropped until my feet grazed the water.

"Please," I begged. "N-not again."

"Answer me."

"I c-can't."

He grinned, forcing Coby's lips into a foreign, cruel

expression. "I'll give you time to think about your decision."

And he let the rope slide between his fingers.

The shock was worse this time, the cold slamming into me. But now I knew what I needed: the ring. My skin numb, desperately needing to breathe, I strained against the leather straps. They'd tightened in the water and I'd weakened. I was helpless as the darkness closed in.

Just as I thought I would pass out, he pulled me up and swung the chair toward him. My body convulsed, but I needed to buy time, so forced myself to speak. "Why did you k-kill them?"

"I already told you. Power."

"But h-how?"

"I was born a ghostkeeper, little Emma," he said scornfully. "And a good one—one of the best. But not like *you.* I've never seen one like you, turning into a ghost—"

"Liar." I slumped listlessly in the chair. "You weren't a ghostkeeper. Dead ghostkeepers can't be summoned."

"I wasn't summoned, I never fully left. I killed myself— they said I'd linger forever, always fading but never gone. Until insanity overtook me, enfeebled me. But look at me now, I—"

"Y-yeah. You're Mr. Sanity."

He slapped my face, but I was so numb that all I felt was a distant stinging. "I am not *feeble.* Nothing—nothing is as powerful as I. It took my death for me to come into my full potential."

"Why did you kill them? Why kill Martha?"

"Poor, pathetic Emma, the lonely little girl pretending ghosts are her family, and a housekeeper her mommy. By killing other ghostkeepers I gain more power—using the focus of the jade amulet."

I gasped.

"Oh, yes. Your mother's amulet. I could only use the design, until you kindly brought me the talisman itself." He opened his mouth and I saw again the jade embedded in Coby's tongue. He wiggled it at me, like some obscene piercing. "And now I walk in living skin."

"But—why my mother's? Why me, all those years ago?"

He pulled me close and I smelled Neos under Coby's body, foul and sulfuric. "Because you're Jana's daughter."

"You knew my mother?"

"I loved her." The knife blade glowed despite the lack of light, and he traced the tip across my neck, then down between my breasts. I felt so vulnerable, and searched his face for some sign of Coby, but there was no gentle sweetness there. "Why do you think I killed myself?"

"My m-mother?" I asked.

"She chose your father over me. I knew her focus so well, it served to anchor me. Then I bonded myself to you, in that storefront—remember me taking your blood? I would've risen to power then, if they hadn't driven your skills out of you. But now your powers are returning, stronger than ever."

"Lucky me," I said, rain sheeting down my face.

"And they'll make me not a ghost, but a god." He slapped

me again, harder this time. "Tell me how you took spectral form."

I shook my head, my teeth chattering.

And he plunged me into the water again. I couldn't see, couldn't breathe. Strapped to the chair, I was shivering and my lungs burned. A moment before I blacked out, the chair rose through the icy darkness and broke the water's surface.

I gasped and coughed, but the instant I caught my breath, he plunged me under again, brought to the verge of drowning over and over.

"Once more, Emma?" he asked. "Or will you answer me now?"

I longed to tell him everything, to end the fear and stop the pain. But I couldn't leave him to kill more ghostkeepers. I couldn't leave him like this, polluting Coby's body. I couldn't leave Martha unavenged.

And I knew how to save myself: by slipping the ring onto my finger.

Only one problem—I couldn't get the ring. The straps around my wrists were too strong.

"Tell me, Emma. Now . . ."—he kissed my cheek and traced a wavy cut across my sternum and my blood dripped onto the dress—". . . or later."

As he cut me, he exposed the wedding band on my necklace, and I panicked. If he realized what it was, I was dead. I needed to distract him, to goad him into dropping me into the pond, to get one last chance to break free and slip on the ring.

Tears welled in my eyes, because I knew I'd fail. I'd tried compelling him and dispelling him, but he was too strong. And I was just a girl. A girl with a dysfunctional family, torn between two boys, and about to lose everything else.

But I was also the girl who could keep ghosts and I had no choice.

So I thought of Martha and the Rake and the original Emma. Of my parents and my brother—and of Bennett.

And I found the sparks inside me. Martha had told me, when I most needed it, my power would be there. I gathered the sparks into a bright ball radiating out from my chest and launched the light at Neos. He wasn't expecting it and I slipped under his protection and battered him with an onslaught of brilliance that made him take a step back.

He winced and shoved at the chair and swung me out over the pond. "Try that again, underwater."

And the chair plunged again into the freezing pond.

Exactly what I'd wanted, to be hidden under the water to get the ring. Except I was so cold I couldn't move my arms, and so tired I couldn't summon more power.

I surrendered. I had nothing left, except desperate pleading. *Please,* I implored. *Please help me.*

I'm not sure if God heard me. But someone did.

Ghosts.

As my body went limp and my brain started to misfire from lack of oxygen, amorphous figures floated in the water in front of me. They glowed in the murky darkness, not looking like regular ghosts. They were less solid, less defined and they drifted through the water like patches of luminous fog. I thought I was hallucinating—until I felt a tingle in my spine.

And in a rush, I knew who they were. The spirits of women drowned as witches. They'd heard my call for help.

They didn't take human form, but a strong current rose in the still pond, and the necklace drifted upward, the ring illuminated in the dark water. The chain slipped over my head and the ring drifted down, spinning and twisting until it landed firmly on my finger and—

A new rush of energy pulsed through me. I turned translucent and felt the water crashing though the place I'd been. I still couldn't breathe, but I no longer needed to. My wrists lifted free of the leather straps as the spirits swirled and faded, and I said, *Thank you*.

I streamed upward toward the surface, and noticed the chair rising behind me. Neos was trying to lift me into the air, for the pleasure of plunging me under again.

Well, he was in for a surprise.

"Are you finished?" he asked, as the chair broke the surface. "Or will you answer me now?"

Yes, I'd answer him. I knew things now that I'd never imagined. I wasn't just Emma Vaile, the girl with boy troubles, SAT-phobia, and poorly fitting uniforms. I was Emma Vaile, who lived and died over two hundred years ago, the most powerful ghostkeeper of her—or any—time.

In my ghostly form I couldn't dispel or compel, so I

flew from the chair and flashed past Neos, hearing his cry of surprise and anger behind me.

I flew faster than I thought possible and felt a wave of evil swooping behind me. He'd summoned a wraith to follow me. It crashed heedlessly after me. Neos thought I was running away—and he was right.

But only as far as the trees. I tore a long thin branch from one and spun into fighting stance. The wraith came flying and skewered itself on the point. I shot bolts of my dispelling power into the branch. Blackness spewed and heaved around me, and I shoved the wood jacked up with dispelling energy further into the thing as the shadow howled and faded. Easy enough, even if it was the first time I'd imbued an object with dispelling power.

One down, I told Neos.

And I flew at him with the branch, freed from the weight and sluggishness of my mortal form, I swirled around him feinting and jabbing. He parried with his knife, but not quickly enough.

I stabbed him in the chest, but the voice that cried out wasn't Neos's but Coby's. I froze. Was I going to win this fight over Coby's dead body?

I couldn't.

I faltered, and Neos attacked. He knocked my branch aside and backhanded me across the face. My body was still that of a ghost, but not to Neos. He could still hurt me while wearing Coby's body. I sprawled to the ground, my vision blurred.

"Now you die," he said.

You'll never learn my secret, I told him.

"Instead, I'll take your death."

He twirled his knife in his right hand, scattering droplets of rain, then grabbed my arm to lift me into his thrust.

And he screamed in pain. Welts rose on his hands where he'd grabbed me—vicious frostbite. Neos was so powerful that ghosts burned him even more than they did me. He'd become a human ghostkeeper in Coby's body and I'd become a ghost. Maybe I could burn his spirit from Coby. The ache would be so great, he'd have to leave. Coby would probably end up scarred, but alive.

I grabbed his arms and pressed myself into him—he bellowed in pain and fury, but remained firmly entrenched inside Coby. He hit me hard, in the ribs and kidneys, but I clung to him, hugged him tighter.

I shrieked with the effort and pain. How much longer? I was weakening. Though he was weakening, too. We fell to the ground, me still clutching him, he still trying to beat me off.

Then I felt his blade cutting into my chest, closer and closer to my throat. I didn't have the strength to resist. Between the torture and the fight, I'd reached my end. I had to get away. I couldn't let him have my powers or he'd be indestructible.

With a tug of will, I wrenched the blade from my chest and threw my spectral body into the air. I hovered over Neos, as he nestled in Coby's body in a heap below.

He looked depleted and spent—still I knew I couldn't finish him.

I will kill more of you, he said, his voice weak but clear. *And I will grow stronger.*

Like a coward, I fled.

29

I didn't fly away—I disappeared.

I felt a longing for safety, for warmth. For Bennett. And I felt myself *shift*, and found Bennett in his bedroom in the attic, poring through an overstuffed notebook.

Bennett, I said.

He didn't hear me—he couldn't communicate with ghosts—but he must've felt me. He glanced up from his notebook and his face lost all color, his eyes were wide with shock and grief.

"Emma!" he cried. "No. *No.*"

He stood and reached a hand toward me, touched the blood that dripped from my chest wound. He pulled back as it burned him. "How could this happen? I don't understand."

I removed the ring. "I'm alive."

"Oh God." He wrapped me in his arms. "Emma, I—"

Dripping with pond water, my ghost gown torn and bloodied, my heart still thundering with fear, I kissed him. He stroked my neck and back, as if reassuring himself I was real, and I clung to him until my knees gave way from exhaustion and relief.

He laid me gently on the bed, and I was smiling and crying at the same time. "I'm sorry," I said, though I didn't know what for. "I'm so sorry."

"I thought you were dead."

"I almost was." I showed him the ring. "This belonged to the first Emma—it turns me into a ghost."

"That's impossible."

I slid the ring back on, watching Bennett marvel at my spectral form. He moved to touch me, but I pulled the ring off before he could, not wanting to burn him more.

"You're impossible," he said, and before I could respond, he kissed me again.

Then I told him everything.

He dialed 911, as I changed from the tattered ghost dress into a pair of Bennett's black long johns and a gray wool sweater. Then we raced downstairs and scrambled into his Land Rover and went back to Redd's Pond.

I prayed Coby was okay. He'd taken a lot of punishment from me, let alone Neos. But he was healthy and strong and deserved to live. I hoped that I'd left Neos too weak to take revenge.

I shifted in my seat. "I shouldn't have left him."

"Emma, there was nothing you could do."

"I could've fought harder."

"Nobody else—*nobody*—could've even gotten away alive. And you kept the ring from him."

But was it enough? I bit my lip and remained silent on the drive through town. As we turned onto the road to the pond, the rain turned into a downpour, diffusing the blue and red lights flashing through the woods.

"They're already here," I said. "The cops."

"Let me do the talking," Bennett told me, as we parked.

"What will you tell them?"

His face was grim. "I don't know yet."

The path was dark and muddy, and I felt the same touch of fear as when I'd realized Neos had possessed Coby. I grabbed Bennett's hand and held tight.

"You're safe now, Emma," he said.

I nodded, unsure, and followed him closer. I expected yellow police tape blocking the scene, but we made it to the water's edge without being stopped.

A flurry of activity. Police cars, an ambulance—even a fire engine, despite the rain. And then I looked closer at the men in hip-boots wading in the shallow edge of the pond.

"Oh, no," I said, tearing away from Bennett. "No."

They were dragging Coby's lifeless body from the water.

I darted through the men and threw myself at him. "Coby, no, I'm so sorry—"

"Miss!" The cops dragged me off him. "Who are you?"

"His friend. Oh, God, I should never have—"

Bennett appeared at my elbow. "Emma, I'll explain."

"What does it matter?" I started bawling. "He's dead."

"Give her a sedative," one of the cops muttered to an EMT. "Teenage girls . . ."

The EMT fed me some pill and I pretended to be calm so she'd leave me alone. I never should have left him. Maybe if I'd given Neos the ring, he'd still be alive. I was the one who should be dead, not Coby—sweet, gorgeous, trusting Coby.

"Emma, there was nothing you could do," Bennett said, putting an arm around me. "It's not your fault."

He shepherded me toward the car, my feet slipping in the mud, tears streaming down my face. Halfway there, we met Sara rushing toward the pond with Coby's mom and dad right behind her.

"His parents got a call at Harry's," she started.

Then she saw my face, and hers crumpled. She groped blindly for support, then fell to her knees, making keening noise of heartbreak and grief.

"You promised you wouldn't hurt him," she finally whispered to me.

"I'm sorry," I said. "I'm so sorry."

"You'll never be sorry enough," she said.

And she was right. Because being sorry wouldn't bring him back.

30

The Knell provided me with an attorney, who made me memorize the story for police questioning:

On our way to the cocktail party at Harry's house, I'd noticed Coby acting strangely. Not at all himself. He was worried about the game—what everyone would think of him if he lost. When he pulled into Redd's Pond, I'd left the car and run back to the museum, where Bennett phoned the police. Because I was worried Coby was going to hurt himself. Kill himself.

So ending his life wasn't enough; I also lied about his death.

The downpour had wiped away all evidence of the fight and though the story seemed a little vague to me, the Knell exerted pressure behind the scenes, and the cops closed the file.

Suicide. At least no one had seen the knife wound in my chest. I couldn't bear for anyone to think Coby had hurt me.

Gossip at school said that Coby had killed himself because I'd broken up with him—I wondered if Harry was fueling it. I actually had a kid ask why I couldn't have waited until after Homecoming to dump him. Didn't I know I'd ruined everything?

So I went from being the most popular girl to the school leper. In the days after Coby died, Harry and Sara didn't wait for me at the school gates. In fact, they didn't talk to me at all. I couldn't figure out how to approach them, how to explain what had happened. To tell them that I cared for Coby, too. I hadn't known him forever, as they had, but I mourned him all the same.

I longed for the comfort of our friendship, to share the happy memories and the grief. But I couldn't blame them for turning away, for hating me.

I would've done the same.

One night, a few days after Coby's death, I found Bennett in the solarium. He hadn't been around, even though he'd been staying at the museum with me and Natalie. I missed him and couldn't take his disappearing act anymore, so after finishing dinner with Natalie, I'd gone to look for him. He stood at one of the windows, staring out at the pitch-black sky.

He watched my reflection in the window as I approached, and his brow furrowed with an expression I couldn't decipher. Then he turned to me. "Did you love him?"

I shook my head. "Not like that."

"Like what then? Did you . . ."

I didn't want to talk about it. What if I had loved him? He'd still be dead and I'd still be responsible. "What does it matter?"

"No, I just—God! I've screwed everything up, Emma."

"What have you done? Everything's my fault."

He shook his head. "I mean between you and me."

"Is there a you and me?"

He gave me a look of such intensity that my breath caught. "All I know is that I'm in love with you," he said, almost angrily. "That the sight of you, the scent of you, the sound of your voice—I can't help myself, I can't stop it, I can't think of anything else. You've made me completely useless."

"Oh!"

"Every time we're together, we fight and you—"

"And I've loved you from the moment I met you. You walked in that door with Max and—I knew."

Bennett finally gave me the look I'd been dreaming of. The one that said, I could kiss you right now, and live with you and you alone, forever. And I returned it full force.

Then he spun away from me. "Don't look at me like that," he said.

"Like what? Like I want you to take me upstairs and—"

He groaned. "Please!"

"What? Don't you want me?"

"Just—just give me a minute." He took a deep breath,

struggling to control himself. I stepped behind him and touched his shoulder. His muscles felt bunched and tense beneath my palm.

And Natalie strolled into the solarium, chewing on one of Anatole's almond cookies. Martha had been right. I'd opened up to Natalie and she'd become a real friend to me.

"Have you told her yet?" she asked Bennett.

"Natalie, get out of here," he said.

"What?" I said to Bennett. "What is there to tell?"

"Oops." She backed toward the door. "Forget I was here." And she tiptoed away.

"What is she talking about?"

"Emma, ghostkeepers can't be together," he said in a strangled voice.

I laughed. "Is that some ridiculous Knell rule? Ignore them."

Bennett turned to me. "I can't."

"You're not serious," I said.

"When two ghostkeepers are together—the more they touch—one of them loses their powers."

"What?"

"Until they have nothing left at all."

"So they can't date or marry or—" I stopped. "What about my parents?"

"Your mom lost her powers to your father. That's what happens to the weaker partner, and your mom's abilities were never strong. That's why she needed the amulet to focus them."

"But didn't she know what she'd lose?"

He nodded. "She knew."

"She loved him very much," I said, thinking also of the original Bennett, who'd sacrificed his powers to be with the first Emma. That's why he'd become a ghost. He hadn't been a ghostkeeper when he died.

"And wanted a family." Bennett looked for a moment toward the garden. "I can't imagine how she must've felt, unable to protect you from Neos once she lost her power."

I nodded slowly. They really had tried to protect me. That's why they'd sent me to the poof, and—and maybe why they'd disappeared, too. Were they still watching out for me?

"I don't care," I finally said. "I'll give up my powers to be with you."

Bennett laughed. "Emma, you're already the strongest ghostkeeper I've ever seen. *You* won't lose anything."

"Oh."

Of course Bennett wasn't willing to sacrifice his powers to be with me—this was his whole world, born a ghostkeeper, working for the Knell. Could I ask him to lose everything for me? Never. Except shouldn't he be willing to give up everything for love? Isn't that what love was?

I was afraid to ask, but I didn't want to start keeping secrets again. So I said, "And, um, I don't suppose you . . ."

"I would, Emma." He took me in his arms and kissed me like I'd never been kissed before and maybe never would be again. "I totally would."

I sighed into his neck. "But?"

"That first murder in San Francisco?" he said. "That was my sister. That's why I've been so busy investigating. I can't stop now. Not until I find Neos."

A few days later, Bennett was waiting for me outside the front gates of Thatcher. Coby's funeral was set for Saturday and school had turned into a living hell. It was a relief to see a friendly face. Bennett wore a navy wool coat, ripped jeans, and teal blue knit scarf. I wanted to hug him. Kiss him. Slide my fingers under the scarf to touch his skin and never let go.

Instead, I said, "Hi."

"Hi, yourself." He smiled, happy to see me. We were always happy to see each other these days, even if we both kept our hands in our pockets.

We headed down the street, side by side, not touching.

"Nothing's ever going to be normal again, is it?" I said.

"Not normal, no." He laid a hand on the small of my back. "But one day, you and I . . ."

I shivered. Still, as much as I longed to feel Bennett's arms around me, and his skin next to mine, I wasn't sure I could let him give up his powers. He'd not only stop dispelling, he'd stop seeing ghosts entirely. Part of him would be missing forever.

Still, that little dilemma could wait. First we needed to find Neos and stop him for good.

"Any word from the Knell?" I asked.

"There's no trace of him yet."

"I think it's time I met them."

"Good," he said. "Because you've got an appointment on Saturday."

I stopped walking. "When did that happen?"

"Today. I couldn't put them off any longer."

"The meeting's here?"

"In New York. We'll take the train."

"Wow." This was unexpected. "Um. You're going with me?"

He grinned. "Of course."

I started walking again. "That's okay then."

We stopped in the village for a couple of red-eye chais, then when we got home, Bennett stepped into the kitchen while I leafed through the mail. Mixed in with the catalogs and bills, there was a thin manila envelope addressed to me.

I ripped open the envelope, and found a single photo.

Of Bennett, at Fisherman's Wharf in San Francisco, which made me think Max must have taken it.

Scrawled across the bottom: *Don't trust him.*

The dot over the *i* was missing. It was my mother's handwriting.

I flipped over the envelope again. There was no return address and it hadn't been postmarked. Did that mean she was in Echo Point? Were Max and my dad here, too?

"What's wrong?" Bennett asked, coming into the foyer.

I crumpled the photo, the words echoing in my head: *Don't trust him.*

"Nothing," I said. "How's that chai?"

ACKNOWLEDGMENTS

Thanks to my spectacular agents, Nancy Coffey and Joanna Stampfel-Volpe; my fabulous editor, Caroline Abbey; and all the other wonderful people at Bloomsbury, especially Raina Putter, Nicole Gastonguay, and Deb Shapiro.

Lee Nichols was raised in Santa Barbara, California—the setting of her adult novels *Tales of a Drama Queen, Hand-Me-Down*, and *True Lies of a Drama Queen*. She attended Hampshire College in Amherst, Massachusetts, where she studied history and psychology. She now lives in Maine and is married to novelist Joel N. Ross. *Deception* is her first novel for young adults.

www.leenicholsbooks.com